OTHER BOOKS BY LINCOLN JAMES

Coming Spring 2026

All We Wanted
A Supernatural Thriller

They make your dreams come true. Then you disappear.

Spring Formal, 1982—a weekend of open bars, rented tuxedos, and
bad decisions at a luxury resort in Las Vegas.
But the casino has unveiled something new.
Buried behind the lobby stands a glass display case housing three
mummified figures adorned in gold:
a ring, a tooth, an eyepatch.
By day, they're on display. By night, they hunt.
They slip into borrowed skin.
They feed on desire, envy, regret.
All they need is one phrase.
I wish.
Because in this hotel, dreams don't come true.
They come for you.

<u>Now Available</u>

The Ninth Layer
A Claustrophobic Survival Thriller

This wasn't a field trip. It was a burial.

It was supposed to be extra credit.
A simple research trip into the caves beneath Pendleton University.
But the deeper Alex and his classmates descend, the stranger things
become. The air hums. The walls glow. And the silence feels alive.
Then the lights go out.
And something starts screaming in the dark.
By the time they realize there's no way back up, the ground itself
seems to shift—breathing—hungering.
In the dark, they know they aren't alone.
And now, they'll have to fight to survive.

Available in print and ebook.

Written Just For You
A Romantic Psychological Thriller

*Some love stories are written in the stars. This one was written in
blood.*

Will wasn't supposed to stay in town. Jean wasn't supposed
to meet him. And the book she gave him? It wasn't meant to be read.
Depoe Bay is a place of whispers—where the fog clings
too close and stories go unfinished. The town says Jean is a
ghost, a siren, a memory that never made it out of the water.
But Will knows she's real. He's seen her. Heard her laugh.
Felt something shift.
And now that he's read her words...He can't let her go.

As the town turns colder, the secrets grow louder—about
the past, the dead, and what love refuses to bury.
Some girls don't make it out of their stories...
But Will's about to make sure this one does.

Available in print and ebook.

All the Time
A Coming-of-Age Sci-Fi Thriller

The past isn't just a memory... It's a trap.

When Carter sets out to reconnect with his dying mother, he never
expects to arrive at her house years before he was born. Stuck in the
past with nothing but his car, a bag of clothes, and a barely working
iPhone, Carter faces an impossible question: how did he get here—
and how can he get back?
Time is slipping through his fingers, and every moment spent in
the past pulls him further from the future he's desperate to
return to.
Caught between what was and what could be, Carter begins to
question if time is something you can outrun...
or if it's already run out.

Available in print and ebook.

Devils Like Us
A Tense, Gritty, Chase Thriller

Some devils hide in the shadows. Others look just like us.

Jason Murich thought he was heading home for a quiet weekend—
until two desperate runaways hijacked his car. Now he's hurtling
through the underbelly of 1990s Los Angeles on a high-stakes chase

that spirals into chaos. As secrets surface and loyalties blur, Jason is forced to confront just how far he'll go to survive.

Gripping and raw, Devils Like Us is a taut psychological thriller that will keep you holding your breath until the final page.

Available in print and ebook.

The Vanishing Eight
A Pulse-Pounding Survival Thriller

Disappearing was only the beginning.

Eight friends. One missing.
The town of Piedmont had always whispered about them—too close, too wild, too perfect.
Then Roy disappeared.
Now, Jonathan is racing to hold what's left of their group together. But the deeper he digs, the more he realizes: Roy's not the first to disappear. And if Jon's not careful... he won't be the last.
In a town built on secrets, nothing stays hidden forever.
And some friendships don't survive the truth.

Available in print, ebook, and audiobook.

FOREWORD

Content Warning

This story contains themes and depictions that may be distressing to some readers, including medical experimentation, loss of bodily autonomy, violence, trauma, and psychological manipulation. There are moments of horror, grief, and violation that may be difficult to read.

Please take care of yourself as you go—pause, skip ahead, or step away if you need to.

A Note on Themes

We Are Human is, at its core, a story about identity, survival, and what it means to still call yourself human after everything else has been taken. Set in a near future where technology blurs the line between body and machine, it follows a young man fighting to reclaim his autonomy in a world that profits from his pain.

This book explores themes of control, memory, grief, and the persistence of the soul. It's about the systems that strip people of their humanity—and the quiet, relentless strength it takes to reclaim it. It's about what happens when survival becomes rebellion, and love becomes the only thing real enough to hold onto.

More than anything, it's a story about being alive. About the courage to exist, even when the world insists you're something else.

Thank You

To every reader who's picked up this book—thank you. You could've chosen anything else, but you chose to walk beside these characters, and I don't take that lightly.

To my friends, family, and early readers: your encouragement made this story possible. Thank you for seeing the humanity in it before anyone else did.

And to anyone who has ever felt changed, used, or lost in the space between what you were and what you've become—this story was written for you.

Respectfully Yours,
Lincoln James

WE ARE HUMAN

LINCOLN JAMES

ISBN-13: 979-8-9985731-5-6 (Hardback edition)

ISBN-13: 979-8-9985731-4-9 (Paperback edition)

ISBN-13: 979-8-9985731-6-3 (Ebook edition)

Library of Congress Control Number: 2025922784

This is a work of fiction. Names, characters, places, and incidents either are the product of the author's imagination or are used fictitiously. Any resemblance to actual persons, living or dead, events, or locales is purely coincidental.

Published by: Lincoln James

P.O. Box 10660 Page Ave # PO 4034

Fairfax, VA 22038-4034

Edited by: E. Lee Caleca

Printed in the United States of America

First Edition: November 2025

CHAPTER 1

THE CLUB SWALLOWED sound like it was alive, a living breathing testament to the tribal depravity of humankind.

The music didn't play—it pulsed, heavy and low, bypassing my ears entirely and vibrating directly through bone and marrow, shaking me almost to the point of being nauseated. Each beat crawled along my spine, settling like frost beneath my skin, hard and bitter. The bass had a rhythm that felt wrong—something ancient, something primal, a heartbeat buried beneath layers of synth, an oppressive animal that made it hard to breathe normally.

Everything was drenched in neon: violent pinks, electric blues, and shades of ultraviolet my eyes weren't meant to process. The lights came in staccato flashes, slicing the crowd into stuttering frames, like a film reel slipping on its spool. Faces blurred in and out of focus, strangers flickering into something less than human. For a moment, everyone in the room looked like they were made of smoke—shifting and intangible, less real with every beat and every passing second.

I stood against the bar, one hand curled loosely around a bottle I had no intention of drinking. It was still cold, condensation dripping slowly down the glass, pooling beneath my fingertips. But it felt unreal, disconnected. Like an anchor from a different world entirely or another lifetime.

2040 had been hell so far, and it was barely August.

Jackson was already halfway gone. He danced with Sophia like they'd never known grief, never buried someone who shared their blood. Jackson's laughter was loud, a little too sharp, cutting through the surreal pulse around us. Sophia's silver dress shimmered like liquid metal, reflecting colors that shouldn't exist, shifting from indigo to violet and back again. Her blonde ponytail whipped in an arc as Jackson spun her, glitter catching in the flashes like sparks flying from steel.

They danced as if they weren't haunted by silence—as if they hadn't lost Liam just weeks ago. Like tonight wasn't supposed to be his birthday.

Just once, I wished I could join them in forgetting. But grief isn't something you dance away. Grief is patient. It waits quietly in that vulnerability, lingering just behind your shoulder, silent and heavy, until even laughter feels like pain.

I looked past the bar, staring into a wall that wasn't a mirror but something darker—a polished, obsidian-like surface threaded with thin veins of something faintly orange, barely visible beneath the club's shifting lights.

My reflection stared back, warped by the movement, uncertain.

The sides of my hair were buzzed close, the top hanging long and straight, black enough to catch the light and throw it back at me. A few strands fell into my eyes, shadowing the exhaustion there.

The rest of me looked like someone trying too hard to pass for normal. But in a place like this, maybe there was no normal.

A fiber-mesh tee clung to my frame, webbed with faint reflective threads that pulsed when I moved. Below that—cargo pants. Scuffed combat boots. The kind of outfit meant for working, not dancing. A cracked wristband blinked weak diagnostics against my skin, the glow stuttering every few seconds like a heartbeat that couldn't decide if it wanted to keep going.

Just hit twenty-three and I was already this worn down. Dark eyes shadowed. Skin pulled tight from exhaustion and unspoken anger.

I barely recognized myself anymore.

Til a little over two weeks ago there were three of us.

Three brothers.

Now there were only two, tethered together by silence and loss, and the ghost of a promise we made Liam months ago.

This whole trip had been his idea, a joke turned tradition he swore we'd honor. He'd planned every detail—the hotel, the restaurants, even this strange, impossible club. He'd counted down days, booked reservations months ahead, crafted playlists we still hadn't found the strength to listen to. Liam wanted all of this. But he wasn't here to see it.

The ache in my knuckles sharpened. Bruises from the gym still bloomed dark across my hands—not from training, not from a fight worth having. Just from hitting the punching bag, again and again, because pain was simpler than memory and more effective at masking it.

"Ty!" Jackson's voice cracked through the noise, too loud, too bright. He lifted a glass, spilling neon liquid over his fingers. "Come dance, man. You're killing me."

I raised my untouched beer, shaking my head once. "Not tonight."

He shrugged, his smile flickering briefly, and spun back into the lights, pulling Sophia with him. They dissolved into the haze of neon and sound, lost again to the maniacal culture we called having fun.

I leaned harder into the wall, feeling the strange material hum faintly beneath my shoulder, a subtle warmth, as if something was moving just beyond the surface.

People around me danced like shadows cast by flame, Plato's cave of falsehoods—bodies jerking in unnatural rhythm, eyes dilated wide beneath glowing contact lenses, faces illuminated by visors pulsing with color. No one seemed fully conscious, just passengers in their own bodies, lost in a dream they wouldn't remember.

And then—

I saw her.

She didn't dance.

Didn't drink.

Didn't belong to the same gravity holding the rest of us down.

She stood alone across the club—half-lit by the lazy rotation of violet strobes, her shape flickering in and out like something not fully tethered to this world. Her body didn't move with the beat. Her chest barely lifted with breath. She just stood there, still as glass, head tilted slightly like she was listening for something no one else could hear.

And she was staring at me.

Not the way strangers scan a crowd. Not the way someone tries to be mysterious.

She *saw* me.

Like we'd met before. Like we hadn't met yet, but would. Like she was waiting for the part of me that hadn't arrived. And then— without a word—she turned and disappeared into the crowd.

I should've let her go. Told myself it didn't mean anything. Just static. Just a girl with good lighting. But there was something in the way she moved. Not seductive. Not playful.

Purposeful.

Like she wasn't crossing a room, but a threshold. And something inside me followed without asking. I left the bottle on the bar.

And I followed.

The crowd pulsed like blood. Lights throbbed in waves, painting the air with color the human brain could not decipher—color meant to disrupt, to create a surreal world where nothing mattered. Fog hissed from the floor like steam from a broken pipe. Laughter tangled with bass lines. But she—

She moved through it like it wasn't real. Like the room made space for her without realizing it had. Every time the strobe caught her shoulder, her jaw, the sweep of her silhouette—something flickered in my memory. Something I didn't have yet. Familiar. Unnerving.

I told myself I was looking for Jackson. That I was just wandering. But then I got close enough to smell her.

It wasn't perfume. Not really.

It was cold. Metallic. Like the air before lightning. Ozone and hurricane clouds, blended with something sweet.

She turned.

Her features were sharper than I expected. Not flawless. Real. The kind of beauty you couldn't recreate—only remember or imagine.

Her hair fell in soft, shoulder-length waves—dark brown, like river rock wet with storm. Light skimmed her skin in fractured hues like broken stained glass—at first pale and white, then blue and gold, all the base layer for the primary violent violet that shaded her hair like unnatural dye. She wore a sheer black top over a bralette that shimmered like copper trapped under tinted glass. Her skirt hugged her waist, slit high and dipped in liquid bronze—its hue shifting with every step, like molten rust in a Marlene Yu painting. Her boots rose to her knees, laced in front, lean and quiet like they were made for darker places than this.

She didn't look out of place. She made the place look wrong. Like the club was some crude replica of a memory she still carried better.

She didn't glow like the others. She swallowed light. Made the neon look pale.

And her eyes—a rich, watchful brown. But beneath them... a glint. Just for a second.

Orange.

Not warm like candlelight. Not soft. A buried ember—pulsing like it had a heartbeat of its own, drawing me in like enlightenment— a knowing I couldn't place. A beat I tried to hold onto.

I blinked.

Gone.

"Hey," she said. Just that. Smooth. Unbothered. Like we'd already met in a dream and she was just waiting for me to catch up.

I looked at her whale-eyed, caught off guard like a deer in head-lights. "You always open with that?"

She tilted her head, eyes scanning me like she was making a mental list. "Only when it works."

The music curved into something slower—sludgy and hypnotic. Her eyes didn't blink. Didn't look away. I couldn't tell if the pulse I felt was the beat, or just something she was doing to me by existing.

"You don't dance," she said.

"Never really saw the point."

"That's because you're watching it from the outside." She stepped closer. "It's different in here."

"In where?"

Her fingers brushed mine. "The static."

I let out a breath I hadn't realized I was holding. "You talk like a cult leader."

"And you follow strangers like you're looking to be converted."

That got a twitch of a smile out of me. "What's your angle?"

She shrugged. "Maybe I like your face. Maybe I'm bored. Maybe I think you're just sad enough to be interesting."

I raised an eyebrow. "Sad's a weird pickup line."

"It's not a line." Her voice dropped a little. "It's a mirror."

I was about to say something—anything—when she held out her hand, ringless, deliberate. "C'mon. Just one song."

I hesitated. Every part of me told me not to move. But then again —every part of me had stopped knowing what the hell it wanted a long time ago.

I took her hand.

She didn't dance with me. She danced like gravity bent differently around her. She moved like she remembered music from a life-time before it was ever written. I tried to follow, but it felt like chasing smoke.

My eyes caught hers—and behind that brown, there it was again.

That strange, simmering orange. Like something buried deep was trying to break through the cracks.

"You here with friends?" she asked, voice lazy, like the answer didn't matter.

"My brother. And his wife. Sort of a... trip. We're up in 1408."

"Romantic," she said flatly. "You look like someone who doesn't know what to do with downtime."

"And you look like someone who doesn't believe in it."

She smirked. "Downtime's for people with little time left."

I leaned in a little. "You always this cryptic?"

She leaned in closer. "You always this fun?"

I huffed out a laugh. "Depends on the night."

She twirled once, pulled me back to her. Close enough that my pulse jumped. "What's your name?"

"Ty."

"Figures."

I gave her a look. "What's that supposed to mean?"

"Nothing. Just... you look like someone named Ty."

"And what do people named Ty look like?"

She traced a finger across my collarbone, just once. "Like they don't know whether to kiss you or kill you."

"Why not both?"

"Maybe it can be." She tilted her head, playful now, but not soft. "What about me?"

"What about you?"

"What do I look like?"

I paused. "Like trouble."

"Good." She smiled, finally. Sharp. Gorgeous. "Then we're on the same page."

I raised my eyebrows for a beat. Just long enough to think maybe this moment was going somewhere.

Then—

"Ty!"

Jackson's voice shattered the spell, cutting through the sound like a dull blade. His hand clapped my shoulder, rum breath heavy and oblivious. "Dude! What the hell, man? We're doing shots, let's go!"

I turned, just slightly, and in that half-second—

She was gone.

I spun back—nothing. No trace. The space where she'd stood now filled with strangers and synth.

Jackson clapped my shoulder, laughing. "You good?"

I nodded, distracted. "Yeah. Just—yeah."

He shouted something else, but I didn't hear it.

Because across the club, by the far exit, I saw her.

She stood in the red glow of the emergency sign like a warning someone forgot to heed. Her silhouette was long, still, unmistakable. Her hand rested on the doorframe. She looked back at me—once.

And there it was again.

That orange flicker. Like fire. Like a memory. Or a warning.

Then the door opened.

And she was gone.

It slammed shut behind her, but the air still buzzed. Like she'd taken something with her. Or left something behind.

I stood there a second longer.

And then the music swallowed me whole.

CHAPTER 2

MORNING HIT like static in my teeth. Not the kind that coaxes you awake with gold and birdsong—but the harsh kind.

Angular. Accusatory.

The air smelled like lime, sweat, and stale regret. I opened my eyes and forgot where I was for a second. The light didn't warm the room. It exposed it.

Sun crawled across the suite floor in long, judgmental fingers. It caught on crushed cans and half-eaten takeout. Confetti clung to the sink. And a smear of something red marked the wall—I hoped it was lipstick. The king bed in the middle of the room looked like a war zone, its blankets twisted into a makeshift fort. Surprisingly, there was no sign of Jackson or Sophia.

The couch groaned beneath me as I sat up. My shirt had twisted halfway around my ribs. My spine ached like I'd gone three rounds with sleep—and lost. No blanket, but someone had tossed me a pillow at least. I'd like to think it was Jax, even if he'd never admit it. The little things meant more now.

Two weeks. That's how long it had been since we lost him. A pillow on the couch shouldn't mean anything—but when someone you love disappears that fast, even dumb things get heavy. The pillow. The trip. The unspoken promise to act like something in this world still made sense.

But grief doesn't honor plans. It lingers. It leaks. And it always wakes up first.

But something else was clawing at the back of my head.

Her.

The woman from the club. That strange stillness in her. The way her eyes didn't only meet mine—they held them. Like she was studying something beneath the surface. I could still feel it—static beneath my skin. Like she'd left a mark, invisible and deliberate, somewhere I couldn't scratch.

I didn't know her name. But part of me was already listening for her.

"Ty..."

The sound came from the floor. More like a groan than a name. Jackson sprawled across the carpet like he'd fallen off the bed and decided to stay down. Liam used to call it his 'plank of shame' pose. One bare foot hooked under the coffee table. The other flopped sideways, defeated—like the fight had left it hours ago.

"You alive?" My voice came out rough—sandpaper and bad air.

He rolled over and buried his face into a pillow. "What time is it..."

His hair was a crime scene. Shirtless. Jeans from the night before still hanging low on his hips, looking like he'd slept through a car crash. Situated in the kind of posture you only hit when your soul is on vacation.

I checked my phone. "Thirteen-hundred. We missed breakfast. Again."

I stepped over somebody's clothes. Not mine. Didn't care whose. The hallway stretched too long, judging, like it knew what waited at the end. Shadows flickered in the corners like they hadn't realized the party was over.

The door was half open.

Sophia sat on the cold tile floor, slumped beside the toilet like she'd made peace with her choices and chosen to mourn them there. Her head leaned against the side of the tub. One false eyelash clung to her cheek like it had barely survived the night. The other was missing. Her once-metallic dress clung in defeat, bunched at the hip like it couldn't hold itself together anymore.

She didn't flinch when she saw me—just blinked once, slow, like my presence had already been filed under "expected."

I leaned on the doorframe. "Morning sickness?"

She blinked. Slowly. "You're funny."

"You alright?"

"Depends. Is the room supposed to spin when I move my eyes?"

I grabbed a cup from the sink, rinsed it twice, and filled it halfway with lukewarm water. Passed it to her gently, like I was feeding a wounded animal.

She sipped it like communion.

"You look weirdly alive," she rasped.

"Didn't drink much."

"Didn't sleep either?"

I shook my head. *Barely ever did anymore.*

"You're the spooky kind of resilient," she muttered. "Like something in you already snapped, and you're just walking it off."

Apt.

She paused, blinked again like maybe that came out harsher than she meant.

"Sorry. That was probably..."

"Accurate," I said.

"Girls probably eat it up. Mysterious. Brooding. Sad eyes. You're basically a noir character."

"Must be why I'm still single. Look, do you need anything, Soph?"

She laughed, rough and real, and swished the rest of the water in her mouth like mouthwash. "If you find coffee, I'll Venmo you a soul."

"Not sure it's worth all that, but I'll see what I can do."

Sophia set the cup down on the floor next to her, pressing two fingers to her temple like she could squeeze the ache out of her skull. Then, she exhaled like the question had been waiting for permission.

"Wait, Ty. Are you—doing okay?" she asked. "With... everything?"

There it was.

The *everything*.

That quiet, brutal word people used when they were too kind—or too scared—to say the real ones.

I didn't answer right away. My gaze drifted past the balcony door, where sunlight poured in slow and gold across the carpeted floor like nothing had ever gone wrong. Outside, the ocean glittered in a world that no longer existed for me. Beautiful. Unbothered. Unfair.

"I haven't decided," I said finally.

Sophia didn't press. She never did. That was her thing—quiet loyalty, sharp eyes, sharp tongue. She could hold space for grief without trying to fill it. It's what made her dangerous in a good way.

She leaned her head back against the tub and stared at the ceiling like it owed her answers. "I think he'd be glad we came," she murmured. "Even like this. Especially like this."

I nodded, but I didn't look at her. Couldn't. My throat was already closing up.

The suite felt colder all of a sudden, like the air had dropped ten degrees between blinks. Liam's ghost wasn't loud. Wasn't angry. Just... present. Like the room remembered him better than we did.

He'd planned this trip like he planned everything—meticulously, joyfully, down to the events and the room keys. Said we needed something to look forward to. Said it'd be good for Jackson. For me. Said he'd meet us here.

He didn't.

He'd survived three deployments in the Second Cold War—came back with medals, a limp, and that far-off stare most vets had now, like they were still dodging drone strikes and navigating ghost towns with radiation bloom warnings. Places so quiet, the silence had weight. Liam told me once you could hear your own pulse echo off broken glass. No one really came back the same—not with their nerves intact, anyway. We thought he was adjusting. We thought wrong.

It'd been two weeks.

Fourteen days since we lost him.

Fourteen days since Liam closed the garage door and didn't come back out.

No note. No goodbye. Only a memory of his laugh, the smell of motor oil and aftershave. I still check my phone like maybe I missed something.

Like maybe I could still catch him in the act of leaving.

But I knew it was stupid.

Downstairs, the convention was waking up. I could hear it through the floor—buzzing, alive, like it had the right to exist without him. Game launches. Indie booths. Cosplay. Whole crowds pretending they'd found a reason to still care about something.

I moved fast and didn't apologize for it. Walked toward my duffel, tugged on my jacket—mesh-shell, lined with reflective thread, hood pulled up over the mess of my hair. No shirt underneath. The cold bit against my skin, but I didn't care. Muscle memory had more to say than comfort ever did. The faint bruises across my ribs caught the light when I moved—shadows of old fights, old lessons. My hands worked quick, practiced. Combat slacks, dusty at the knees. Laced my boots like I was about to fight someone. Maybe I was.

Sophia caught my eye in the mirror.

"He was getting better. You remember that coffee maker? The one we said had a vendetta? He fixed it. Even made us that terrible hazelnut stuff he liked—said it tasted like hope and battery acid. And he laughed. Not forced, either..." She drifted. "Really, Ty. He was trying. I really thought..."

Her voice trailed off.

So did my breathing.

I hated how calm she sounded. Hated that part of me wanted to believe her. But if I believed her, I had to believe we let him slip through the cracks smiling.

There was a buzz behind my eyes—low, rising. I should've agreed. Should've let it pass. But the second she said his name like that, like he was already a story we were moving past... something cracked. A hinge swinging too fast. A fuse burning too low.

And I said—

"You really thought what?" I asked, sharper than I meant to be.

She turned, caught off guard. "I meant—he seemed okay. He was trying. You saw that, right?"

There it was again. That soft certainty. Like if we said it enough, it'd make it true—that Liam had been okay. That we hadn't missed the signs. Like it mattered one way or the other. And now she was trying to package the mess in past tense, like it wouldn't keep me up at 2 AM.

"Yeah," I said, too fast. "He tried. And he still died."

She looked like I'd slapped her. Not angry. Just tired. Her hands dropped to her lap, like she didn't know where to put the weight of what I'd said.

"I'm sorry," she said. "Me and Jackson, we're just—worried about you."

I didn't answer. It wasn't her fault. But the truth was: I needed someone to blame. And blaming Liam didn't work. He'd been too good. Too careful. Too good at hiding the cracks. And I was the only one who could've seen the signs.

Still, we all missed them.

I stared at her like I was waiting for a better answer, knowing there wasn't one. Just sorry. Always sorry. Like the word could patch bullet holes if you said it right.

I zipped up my jacket. My hands fought me the whole way, twitching just enough to make the zipper stick. Just enough to know I wasn't alright. Just enough to pretend I was.

I clenched them into fists, hoping that would steady me.

It didn't.

"I'm heading out," I said, voice flat.

"Where?"

"Gym."

"You sure that's—"

"Yeah." My voice cracked a little. I ignored it.

I grabbed my keycard off the counter and stepped into the hallway before she could ask anything else. The door clicked shut behind me, closing any thought that might have followed.

I took the stairs two at a time. My heartbeat pounded like it was trying to outpace me. Digital ads flickered along the hallway walls — full-length panels that used to sell vacation bundles and smart beverages but now glitched between broken pixels and static bursts.

I didn't stop. Not until I hit the first floor—past the rows of pop-up promo booths clogging the lobby like tumors, each one glowing in chemical neon. Tall LED banners screamed PRODUCT NAMES like they were gospel:

NEUROBURN PRE-WORKOUT // MILITARY GRADE FORMULA // LIMIT 2 PER GUEST

A cartoon soldier flexed on screen, pupils glowing neon blue, a trending misnomer for being hip. A line of teenagers in chrome jackets waited for free samples, scanning QR codes with chipped nails and glazed eyes. Someone in a branded mech-hoodie shouted about a VR tournament, promising reflex boosters and discount codes to the winner.

Past them, booths for streamers and e-sports teams flickered with glitchy holograms—bright as a carnival, empty as a morgue. A giant rotating banner read:

WRAITHCON 2040 — FUTURE OF TECH // FUTURE OF PLAY // FUTURE OF YOU!

The tagline kept looping, like it was trying to convince itself. Nobody looked at me as I passed. They were too busy watching screens. Watching themselves on screens. Watching for something to believe in.

I kept walking.

Finally, I found the offshoot hallway that led to the hotel gym.

The door scanned my wristband before unlatching with a tired beep, like even the lock wanted to clock out. Inside, the gym was small. Empty. Blessedly silent.

A row of virtual spar rigs lined the wall — glossy black pads that were supposed to simulate opponent impact and adjust difficulty using biometric feedback. Half of them flickered with red OUT OF SERVICE text, and one was duct-taped across the sensors like someone had punched through the calibration screen and the hotel gave up trying to fix it.

I let the door slam shut behind me.

I stood there for a moment. No sound. No questions. Just me and the hum of induction lights and rubber floor tiles that smelled like old sweat and bleach. The kind of place built for people who needed to fight something—anything.

Then I pulled out my phone.

Liam's name was still in my favorites. It felt wrong to take him out of it.

I stared at the screen.

Then I hit play.

"Hey. It's me. If you're screening this, I swear to God—pick up the phone, asshole.

I booked the room. Outer Banks, just like we said. Beginning of August. Same place as last time, with the fire pit and the good pillows. Jackson already said yes, so don't be the weak link.

And for the love of everything holy—bring your own protein bars this time. I'm not carrying your low blood sugar ass through another hike. I mean it."

A pause.

The kind that wasn't written into the message, but bled into it anyway.

Like he wanted to say more. Or maybe didn't know how.

"Anyway. Just wanted to say I'm excited. Think it'll be good for us. I need this. I think you do too."

A breath.

"Love you, Ty. This is gonna be a good one. Just... don't bail, okay?"

His voice cracked a little at the end. I hadn't noticed that before.

In my head, I saw him laughing in the kitchen, stirring burnt coffee with a pencil like it was a potion. Alive. Annoying. Mine.

I sat on the bench and let the silence crawl back in.

Then I wrapped my fists, set the timer, and started hitting the bag.

Hard.

The bag didn't hit back. But it didn't have to.

Grief hits softer than fists—it never misses but somehow always has the same impact.

CHAPTER 3

THE BAG SWUNG, talking back to me like it was trying to tell me something. So I shut it up. Again. And again.

Jackson's face. Sophia's voice. Liam's shadow.

He used to say the gym was "where boys went to bleed without crying."

I used to laugh at that.

Now I just hear it in his voice—hoarse, bitter, stuck somewhere between a joke and a warning.

The hood of my jacket slid farther off my head with each swing, fabric snapping against my sides, swaying like a shadow trying to keep up. Sweat slicked across muscle, skin growing hot against the cold mesh shell. The reflective thread caught the dim light with every punch, flashing like a warning before disappearing again. Lightning in the middle of a storm.

Then there was that girl with the neon eyes.

All of it buzzed in my head like radio static that wouldn't die.

My fists were too slow to catch it, but I threw them anyway.

Jab. Hook. Breathe.

Jab. Hook. Breathe.

Except I couldn't. Not really.

Everything felt loud. Not just the sounds—the air itself. The kind of loud that made your skin itch, something you knew was there but couldn't see.

I didn't want to be here. I knew that the second I walked into this hotel. But here I was, pretending it helped. Pretending any of this worked.

The TVs made it worse.

Wasn't the volume. It was the presence. Like they were watching me watching them.

Every wall had a screen. Every screen had a war.

Muted footage looped like a broken prayer searching for retribution. Or was it forgiveness. Another city turned crater. A half-collapsed station pouring bodies and smoke into the street. Some anchor in a suit, eyes too bright, talking about civilian casualties like they were market trends.

The subtitles ticked along the bottom like wooden soldiers who couldn't stop.

"...retaliation in Sector 6B... fifth civilian strike this quarter... Allied Western Forces blame East Coalition separatists..."

Same script. Different victims.

I stopped keeping track of who fired first. Only kept track of who didn't come home.

I ripped the wraps off my hands, jammed them into my back pocket. My shirt clung to me like I owed it money. My arms ached, my knuckles burned. But none of that hit as hard as what I saw next.

A woman on-screen. Crying. Screaming.

Face streaked with dust. Hands shredded from digging someone out—maybe herself.

Three seconds. That's all she got before they blurred her out. Then came the drone shot. Wide. Cold. Clinical. Just another day in hell.

That old feeling hit me again. Right in the throat. Not panic. Not rage. Just that hollow sort of grief that fills a room before you even realize you're alone.

I wasn't gonna cry.

I didn't wanna cry.

I just wanted out.

Along the center wall, a massive holo-banner glitch-flashed every few seconds:

TRAINING APPROVED BY THE U.S. URBAN DEFENSE PROGRAM — PROUD PARTNER SINCE 2034

Like it meant something.

Like that stamp of government approval could hide the rust creeping up the dumbbell racks or the locker doors hanging off their hinges.

A couple meatheads wandered in behind me—laughing, checking themselves out in the mirror, blasting whatever garbage passed for music. One of them took selfies under the banner, tagging themselves like being here meant they were part of something bigger than a forgotten gym on the edge of a dying city.

I had enough.

I grabbed my bag and bailed.

The hallway outside was colder than I remembered. Or maybe it was just the sweat. I should've gone left—toward the lobby, the elevators, the part of this place pretending to be normal. But something made me turn right instead.

The carpet dipped into the back wing of the hotel. The convention center.

I didn't have a plan. I just needed to move.

And that's when I saw them—through a glass divider. A crowd. Neon lights. Rows of booths. Holographic signage glitching like it forgot how to be happy. The low hum of fake joy.

And for a second—just a second—I saw Liam again.

Fifteen. We were at Comic Nexus in Richmond. He wore that stupid Mega Mecha 5 helmet all day, even though it made his ears red and smelled like dried glue and spray paint. He grinned the whole time. Before the war. Before the meds. Before he stopped laughing altogether. I swallowed the memory like a pill with no label.

"Fuck it," I muttered.

I had time to kill.

So I disappeared into the mob.

The convention level looked like a high school prom that got too much money and not enough vision.

Strip lights flickered overhead like they were trying to have a seizure. Rows of booths stretched out across the floor—makeshift monuments to lag, neon, and secondhand ambition. Monitors buzzed. VR headsets blinked. None of it felt real.

Indie game expos in 2040 looked exactly the way they did in 2030—just more wires and less wonder.

When I was thirteen, this kind of place felt like magic. Now it just felt loud.

Not the kind of loud you hear. The kind you feel. Like the constant static that crawls under your skin when there's no way out.

Everywhere I looked, somebody was plugged in. Headsets on. Eyes glazed. Half of them twitching in place like they were dreaming with their eyes open. The other half wandered between booths, swiping through demos like they were shopping for personalities.

A vendor bot rolled past me—slow, boxy, covered in peeling decals and overconfident branding.

One sticker read: REFUEL // RESTART.

Two blinking buttons below: CAFFEINE or ELEC-TROLYTES.

Great. Choices.

Overhead, massive screens played silent trailers on loop—CGI avatars screaming into broken landscapes, glitchy worlds folding in on themselves, marketing taglines flickering like bad prophecies:

OFFLINE IS OBSOLETE.

I didn't know what I was expecting. But it sure as hell wasn't this.

This wasn't for me.

Too much flash. Not enough soul.

Even the glitches felt rehearsed. Like the fake had infected the errors too.

Still, I hadn't come here looking for anything. Not really. I just needed to not be somewhere else.

I stood still for a second, letting the room spin around me. Letting the noise blur. Letting the weight in my chest settle, even if just a little.

The air reeked of synthetic vanilla and warm plastic. Somewhere nearby, a VR headset caught a glitch—one of the avatars froze mid-scream, its mouth stuck open, pixelated blood flickering at the corners. It stayed like that. Just vibrating slightly. Like it knew I was watching.

And behind me, a booth screen flashed static for a second. Just a flicker. Like something—or someone—was trying to make contact and changed its mind.

I turned to look, but it had already reset. Just another branded trailer for some tech I'd never need.

Still... I swear, for half a second, it felt like something was watching me back.

I moved past a kid—maybe fourteen—cackling as he played a VR shooter where you mow down civilians in a metro station.

His avatar wore riot gear. His hands twitched on imaginary triggers.

A few feet away, two devs bragged about dopamine loop retention like it was a badge of honor.

I didn't blame the tech. I blamed what people did with it.

That hollow spot in my chest widened. And that's when I heard it—

"You're Ty, right?"

The voice wasn't loud, but it landed. Controlled. Velvet-lined, with a sharpened edge underneath.

I turned—and there he was. Standing like he'd always belonged there. Like he'd been waiting.

Early thirties, maybe, but built like the kind of guy who jogs at dawn and never sweats. Blond hair slicked back—not greasy, not loud. Intentional. Classic. His jaw could've been chiseled into a cologne bottle.

He wore a slate-gray cashmere sweater, fine-knit, the collar of a crisp white shirt just barely peeking above it. Charcoal dress pants, perfectly pressed, the kind that never wrinkled no matter how long you sat in them. Polished oxfords that caught the light without showing a single scuff. Everything about him was understated wealth —old-world grooming meeting new-world precision. Even the faint scent of cedar that hung around him felt engineered.

His eyes were gray. Not cold. Not warm. Just precise. Like he was already downloading everything about me and deciding what parts to keep.

His badge read:

DR. N. WILDER – Dev // VRX Labs

Of course it did.

He smiled. Subtle. Like we'd just run into each other at a party neither of us wanted to leave.

"My friend spotted you last night," he said, tone dipping low enough to feel like a secret. "Said you danced with her."

My stomach kicked. I didn't move.

"She moves like something else," he added. "I told her to work the room, not steal it. Guess you surprised her."

I didn't answer. But I remembered.

The perfume like electricity. The way she looked at me like she already knew how I'd end.

He let the silence stretch, then filled it with a little smirk.

"She said you were worth remembering."

I crossed my arms. Habit. Armor.

"You always make a habit of sending girls to scout for you?" I asked.

He chuckled. "Only the remarkable ones."

The grin stayed—tight, measured. But not forced. He didn't seem like he was selling anything. Just enjoying the game.

"Pleasure to meet you," he said, offering a hand.

His shake was confident, not crushing. Just enough pressure to show me he didn't flinch.

"I run a local outfit here in town. We're developing tech that hasn't made it past the rumor mill yet."

"And what, you looking for play-testers in hotel lobbies?" I said, eyebrow raised.

"Something like that," he said, eyes narrowing. "But we're not talking another brainless shooter or aimless sandbox. This is different."

He stepped half a pace closer, voice dropping—more intimate than secretive.

"Full-immersion. Deep-scan. What we build doesn't just react to you. It learns you. Rewrites the line between experience and memory."

I gave a short laugh. "Sounds like a therapy session with better graphics."

"Depends what you're trying to forget," he said.

We stood there. Not speaking. Just letting the moment stretch taut.

Then, casual as a shrug, he added, "She's around, by the way. If you were hoping for another glimpse."

The words slid under my ribs before I could brace.

The memory of her burned like a fever dream. I wanted to forget it. And I wanted it back.

My voice came out drier than I wanted. "Who is she?"

His smile was unreadable. "Someone who wants to see you again. Eventually."

Eventually. Like fate with a soft timer.

His eyes stayed locked on mine.

Then he asked, softer now. Sincere in a way that made me pause:

"Look around, Ty. What do you see?"

I turned.

The convention space flickered like a broken dream—neon

bleeding into carpet stains, booths buzzing with noise no one was listening to. Headsets on blank faces. Trailers screaming through muted speakers. No one talking. Just escape.

"People running," I said. "From something. Toward something faker."

He didn't flinch. But something shifted in him. His shoulders pulled straighter, like he'd just heard the right answer.

"You're not like them," he said. Not in admiration. In recognition.

I didn't want to be. But I wasn't sure what I was instead.

I stayed quiet.

He looked down, then back up with a spark in his eye that was part invitation, part challenge.

"Are you ready to see something real?"

I should've said no. Should've told him to shove his mystery tech and movie-trailer monologue.

But the truth?

I was tired of the fake.

Tired of pretending that any of this mattered—that you could scroll through grief or sweat it out of your system. Tired of noise that never stopped, people who never really looked, headlines that looped like static.

He had predator eyes, and I still wanted to say yes. Because pretending not to see the monster is worse than looking one in the eye.

He didn't press. Just watched. Like he was waiting for me to catch up.

If it was a trap, fine. At least it wasn't a loop.

At least it was something.

I sighed, long and low. "Alright, *Doc*," I said. "Let's see what you've got."

CHAPTER 4

I TOLD myself I wasn't curious.

Not really. Just enough to kill a few minutes. Just enough to lie to myself about why I was here.

If I was being honest, I figured I was doing it for Liam. Or maybe to avoid thinking about him.

He was two years older than me, and for most of our lives, he carried the world like it was something you could pause. He lived in games—not just as a player, but as someone who *belonged* there. Fantasy worlds made more sense to him than the real one ever did.

After the war, he didn't come back all the way. His body made it home, but something else stayed out there. He stopped posting. Stopped showing up. But sometimes—when he had a good day—he'd send me a link. A patch. A screenshot of some side quest I'd never finish.

That was his way of saying, *I'm still here.*

Until he wasn't.

I couldn't even tell you why I thought of dropping by his house that day, but I found him in the garage. No note. Didn't even lock the door.

He just... stopped. Propped up. The damn thing still around his neck.

Mom said it must've been sudden. The police called it clean, but I hate that word. And Dad stopped being himself all at once, like that day was the day he died too.

There was a folded towel on the workbench, like maybe Liam didn't want to make a mess. Like he still cared.

But I always knew something was up long before that.

The way he flinched when someone dropped a plate. The nights he slept in his truck. The mornings he couldn't look me in the eye.

He didn't die that day. Not all at once.

He left in pieces.

Jackson thought this trip would help, but I think he just wanted to keep moving too—like if you never stop walking, the grief can't catch up.

But I stall.

I linger in rooms long after everyone else leaves. I replay conversations in my head until the dialogue breaks.

So yeah. Maybe this was stupid.

But part of me needed to see the kind of place Liam would've loved.

And maybe I was still thinking about her. The girl from last night. The way she looked at me—like she already knew I didn't belong here either. Like she was proof there was something behind the screen. And if I had the chance to see her again...

I wouldn't turn it down.

Doc's badge caught the light like a scalpel.

He led me down a side hall that curved behind the convention floor—wide enough for foot traffic but too narrow for comfort, still humming with leftover energy like a battery almost dead. Cosplayers drifted past in half-costumes and half-lidded eyes. A girl in fox ears brushed my shoulder without looking up. A guy with glowing boots laughed too loud at something that wasn't funny. The neon here was sickly and weak, like old Life Savers left too long in the sun.

The farther we walked, the more it shifted.

The hum of the expo thinned behind us until it was just our footsteps and the buzz of old fluorescents that had picked up a mean edge. No exit arrows. No security. Just blank concrete swallowing sound.

I started to feel it in my stomach—the party's over but no one's told you to leave yet.

Doc didn't speak. Didn't look back. He moved like this hall belonged to him, like he'd walked it a hundred times. I was trying to memorize each turn. Left. Right. Left again. By the third bend, the crowd was gone. No chatter. No blinking bracelets. No half-dead vendors hawking keychains. Just the smell of bleach hiding under metal.

I thought about Liam. About how he'd told me once that every room has a way out, you just have to find it. But the hall kept bending and all the exits kept vanishing. I kept walking anyway. Because I wanted to know. Because this guy seemed like the only one in the building not pretending.

Then the hallway spat us out into a back lot.

Storm clouds had bruised the sky purple, low and wet, the smell of seaspray lingering like yesterday's cocktail. No lights out here, just broken shells and crushed dune grass. I could hear the ocean but not see it, just smell the brine curling in on the wind. Seagulls spiraled overhead like they were waiting for something to die.

The Outer Banks used to feel like escape. Now it felt like something waiting to collapse.

His van sat alone at the edge of the lot. Long. Matte black. No windows. A license plate sitting crooked in the windshield. Government or just trying to look like it.

He unlocked it with a blink.

I stood there a second too long. A voice in the back of my head whispered 'turn around'.

But I didn't.

Doc looked... *normal* — but the kind of normal that came from money and mirrors, not nature. Fit, but not built. More model than fighter. Slick blond hair pushed back just enough to look effortless, gray eyes that didn't blink as often as they should. He had that curated stubble, the tailored casual clothes, the posture of a man who'd been told he looked good from every angle and believed it. The kind of guy who belonged in a magazine spread about "the most eligible tech bachelors." Not someone who'd win a fight in a parking lot.

My brain did the math automatically—the way it always had back in the ring. Weight class. Reach. Center of gravity. His stance was relaxed, no guard, no tension in the shoulders. He didn't square his feet or track my hips. Either he'd never thrown a punch in his life, or he'd never had to.

If this goes sideways, I can take him.

The thought came fast. Confident. Dangerous. A reflex born from too many nights in gyms that smelled like blood and artificial air fresheners. *Chin. Ribs. Inside elbow for the disarm.* I didn't even realize I'd mapped his weak points until my hands relaxed.

"You still with me?" he asked. His voice was smooth, like silk over a knife.

For a heartbeat I swore I heard Liam. Not the words—just the shape of them. Like a ghost hiding in the metal hum.

I stepped closer anyway. Because maybe ghosts were easier than what I'd left behind.

He slid the van door open.

Cold air spilled out. Sharp. Too clean. No dust, no sweat, no sign of a dozen other people before me. It smelled like nowhere.

I hesitated. One step. Then another.

Inside was a room that didn't belong in a van. The air had that sterile, electrical smell—like a hospital built from schematics but never actually lived in. Panels lined the walls. Black screens blinked to life the second I stepped in. No seats. Just cables. Floor lighting.

One padded wall. And a single headset resting in a molded indentation, waiting.

No branding. Just black chrome and veins of orange light pulsing like a heartbeat.

I stared.

"This the part where I disappear?" I asked. Tried to smile like it was a joke.

Doc's smirk was small, almost fond. "Only if it works," he said.

I hovered in the doorway, heart hammering like a moth against glass. The air in the room felt heavier than it should — still, electric, like somebody had left a current running under the floorboards.

"Go ahead," the man said, reaching for the headset like this wasn't a command but a formality. His tone was light, but his eyes didn't move.

I stepped inside.

That's when I noticed it — a thin red smear tucked just under the floor panel. Paint, maybe. Or something worse. My feet hesitated before my brain did.

I thought about walking out. Didn't. Too late anyway. I'd already said yes.

He tilted his head. Not much. Just enough to make me realize he'd noticed.

"You okay?"

I nodded too quickly. "Just... smells like burnt plastic. Like something shorted out." My voice wavered.

He didn't answer.

The device sat in his palm like something alive. Sleek, surgical, black mirrored lenses that stared back like waiting eyes in a dead doll. No straps. No wires. Nothing to hold on to.

I took it. It was lighter than it looked — cool against my fingers.

The headset seemed to exhale as it neared my face, as if it had been breathing without me, a low hum threading under the skin of my palms. Not a boot-up chime. Something quieter. Lower.

Then the lenses lit up.

The van faded. The walls dissolved. Whatever room I'd been in —whatever man had been standing beside me—was gone.

Just me. And her.

A face formed from pixels. Not a person, but a memory pretending to be one. Red hair floated unnaturally, as if she were caught in an underwater grave. Her skin glowed porcelain and wrong. Her mouth opened and shook but made no sound.

A scream trapped behind glass.

Static hissed in my ears. The screen pulsed. Broken text flashed across the display:

"THERE'S STILL TIME."

My blood went cold.

"Jesus," I breathed. "Is this... a horror game, Doc?"

Silence. Then a shift somewhere behind me. "Something like that," he said at last, watching me the way people watch a fuse burn down.

And then: "Why do you keep calling me Doc?"

The chill that ran through me wasn't from the air. My mouth opened, then closed.

The badge. VRX Labs. Dr. Wilder. He'd never actually said it. Not until I did.

"I mean—" I forced a breath. "Your badge said—"

"There are a lot of badges in this place," he murmured. "People like labels. They make you feel safe."

He stepped back just slightly. Just enough for the distance to settle like a weight.

"Do you feel safe, Ty?"

My heart thudded hard.

The silence shifted. A hiss. Or maybe a breath.

I started to pull the headset off—

Pain stabbed into my neck. A syringe. A freezing sting, like a wire had just been threaded through my spine.

My whole body jerked once, then locked.

The headset slipped from my fingers and hit the floor. I couldn't follow it. Couldn't scream. Couldn't blink. But somewhere, buried deep, something in me still shouted: move.

I couldn't. There was no fight. Just paralysis. Pressure. The faint sound of my own pulse filling my ears.

My vision blurred at the edges.

I couldn't see him—but I could see the wall.

And in its reflection, the man was still there. Watching. Waiting. Like he'd never moved at all. Smiling. Just enough to make me hate myself.

Like this had been the plan. Like he didn't take anything I hadn't already offered.

Because monsters felt more honest than ghosts.

Then the door slid shut behind me.

CHAPTER 5

TIME DIDN'T PASS SO MUCH as it fractured.

Not like a clean break. More like old ice giving way under boots that don't belong — soft cracks spreading out, invisible until you're already falling.

Everything felt out of order.

Like I'd woken in the middle of someone else's dream. Like scenes shuffled out of a reel: a flicker of light, then black, then something in between that didn't have a name.

Metal under my cheek. Warm, like it had been holding the sun for me. Except the hum beneath it wasn't sunlight. Tires rolling. A low, uneven rhythm. Every bump was a jolt inside my ribs, sparks against machinery that wasn't supposed to be there.

I didn't know how long I'd been under.

A nap. A day. A lifetime.

The light never changed. That dull gray that doesn't belong to morning or night. Could've been dawn. Could've been ten years from now. It didn't matter.

When I tried to move, my body reminded me it had opinions. Sluggish. Wrong in ways I couldn't name, like a jacket that used to fit and now cut in all the wrong places. Fingers twitched like they were waking up from their own bad dream.

The world came back in layers.

Grimy floor smeared with oil.

Dark stains that had history.

A smell like burned plastic baked into the walls. It clung the way some fears cling — even if you wash, it's still there, stitched into your clothes, stitched into memory.

My shirt was damp. Not from heat. From sweat that had gone cold. The kind your body makes when it's been afraid too long and just decides to get lazy about it.

And then—

Her.

Red hair. Suspended. A headset clamped over her head. Mouth open, caught in the act of screaming. Except the glass between us didn't care what she was saying. Didn't care if sound existed at all.

Had that already happened? Was it happening now? Or still coming? Time folded in on itself. My brother used to say fear does that — it crumples time like laundry, except bloodier, heavier. I laughed at him back then, a sort of nervous laugh, not because he was wrong but because sometimes it was easier to laugh than to acknowledge the truth.

Maybe I was back in his garage. Maybe I'd never left. Maybe I was still holding that towel he used to wipe the oil off his hands, pretending he'd come back down the stairs. Pretending nothing had snapped when he—

No. Not now.

The shift back into the present was brutal. My ribs ached, my vision lagged at the edges like I was still buffering.

Then I heard it.

Music.

Low. Wobbly. Like it had been playing forever in an empty room. The kind of sound you find long after everyone's gone.

ABBA, maybe. Something bright, something too clean and innocent for this place. Synths clawing through static like they didn't realize they were soundtracking a funeral. Joy in the wrong place. Joy after the end of the world, like an activist protesting the obvious.

I turned my head, slow. Too slow. Felt like moving underwater.

Through the divider I saw him.

The Doctor——or the man who wanted me to believe he was one. His hand was on the wheel, the other tapping out the beat against his leg like he'd been born to it. Humming along.

Not the hum of a man with a plan to save you.

The hum of a man who'd already knew——had decided——how this story would end, and was patient enough to wait for me to notice.

The dash-light washed his face in a sickly glow, too clean to belong here, a disconnection I couldn't place.

He sat in the driver's seat like a photograph of a person instead of the person himself.

Hair perfect. Collar pressed. Skin pale in that not-quite-alive way that photographs well but feels wrong in real life. He was the kind of guy toothpaste ads picked when they were looking for "trustworthy" where trustworthy didn't exist.

Nobody that clean ever is.

The worst part wasn't how calm he seemed. It was how prepared. Every blink. Every steady breath. A performance. A script he'd practiced for years, word by word, until he could wear it like a face.

"Are you ready for something real?"

The voice floated out of him, and for a heartbeat I didn't know if it came from his mouth or the inside of my skull. It landed in the pit of my stomach like a dropped stone. Whatever it meant, it wasn't good. It didn't *feel* good. It felt like misdirection.

The windshield cleared as if a curtain rose on a play I'd never agreed to be in. Outside, the world passed in stitched-together fragments — not fast, not slow. Just broken. Salt-stained roads shimmered with ghosts. Sidewalks that had drowned a decade ago and never came back. Chain-link fences twisted like grave markers for storms no one named... or witnessed.

We rolled past the arcade. Still standing. Still trying. Windows punched out — hollow sockets staring at nothing. Its sign flickered like a dying code, like it wanted to spell help but forgot how.

The rest of the town wasn't destroyed. Just abandoned in that quiet way where the people leave but the bones stay behind, still trying to look alive.

The last light before the dunes was a neon fishing dock. Half-lit. Still blinking.

Even ghosts have routines.

My heart kept count of every landmark. Every bump. Every loose wire rattling inside the van. Not because I wanted to. Because it was the only thing left to hold onto.

Inside, the van was its own grave. A light flickered in a cracked casing near the ceiling. A cooler sat duct-taped shut like something alive was inside that might escape. Precious cargo that couldn't be spilled A tray of syringes rolled lazily with each turn, clinking like wind chimes in hell.

A rag. Grease-stained. Forgotten.

And a glove. Small. Worn. Curled in the corner like an animal that had given up.

I catalogued it all like evidence. Because maybe that's what it was — a record of what came before. Or a warning for what was coming next.

Outside, the sky looked sick. Not storm-sick. World-sick. Greenish and bruised, like it had held its breath for so long it forgot how to exhale. Clouds sagged low, heavy and unmoving — an atmosphere that wanted to pin us down.

The ocean peeked out behind the dunes. Closer than it should've been. Too close. Like it had been creeping forward for years and nobody had the time or the guts to stop it.

And the heat—

It wasn't sunlight.

It was weight.

Thick. Personal. The sun had made up its mind about us and we didn't get a vote.

The van slowed.

The windshield sharpened, refocused, and there it was.

Not a house.

Not really.

A growth. A shape the land hadn't asked for.

Three stories of rot and surrender. Wood faded to gray by salt and time. Siding peeled off in long, curling strips like dead skin. No path. No welcome. No signs of life. Just a shape squatting in the sand, waiting for something to crawl back inside.

And that turret in the back?

Not a lighthouse. Not anymore.

Just a vertebra from something bigger — something that once guided people home and now only watched them drown.

It hadn't been built.

It had been left.

Forgotten.

Or maybe remembered too well.

My pulse spiked. My body agreed.

I shoved myself upright, ribs screaming *don't*.

Did it anyway.

My arms shook like old radio towers in a storm, shuddering under some invisible signal. My knees buckled, not because I was weak but because gravity suddenly felt like an idea I'd forgotten how to believe in. The van wasn't a van anymore; it was a wave I was trying to run through. Heavy. Dragging.

I lunged for the back doors anyway.

The van swerved hard, tires howling like they were in on the joke. The floor tilted and vanished from under me. Shoulder first, then head. Metal against bone. White noise exploding behind my eyes. The pain wasn't blunt—it was sharp, personal. Like it knew my name.

I slid down the wall, skin against cold steel, a thing discarded.

Around me everything went airborne—syringes, coolers, reality itself, all floating in the split-second before gravity reclaimed it.

The driver's door opened. Hinges creaked. Footsteps outside. Sand crunching slow and steady, like the countdown before a gunshot. He was coming.

I tried to move. Tried to breathe. My body answered in small twitches, like it wasn't sure if it belonged to me anymore.

Then the rear doors burst open.

Light punched its way in—hot, accusatory. The kind of light that makes everything uglier. And there he was. Smiling. Like nothing had gone wrong. Like this was all a stage cue.

"You shouldn't be awake," he said. His voice was soft, almost amused.

He climbed inside quick and smooth, movements like liquid. Confidence built into his bones.

I scrambled back on instinct—a roach scattering from kitchen light. My hand hit something small and sharp. Syringe. Didn't think. Just swung.

The needle scraped his face, then jabbed his ribs, then buried itself again. Each stab sent a jolt through my arm like I'd punched a live wire. Bright, electric. Too fast to feel good. He grunted and staggered—just enough to look human.

And I ran with it.

Hope flickered up for half a second—stupid, bright hope. Long enough to lie to me.

I pushed myself up. Knees shaking like bad signals. Muscles lagging like a scratched record. Didn't matter. I moved. One foot. Then the other.

I shoved through the open doors and sunlight hit me like a slap.

Outside: nothing. Just road. No houses. No fences. No help. Blacktop carving a line through sand and silence.

Didn't think. Didn't breathe. Ran. Boots hit pavement, legs screaming, lungs pulling air like broken machinery. Half-sprint, half-fall, like if I stopped, I'd never start again.

The wind clawed at me—not a breeze, a warning. It didn't whisper go; it screamed you're already too late. The heat pressed down my neck, not sunlight anymore but a fever, a punishment.

Vision narrowed. Not dark, just closing in, like the world was tired of playing pretend.

I should've stopped. Should've stayed home. Should've bailed on Jackson. Should've seen it coming.

Liam would've. He always did.

Don't trust anyone who acts above it all, he used to say.

Anyone who looks like they've got answers? They're hiding something worse.

I didn't listen then either. So I kept running.

My legs weren't legs anymore. They were panic. They were guilt. They were the last echo of go before the ground rose up to stop me.

"Keep going."

I heard it. My voice. Or maybe his. Didn't matter. It was all I had.

Twenty yards. Maybe. The road curved. Freedom curled around it like a secret.

Then he hit me.

Not a hand. Not a snatch. A full-body collision, like a car. Like gravity owed him a favor.

I didn't fall. I crashed. Chest against asphalt. Air gone. Teeth clicked like they were trying to bite the panic back in.

I opened my mouth to scream. Nothing came.

So I shouted anyway.

"LET ME GO!"

It didn't come out brave.

It came out ugly. Raw. My voice cracking against the night like it didn't belong to me anymore. I kicked, twisted, clawed at the pavement like maybe it would side with me, open up, swallow me whole, anything but leave me there. My nails scraped asphalt until sparks of pain danced up my fingers. Nothing gave.

He laughed—not mean, not loud. Just even. A sound without edges. Like I was a minor inconvenience. Like he was checking his watch, waiting for me to run out of air. Like I was late to my own funeral.

Then his arm looped under my chin. Another across my chest. His grip wasn't mechanical. It was personal. A practiced squeeze. The kind you don't forget once it finds you.

"She was right about you, Ty," he murmured into my ear. Too close. Too familiar. His breath damp and steady. "You're going to be fun."

My stomach flipped, bile clawing up my throat. My skin rebelled, crawling against itself like it wanted to run away before I could. Everything in me screamed no, but the sound stayed trapped behind my teeth.

I fought back anyway. Every muscle. Even the ones that had already quit. My fists found his ribs, my knees his thighs. He didn't flinch. He didn't need to. He was stronger—not in a gym-rat way, but in the way of someone who's done this before. Someone who's practiced. Someone who already knows how it ends.

My body twitched once, then folded, everything dimming like a switch flipped somewhere I couldn't reach. Thunder cracked overhead, rolling down the beach like the world was tired of watching. Light flared behind my eyes—white, red, black. Colors meant for warnings. Or endings.

And then—

Music.

Somewhere under the static behind my eyes, it rose again: that same warped disco track. Upbeat. Relentless. Wrong. A party song in a mausoleum. The kind of song that loops in a place where no one survives long enough to hear the last chorus.

His breathing stayed steady, possessive, like none of this mattered. Like I was already his.

I went limp. My heels dragged twin grooves in the sand as he hauled me backward across the beach, back toward the van. Not like a prisoner. Not even like a body. Like I was a piece of the plan falling neatly into place. Like the game hadn't ended at all. Just unlocked a new level.

CHAPTER 6

I woke to humming.

Not the van. Not a machine.

Something smaller. Closer.

Like a tune that had crawled up the back of my skull, curling through bone and nerve the way ivy sneaks into brick.

A child's tune. Soft. Sweet. Almost kind.

Almost.

It kept looping, folding over itself. A warped record. A lullaby sung in a room where the child had already left. Safety rewritten as something else.

I didn't move. Not at first.

Wasn't sure if I was lying on the floor or if the floor had swallowed me whole. My body hurt in a way that didn't belong to bruises. This was the deeper ache—the kind you inherit, the kind that grows in marrow and stays even when the skin forgets.

Somewhere under the hum, a buzz lived in my ears. Thin and high, like the ghost of a scream left behind after an explosion. My mouth tasted like metal and melted plastic and something bitter beneath it all, the taste of a lie you've believed for too long.

I lifted my cheek from the floor. The sound it made was like duct tape ripping from skin—a sound I'd only ever heard once before, when Liam had peeled gauze from a wound he wasn't ready to show me. *Don't look. It's worse when you look.*

There was a whirring then. Small. Deliberate. Not my brain. Something outside of me. A breath that wasn't a breath. A lens rotating in its socket. Something watching.

I opened my eyes.

The bay windows blinked back at me, blinds half-closed like tired eyes behind heavy lashes. Daylight slanted in crooked, making shadows that didn't match the furniture. Rain tapped the glass in a rhythm too calm to trust, steady as a clock in a house with no clocks. It didn't care if I noticed. It was going to fall either way.

Across the room—a door.

Too smooth to be wood anymore. Layered with paint until the grain drowned. Corners bubbled from moisture. Black-green bruises climbed the hardwood like mold had learned to breathe.

It didn't look shut.

It looked sealed.

To the left, a built-in closet. Slats snapped like ribs in a tight grip. Like something had tried to force its way out... or in.

The walls had once been pink. Muted, waiting-room pink. Not cheerful. Not quite sad. Time had curdled it into flesh near the ceiling, bruised brown near the baseboards. Shapes bloomed in the stains that I didn't want to name.

And then—

The dolls.

Every shelf lined with them.

Neatly arranged. Legs crossed. Eyes open.

Frozen in poses that were almost polite.

One smiled too wide, its mouth fixed around a secret it would never tell. Another was still in its packaging, arms bent under warped plastic like it had tried to claw its way out before time stopped.

I sat up too fast. The room tilted, then swayed, as if it wanted me gone, wanted to vomit out a bad seed.

The humming grew louder. Not from the dolls. From the walls. Like the house itself was breathing, waiting for me to match it.

I forced myself to stand. My body still felt wired wrong—nerves misfiring, muscles lagging behind thought like a buffering video in hell. My jacket hung heavy on me, hood brushing my face. My boots —gone. Socks were filthy, sticking to the warped floorboards. For the first time in years I felt unarmored, like I'd been peeled down to my softest part and left there.

You're not dead yet, Ty.

But it didn't feel true.

I staggered forward, unsure if I was looking for an exit, a weapon, or just proof that I still belonged to the world.

The rain was a steady hiss against the windows, tapping like fingers that didn't want to be let in. Just wanted to antagonize. Each drop felt louder in here. The air was close. Dust and rot clung to my tongue like tarnished pennies bleeding copper and zinc.

And then I saw it.

Tucked into the far corner beneath a crooked shaft of half-light, slumped like it had been waiting for me, was a dollhouse. Handmade. Two feet tall. Familiar in a way that made my stomach go tight.

Not just a toy.

This house.

The turret. The sagging frame. The rot in the corners. Every detail nailed down like it had been carved from the same wood. Someone hadn't just built it from memory—they had lived it. Worshipped it. Documented every inch like a confession.

I moved closer, careful, the way you do when you're sure something's breathing but pretending not to. The closer I got, the worse it felt. Too detailed. Too loved. Every room accounted for, every window placed with a reverence that didn't feel like nostalgia so much as hunger.

The rain rattled harder.

I reached out. One of the walls swung open on a hidden hinge, slow as a jaw unhinging.

Inside—

Not furniture. Not tiny beds or smiling plastic parents.

Wallets. Phones. Jewelry.

A locket etched with a name I didn't recognize but felt like I should. A cracked phone screen lit up briefly, just enough to show me a boy's face—maybe fifteen. Brown hair. Birthmark on his jaw.

He looked like me.

Too much like me.

My throat closed. I reached deeper. More phones. More wallets. My breath came faster, shallower, hands moving without my permission. Panic making me clumsy.

One phone still had a charge.

I unlocked it—no password—and typed the only number I remembered.

It rang.

Once.

Twice.

"You've reached the number for—"

Come on. Jackson. Pick up.

I tried again. Twice. Voicemail.

Third time—

"Hello?"

Her voice. Sophia.

It cracked through the speaker like a ghost breaking the surface of water.

"Sophia! It's me—it's Ty—I—"

"Ty?" she asked, confused. "Where are you? Why are you calling us from—?"

The phone went black.

Just like that.

Gone.

I stood there holding it like it owed me something. But it didn't. It never would.

How many kids had stood here before me? How many thought

they were clever for opening the dollhouse? How many dialed someone who loved them only to hear the line die mid-sentence?

Something inside me cracked.

"Fuck!"

It tore out of me jagged, desperate. Not a curse. More like a prayer that didn't know where to land.

I hurled the phone across the room. It hit the wall with a sound I didn't want to name. Scattered bone. Glass. Memory.

And then the silence came rushing back.

The rain. The hum. The smell of dust and old metal.

The dolls still watching.

The house still waiting.

Then—

A sound.

Thump.

From above.

Or maybe below.

And a second later—

The closet slats shifted. Just slightly. Just enough to say:

You're not alone.

CHAPTER 7

IT WAS SOFT, but I heard it. A shuffle—barely audible over the electric hum in the walls and the taps of rain at the window. Wasn't the dolls. Wasn't the door. It was somewhere else. Smaller. Intentional.

From the closet. One of the panels hung crooked, barely attached, like a rib cage peeled back.

I froze.

There was no rush. Not this time. My pulse crawled up the back of my throat, slow and cold. I turned toward the sound.

And saw it.

A shape crouched behind the slats. Not moving—just... waiting. Low to the ground. Tucked into the dark like it belonged there. Like it had been there a while.

I didn't call out.

Didn't ask if anyone was there. Just stepped forward, the soles of my socked feet kissing the floor with the softest tap. My breath felt like too much noise. The closer I got, the smaller I felt.

Whatever it was, I told myself I could take it. But I didn't believe it. Not here. Not in this house.

I reached for the knob.

It gave with a tired groan, like it had been opened too many times for all the wrong reasons.

Then—

"Please! Please—don't hurt me!"

The voice hit me harder than any ghost ever could. Young. High. Cracked from crying too quietly for too long. A girl. Ten, maybe eleven. She pressed herself against the back of the closet like the walls might open and take her somewhere safer.

Her hair was neat. Too neat. Brushed into long dark ribbons like someone had done it for a pageant, not a school photo. Her dress had little strawberries on the hem, clean and stiff like it had been ironed for inspection. White socks. Shiny black shoes. Pristine.

Wrong.

She didn't look like she lived here. She looked like she'd been presented here. Lightning illuminated the windows, slicing through the decaying space in fractured lines of white.

I dropped to a knee, palms out, like she was a frightened animal. Or maybe I was.

"I already have a brother," she whispered, voice quivering. "His name's Nathan. He's in fifth grade but acts like a baby."

She sniffled. "I have a dad. And a dog. And I just want to go home."

I didn't reach for her. Didn't move closer. Just let my arms rest on my knees. Let my voice come out calm. Gentle. Real. Thunder rolled in the distance.

"What's your name?"

She hesitated.

"I'm not supposed to say."

"Okay," I said. "You don't have to. But do you know where we are? How long you've been here?"

She looked around, and it hit me—she hadn't really seen the room until now. Her eyes drifted to the wall-mounted camera, then caught on the dollhouse. She stared too long at the second-floor bedroom.

"Why am I back here? I haven't been here since the first night," she murmured. "Since they wanted me to see myself— what they wanted me to be."

"Don't worry, it's just me," I said.

She sniffled, wiping her nose with the back of her hand like it was muscle memory. I reached into my jacket and tore the inner seam loose, holding out a scrap of lining.

"Here. It's clean. Or, clean enough."

She took it like it was the first gift she'd ever been offered. Like it meant something.

"You remind me of my niece," I said, quiet. "She's smart. Smarter than me most days."

Something flickered in her eyes. Recognition, maybe. Not of me —but of being remembered. Of someone out there still knowing who you are.

"Let's get you out of there," I offered gently.

But she shook her head, hard.

"No. I can't—I can't go out there."

"It's okay," I said. "There's nothing out here. No monsters. I promise."

She didn't answer.

I waited with her.

Eventually, she shifted forward. Slow. Careful. Her eyes never left the dollhouse.

We sat side by side. Her arms wrapped around her knees, mine pulled in close. Neither of us looking at each other. Both listening.

She pressed the scrap of jacket to her nose. Breathed it in like it might smell like someone's home.

"You're the first real person I've seen," she said, almost like a joke. Almost.

"What do you remember before this?" I asked.

Her eyes ticked toward the camera, then back to me.

"There was a car. I was walking home from school. I think... I think it was a van."

My stomach turned.

"Me too," I said. "Where's home for you? Are you from here? The Outer Banks?"

She gave a slow nod. "Yeah, me and my family. My address is 14—"

A small red light on the camera blinked. Slow, then faster.

She stopped. "Wait... No! Did I do something wrong?"

A noise cut her off.

Low. Mechanical. A groan. Not fast. Just enough to shift the light.

We both turned.

The door beside us had cracked open—just an inch—but the sliver of darkness it spilled was enough to make her shrink.

A shadow stretched across the floor, inching toward her like a leash.

She flinched. Kicked backward. Her hand shot out—grabbed the closet frame—but the hand found her wrist.

"No—please, I'll be quiet—I'll be better—" she gasped. "I'll be good."

She smiled—just for a second. Like it was part of the routine. Like someone had told her that if she smiled, it wouldn't hurt as bad. But her lip betrayed her. Trembled. Cracked open on the word good like she didn't believe it either.

The hand didn't yank. It didn't claw, or snatch, or tear.

It guided.

Slow.

Practiced.

Almost... gentle.

And somehow, that made it worse.

Like she wasn't a person—just a prop in someone else's play. A figurine returned to its shelf.

Something inside me cracked. My knees almost buckled as I surged forward, teeth grit, throat raw.

"NO!" I shouted, voice splitting open on the way out. "Let her go!"

But the room didn't flinch. The walls didn't echo back.

It was like I wasn't in it anymore—just some faded thing screaming behind the glass of a bad dream.

The girl thrashed once—screamed, high and desperate. I lunged, hand out, reaching—almost caught the sleeve of her dress.

Almost.

She vanished through the door in one blur of motion. Like she'd never been there.

"LET HER GO!"

My fists slammed into the door hard enough to shake the frame.

Metal. Not wood. Not something you could kick through like in the movies.

It gave nothing back—no rattle, no echo—just a deep, dull thud that swallowed my voice whole and returned only a shock and vibration that ran through my fists and up my arms.

The scream inside my chest hitched, collapsed, came out as breath too fast, too loud. My body couldn't decide if it was fighting or falling apart. My knuckles scraped; my shoulder ached.

Outside, the storm clawed at the house, wind slamming branches against the siding, thunder rolling so close it shook the floorboards. But none of it mattered—the real violence was already inside. The scream cut off mid-breath. Gone. Like somebody had pulled the plug. The silence after felt like a trap.

Then the door clicked.

Soft. Final.

A mouth closing. A coffin sealing.

I lunged again, slower this time, like I already knew it wouldn't matter. My palm hit the metal and stayed there, fingers clawing for anything to grip. Too late.

I yanked the handle. Slammed my shoulder into it. Nothing. My breath came in ragged bursts, ugly and uneven, the sound of a boy trying to be something more than a boy.

"OPEN IT!" I shouted, the words half-choked, half-gutted. "Come on—OPEN IT!"

Nothing answered. Not a voice. Not footsteps. Just silence. Not the comforting kind—the kind that feels intentional. The kind that means you're not alone, but no one's coming.

I turned in circles, eyes darting from the camera to the closet to the floor. Looking for anything. Some sign this hadn't just happened.

I lunged for the closet first—ripped the door open so hard it rattled against the wall. Empty. Just a tangle of dust and wires, an old vent shaft behind the panel. Too small for anyone to crawl through. I banged my fist against it anyway, just to hear something move.

Then the main door. I gripped the knob, twisted until my wrist screamed. Locked. I slammed my shoulder into it once, twice—nothing. It didn't give. The metal was cold. Not like something locked. Like something sealed.

My breath hitched. I pressed my ear to the wood, listening for anything on the other side—shoes, breathing, footsteps—but there was nothing. Only the faint static of the cameras overhead, like they were waiting to see how long it would take me to break.

I spun back toward the center of the room. Nothing left. Just the space she'd been sitting in. The air still shaped like her.

The dolls in the corner stared back. They didn't scream. They never did. And neither could I.

I'd promised her she was safe. Promised I'd help. And she was gone—because I wasn't fast enough. Because I wasn't strong enough. Because I thought I had more time.

The shame burned hotter than the helplessness. Deeper. More permanent.

I slammed the door again—harder. It didn't move. Looked like wood but felt cold. Too cold. Not like something built to open—something designed to trap.

My fingers traced the edges, scraping seams, searching for hinges. It was fake. Like everything else in this place. Built to look like it could break, but couldn't.

My chest started to shake. My breath rattled in my lungs. Still—no footsteps. No scream.

Just... nothing.

It hit me then, the way it hit me when they pulled the sheet back from Liam's face—not fast, not loud. Just final.

My knees gave. I dropped back onto the hardwood, the boards cold and unwelcoming under my spine. Didn't want to hold myself up anymore.

The girl's shoe had come off in the struggle. It lay a few feet away —upturned, glossy, too small, like it was still waiting for her to step back into it.

I kept hearing her voice in my head: "I have a dad. And a dog." Like if she listed them out, it would make her real again. Like it would keep her safe. But it didn't.

"Hold it together, Ty."

I said it like a prayer. Like Liam might hear it, wherever he was. Like maybe that mattered.

I hadn't saved him either. What was the point of being strong if I was always too late?

The silence pressed in. Louder now.

I stared at the door. Waited for it to breathe. It didn't.

"You're okay," I whispered. "You're still okay."

But I wasn't sure I believed it.

Somewhere in the walls, a hum rose—faint, like a lullaby twisted through static. Or maybe it was just in my head.

I looked up. The camera was still there. Watching.

And for the first time since waking up, I didn't try to posture. Didn't try to act calm. Or angry. Or strong.

I let the fear settle in. Just a little. Like water finding a crack.

Because whatever this place was, it wasn't improvising. It had done this before.

And I was already behind.

I didn't have a plan. Didn't have backup. And whatever they were waiting to see from me?

I think it had already started.

CHAPTER 8

THE CAMERA DIDN'T BLINK ANYMORE. DIDN'T whir. It just sat there in the corner like it had been carved into the wall, a single black eye watching, waiting, sure of itself. Predators don't pace when they've already cornered you.

It wasn't observing. It was studying. The way a surgeon studies a body before the first cut. The way a kid watches a moth in a jar, already knowing it's not getting out.

Something tugged at the back of my skull, invisible but there, a thread pulling tight. No matter where I stepped, that eye followed. My chest cinched smaller, breath coming in damp, shallow pulls. This wasn't a room. This was a trap. Or a jar where moths were studied.

A whisper rose under the noise of my heart: *This place was made to break you.*

And maybe it was.

And maybe I'd let it.

No.

Not today.

I bolted.

The bay windows yawned ahead like mouths too wide to scream.

Fog smeared across them in long white streaks, claw marks from something trying to get in or something trying to get out. Outside, the storm had gone feral—the sky a sick animal gray, the sea hurling itself at the house in grief-soaked rage.

I slammed my shoulder into the window frame. It rattled, but it didn't budge. Bolted. Of course it was.

The wallpaper closed in on me, soft pink turned strangler's noose. The corners bowed inward, shadows leaning like eavesdroppers. Everything felt too quiet and too loud at the same time. Lace choking me.

Nothing here could save me.

Except—

The dollhouse. Squatting in the corner like a knowing little altar. Its turret gleamed faintly under the storm light, as if it had been waiting for me, for this moment.

I grabbed it. It was heavier than it looked, a brick disguised as a toy. It slammed into my ribs like a pipe but I held on, staggered back, and with everything I had left I hurled it at the glass.

The window screamed. Teeth exploded outward, shards spiraling like they were fleeing. Rain punched through the breach, wet and furious, curtains whipping into the air like ghosts trying to escape their second death.

The storm entered the room like it had been waiting too. Everything roared. Even me, maybe.

I climbed onto the sill. Fingers slick with rain. Heart hammering so hard it shook my vision. I glanced back at the camera one last time —its dark lens, patient and still—and then at the slick roof and the void below. One wrong move and I'm gone. But maybe I'd already be dead either way.

I jumped.

The roof hit like punishment. Hard. Cold. Unforgiving. My knees crumpled on contact. One foot slipped, a tile skidding out from under me and vanishing into the dark.

"God—" My palms slapped the slope, skin scraping raw on shingles. I pressed myself flat, chest to the cold roof like I could merge with it. Rain whipped across my face. The wind tore at my hood, plastered my hair to my forehead. My socks slid uselessly, no grip. Crawling on ice.

"Enough," I hissed. I hooked my thumbs into the wet cotton and yanked them off, one after the other, flinging the sodden lumps into the void. Bare feet slapped against the roof, cold and rough, but at least I could feel the ridges now—the grit, the anchor points.

I started crawling again. Crawl. Grip. Breathe. Don't look down.

But of course, I did.

The drop looked worse than I thought.

Three stories, maybe more. The courtyard below opened like a wound—mud, glass, and twisted iron fencing glinting up at me through the rain. It all looked sharp enough to swallow me whole. Even if I timed the fall just right, even if the wind was kind... I wouldn't make it.

Still, I looked. Scanned the roof for another way down. A trellis. A pipe. An awning. Anything that wasn't suicide in disguise.

Nothing.

Just the turret above me, jagged and cruel against the storm. Beyond it, the slate peaks stretched into the dark, slick with rain and tilted at angles that made my stomach turn. Maybe if I crawled toward the north wing, I could find a gutter—

Lightning tore the sky open.

And for one heartbeat, I saw him.

A figure, standing at the far edge of the roof. Still. Watching.

His outline flickered between frames, as if the storm itself was stuttering.

"Liam."

My brother's name crawled out of my throat before I could stop it.

I blinked—

Gone.

Just a flash. Just the drugs, I told myself. But my blood didn't believe it. My heart didn't either.

I turned away, crawling fast now, my palms slipping against the wet slate. My shoulder caught on a bent antenna, the metal groaning, scolding me for trying. The wind came next—a full-body shove that nearly sent me off the roof. My chest hit the tiles hard enough to knock the air from me.

No way down.

No way out.

The house wasn't letting me go.

Rain poured into my eyes, into my mouth. It crawled under my skin, found every place I'd tried to hold myself together and pried it open again. I didn't want to go back inside. But I couldn't stay here.

And then the scream.

Not mine.

Not the wind's either.

Hers.

It was the girl.

The sound carved into the back of my skull, playing on repeat in the storm.

I wasn't going to end up like her.

I swore it.

I turned, slow, gravity pulling at every limb like it wanted to keep me here. Crawled forward until the roof tilted again beneath me, the angle changing as if the house was leading me somewhere.

And that's when I saw it.

A window.

Long. Low. Trimmed in brass too fancy for a place that stank this much of rot.

I dropped flat, peering through the glass.

And froze.

A shadow moved behind it—smooth, deliberate. A woman gliding through the hall like she owned the ground she walked on. Her heels clicked against marble in an even rhythm. Her hair—shoulder-length, dark and wet-looking even in the light—caught the faint glow of a chandelier above her. She looked too perfect to belong here. Too deliberate to be a ghost.

The woman from the club.

She wore a cropped graphite jacket, the kind that shimmered faintly when it caught the fluorescents. Underneath, a slate halter top hugged her shoulders—simple, sleeveless, sharp at the collar. Her pants were high-waisted and matte, slit just enough at the ankle to show the glint of metallic straps from her heels. No jewelry. No excess. Every line of her looked clean, efficient, deliberate.

She didn't look lost.

She looked like she'd been waiting for me.

Her voice returned in my head, smoke-thick and certain:

"You follow strangers like you're looking to be converted."

Was she part of this? Had she always been?

Then came the doctor's echo, grinning through my memory:

"She's around, by the way—if you're hoping for another glimpse."

Not a warning. Or a comfort. A setup.

Heaven dangled in front of me, close enough to touch.

Close enough to make hell feel personal.

I watched her go.

One step.

Two.

I found another window—narrow, dark, rimmed in grime. A bathroom. The frame smelled of rust and rain.

I climbed up, bracing my body against the sill, letting the wind steady me the way a ship steadies a sailor. My fingers dug into the wood. My pulse counted itself in my ears. Five heartbeats. Six.

Then I kicked.

The first hit cracked the glass, a sound like a bone giving way under pressure. The second blow sent shards cascading inward, glittering for a second before vanishing into the dark. I pulled out the sharp remnants and ducked through shoulder-first, elbow slamming against porcelain. Pain bloomed sharp and white at my arm. I didn't yell—just bit down until the scream came out silent.

The floor caught me. Cold tile. Broken glass. I stayed there for a second, palms against grit, rain still clinging to me. Behind me the storm hissed through the broken window, but inside... inside it was worse. Silent in a way that wasn't peace. Silent like a mouth waiting to open.

It felt like the room wasn't empty at all, but patient. Listening. Waiting for a squeak of my shoe, a breath drawn too loud, the moment I'd let myself believe I was safe. Not watching me—watching me notice.

Anyone here would have heard me breaking that glass. I rose slow, like sudden movement might wake something curled just out of sight. The cold tile vibrated faintly under my feet, a hum I could barely feel but couldn't un-feel. Old wiring, maybe. Or a heart, somewhere in the walls. Not mine. Just like the van.

My knees almost buckled. The room tilted, then righted itself. Across from me, a cracked mirror held a version of me I didn't want to see. Blood at my collar. Rain dripping from my jaw like I was leaking. My eyes too wide, too white. Like I'd been scraped out and only the fear had been left behind.

It didn't look like me. But it was. Whatever pieces of me were still left to fight with.

I told myself it was enough. I was out of the room. Off the camera. For now.

But my lungs wouldn't listen. They kept dragging air in like I was still on that roof. Still in the storm. Still falling. The panic had planted itself under my ribs and refused to leave, like it knew something I didn't.

Above me, the fluorescent light buzzed like a mosquito trapped in glass. The sink dripped. One. Two. One. Two. The rhythm of something alive and waiting.

I turned slowly, scanning. Corners. Vent grates. Shadows. Nothing obvious. Nothing visible. But the feeling deepened anyway.

It was like standing in a church after midnight. You couldn't see the presence—but it saw you.

It always saw you.

I didn't know where I was in the house. Didn't know how far I'd gotten or who else might be here. Didn't know if the girl was still breathing or already behind glass.

And for the first time since waking up in this nightmare, I didn't even have the illusion of control.

But if they'd built this house to break people like me, then they'd made one mistake.

I was already broken. And now I burned.

CHAPTER 9

THE HOUSE FELT wrong the moment I stepped inside. Not wrong like rot, not yet—wrong like a stage set. Everything too neat, too still, too arranged, like someone had studied "comfort" from a TV show and tried to recreate it with paper props. Like a dollhouse.

Cold air hissed from a vent overhead, artificial and thin. It cut through the wet clothes clinging to my skin, each recycled gust crawling up my spine until goosebumps prickled over my ribs. My jacket hung heavy with rain, cuffs dripping onto tile. It felt like the house was tracing its fingers over me, trying to anticipate what I'd do.

Down below, something kept whistling—machines, steady and low. A rhythm that wasn't quite alive. Like the house was breathing for someone who couldn't anymore.

I wrapped a towel around my hand until it bit into my palm. The sting grounded me. Better than the numbness. Better than the silence.

Light caught on something near the sink. A shard of glass. Long, jagged, waiting. I crouched, picked it up. Cold. Solid. A lie I could hold. A weapon. Maybe a ticket out.

That's when I heard it.

Click.

Click.

Click.

Footsteps—sharp, deliberate. Not panicked. Not searching. Just... arriving.

The doorknob turned. Slowly. Lazy, like it thought it was in charge.

I hid. Held my breath.

She stepped into the bathroom with a sound like punctuation, heels tapping the tile one at a time. She didn't glance around. Didn't hesitate. She already knew the shape of the room.

"Aw, look at you..." Her voice was dipped in sugar and scorn. "Bleeding all over my floor like a little Jackson Pollock."

She crouched, pinching a shard of glass between her fingers the way some people hold a cigarette. She turned it, watching the light bounce, her smile flickering—thin, dangerous, almost human for half a second before it calcified again.

"You've got nerve," she said, her voice velvet over something sharper. "Stupid, reckless nerve. I like that. Reminds me of the boys back home who thought they could save me."

She leaned in closer, eyes glinting. "They all disappeared, too."

Her shoulders rolled beneath her cropped jacket as she rose, heels clicking soft and slow as she crossed to the tub. Each step was a circle, a cat stalking a bird that thought it had gotten away.

She stopped in front of the curtain.

I went still, breath locked in my throat.

With a whip-crack she yanked it open, the rings screaming on the rod.

Nothing.

Her shoulders dipped. Barely.

"Cute."

She clicked her tongue, blowing out a bored puff of air. "God, I'm getting rusty."

She turned from the tub, heels clicking toward the hallway, her attention already gone.

That's when I moved.

I lunged from behind the door, the shard clenched in my hand like a promise I couldn't take back.

It wasn't clean. It wasn't noble. It was everything I had left.

The glass sank into her back with a wet, tearing crack.

She gasped—strangled, startled. Her arms shot up like she thought she could grab time midair. She staggered toward the stairs and the banister caught her too late. Her heels slid.

Her body twisted and then dropped.

She hit the stairs hard—once, then again. Her head struck the edge with a sound that seemed to belong in a house like this. A dull, final crack. Like the world letting go.

She tumbled the rest of the way, limbs folding beneath her, boneless, weightless. A marionette with its strings freshly cut.

She landed at the bottom of the stairs like the house had spit her out.

One arm bent under her. The other flung wide, fingers crooked like they'd tried to grab hold of air and found nothing. Her hair spilled across her face like a curtain, still catching the weak light from the chandelier above but dark now, sticky with blood.

Her eyes were open.

Not blinking. Not pleading. Just... open.

I didn't move. Couldn't tell if I was frozen or braced. My body thought it was shock, but it wasn't. Not yet. It was that pause before you know what you're looking at.

She didn't twitch. Didn't breathe.

Just stared—still calculating, still present in a way corpses shouldn't be.

Was she dead?

I stared longer than I should've, waiting for a blink, a shudder, anything to tell me I wasn't standing in the middle of a nightmare. Nothing.

I inhaled, shallow. Careful. Like even my breath might wake her.

She looked arranged. Too still.

Like something meant to be found.

Like bait.

She had to be, right?

God, I needed her to be.

Because if she wasn't—

No. Don't think it.

But the thought slid in anyway, cold and sideways:

What if she was alive?

What if she was an innocent in all of this and needed help?

No. She knew.

I stepped back. Half a step. Then another. Watching. Waiting. Her head had hit the stairs—hard enough that the sound was still in my teeth.

But it wasn't the same.

Not like Liam.

He chose it.

And I missed the signs.

My stomach rolled, not because this reminded me how it happened, but because it reminded me I hadn't stopped it. That same breathless hush after. That same stillness pressing behind your ribs like smoke. That awful, aching unknowing. The moment when you realize you can't take something back.

She wasn't moving.

Neither had he.

Not when I found him.

Just the wind in the garage.

And that same goddamn question, heavier than the rope:

Is there anything I could've done differently?

I blinked. The image fractured. This wasn't then. This wasn't him. But my body didn't know the difference.

What if this was that moment?

The space between pain and response.

Between survival and death.

I edged toward the stairs. Slow. Careful. Like even gravity might betray me if I wasn't deliberate.

She hadn't moved.

Crumpled at the bottom where the stairs gave her up. Limbs splayed, too limp to be conscious. Too careless to be faking it.

But it wasn't the posture that got to me.

It was her face.

Not the blood. Not the bruises.

The vacancy.

Her eyes were open. But they weren't seeing anything.

Yet that orange flicker behind her pupils remained—weak, buried, but there. Like the orange lights in the van.

I stepped down. Each stair creaked, warning me of what I might find. My pulse thudded in my ears. Not from fear. From the possibility.

What if I had to finish it?

What if she blinked?

What if she smiled?

Halfway down, I stopped.

Her hand lay twisted on the floor, fingers bent at angles no one uses while living. Her wrist had already gone a color the living don't wear. Her cropped graphite jacket had slid halfway off one shoulder, flecked red where splinters had caught her skin on the way down. Beneath it, the slate halter clung tight, one strap torn, a smear of blood crossing it like someone's signature. Her high-waisted pants were bunched at the knee, scuffed and wet, one metallic heel strap snapped so the shoe dangled crooked from her foot.

No movement.

I reached the bottom. The machines deeper in the house kept humming—low, steady, constant. A pulse of something manufactured. Almost like a countdown.

The house exhaled, crooked and uneven, like even its walls were trying not to be heard. Dust drifted from the rafters in slow spirals. Each creak of the floor felt like a throat clearing in another room.

I crouched beside her, hand trembling within the wet towel. Up close the damage was worse than the fall itself. The side of her skull had caved just slightly, as if the house had tried to finish what gravity started. A single thread of blood slid down her cheek, too thin to be called a wound, too perfect to be called anything but a tear someone else had cried for her.

I wanted to look away. God, I wanted to. But I didn't. Not because I thought she might wake up — she wouldn't — but because something inside me already had. Something cracked open when she hit the floor. Something that had been buried since before the funeral.

I didn't move. Couldn't. My hand clenched tighter around the towel, warm and wet and darkening in the dim light. It wasn't fear that kept me there. It was something else. A feeling that had no name, only a pulse. Power — not clean, not the kind that comes with forgiveness — but real. Mine.

Her perfume still clung to the air, sweet and antiseptic, powdered sugar over bleach. It smelled like every secret this house had tried to bury.

I leaned in, fingers trembling as I pressed two against her twisted neck. *Just like his.*

Nothing. No pulse. Only the frantic drumbeat of my own heart reminding me I was still here. She wasn't.

For a moment I just stared at her, at the girl I barely knew. Not even a name, just her voice on the dance floor, her smirk in the dark, her hand on my chest like she was choosing me for something I didn't understand.

Maybe I like your face. Maybe I think you're just sad enough to be interesting.

Whatever game she'd been playing, it ended here. And still, some part of me wished I'd known her better, if only to mourn her properly.

She'd made her choices. So had I. And now we were both paying for them. The truth settled in, cold and steady as the boards beneath us: I wasn't the one being hunted anymore. I wasn't afraid. I was dangerous.

I stood. My legs were working. My heart was pounding. I could run. Bolt through the hallway and never come back. Be free of this house and everything inside it.

Then I heard it.

Not her.

The girl.

A voice, a cry — alive, echoing from somewhere deeper inside.

I froze, caught between the front door and the scream. Between what was safe and what was right.

"You don't even know her," I whispered to myself, but the words felt hollow, like excuses I'd already worn out. If I left, I'd take that sound with me forever.

I told myself to leave and get help.

I didn't.

It came again, clearer this time, trembling through the walls. My whole body surged like a wire finally plugged in.

And I made my choice.

Somewhere inside this place, someone still needed me. And now I knew — finally knew — that I could be dangerous for someone who needed it.

CHAPTER 10

I BOLTED toward the screams and the sound of the machines, that low whine cutting through the silence like a mosquito in my skull, and followed them deeper into the house.

The main level looked...normal. Too normal.

A living room staged like it was waiting for a family that would never arrive. Plastic flowers perched stiffly on the end table, their petals dulled with age. A clock ticked but its hands were stuck, frozen at the wrong hour, like time had given up here. Books lined the shelf by color, not by use, spines uncreased, their order too neat, too intentional.

No dust. No fingerprints. No sign that anyone had ever sat in the chairs, touched the doorknobs, lived here.

It felt curated. A memory of a home instead of the thing itself. Like someone had studied a photograph of comfort and rebuilt it from the outside in, every detail correct but lifeless.

The air was stale. Sweet in places, as if perfume had been sprayed days ago and left to rot into the walls. I caught myself listening for something human — a fridge hum, floorboards settling — but the silence pressed back too heavy.

Even the photos were wrong. Black frames lined the wall, their glass gleaming, but inside were only landscapes, empty beaches, cities with no people. Not a single face stared back.

The hallway stretched on longer than it had any right to. White walls, too clean. Not clean because they were cared for—clean because they'd been scrubbed into submission. Sterile. Deadened. That kind of false cleanliness that made me think of morgues.

The air shifted colder as the floor sloped down, pulling me toward the basement.

Stairs waited at the end, spilling blue light from the doorway below. It pulsed faintly, electric and alive, wrong in a way my body knew before my brain could name it. Every step I took down creaked like it was betraying me, but I couldn't stop.

Was this all planned? Was I *supposed* to go down those stairs? Expected to? Did he know the end game even now?

The sound grew sharper as I descended. A high-pitched whine. Machines working too hard on something that shouldn't exist.

When I stepped into the room, it hit me like a fist.

It looked like a surgical suite born in hell.

Monitors blinked with data that raced too fast to read, like the numbers themselves were panicking. Panels hummed low and steady, as if conspiring with one another. The stench hit next—bleach and blood, copper and chemicals clawing for dominance until it felt like I was breathing poison.

And in the center—

Him.

The Doctor.

Scrubs clung damp to his body, half-hidden beneath a butcher's apron lacquered in red. It hung heavy and glossy, like he'd dipped it fresh into a vat of paint. A headlamp buzzed faintly above his brow, its jittering beam sweeping restless circles across the walls. His gloves were soaked through, blood trailing from the fingertips, crawling down his sleeves to drip into the pools already darkening the floor.

But he stood there like none of it mattered. Like the blood wasn't his problem.

He smiled.

"Ty." Smooth. Warm. Almost gentle. My name in his mouth sounded less like a threat and more like a welcome.

He didn't move fast, didn't posture. Just spread his hands slightly, like he'd been waiting for me all along. "You made it."

My grip tightened around the shard, glass biting into my palm. The sting kept me from shaking. "Where is she?"

Behind him, the dentist's chair gleamed beneath the lamp. Stainless steel arms. Leather seat. Straps dangling, swaying faintly as though they'd just been unbuckled.

Empty.

Just blood. Running off the seat in thin rivulets. Fresh, steady, like a metronome keeping time.

His eyes tracked mine. He tilted his head, almost tender, and adjusted his lamp so the light cut directly across the crimson. "You've got good instincts," he said softly, as if admiring me. "But you're looking in the wrong place."

My chest tightened.

He smiled again, smaller this time, like a secret he was letting me in on. "She's right beside you."

I turned—

And saw her.

The girl.

Or what was left of her.

She was curled at the base of the door, discarded like garbage, crumpled in a heap no body should fall into. Her limbs bent at angles that spat in the face of anatomy, one shoulder crushed beneath her weight as if it had caved in. Her jaw hung open, swollen purple and slack, wobbling faintly when a bubble of air rattled out of her throat. The sound was small. Almost apologetic.

Her hair was a snarl of red and black, the bow still clinging to one side like it didn't understand it was supposed to let go. The dress with the strawberries on the hem was soaked through, clinging to her little body in dark patches that turned the fruit a sick, bruised brown. One white sock had slipped down to her ankle, ringed with blood. The other was gone. Her remaining shoe—that shiny black thing that caught the light like a mirror—was spattered and cracked, tossed halfway across the room.

A bare leg jutted out at a cruel angle, the foot twisted backward, pale toes curled as if she'd fought until the very end. She hadn't been laid down. She'd been dropped. Tossed aside. Like a doll someone had ripped open to see what was inside and then lost interest.

Drips pattered steadily onto the tile, a thin rhythm keeping time with the pounding of my heart. The room closed in, every wall pressing against me, suffocating.

Her voice came back to me, clear, alive, and it made the bile surge higher.

"No. I can't—I can't go out there."

"It's okay," I said. *"There's nothing out here. No monsters. I promise."*

The echo rang too loud in my head, crueler now than anything the Doctor had said. My legs froze into ice. My throat burned, heat and bile warring until it tasted like copper and bleach on my tongue.

Her eyes—God, her eyes—didn't land on me. They stared through me, past me, seeing nothing.

A vacancy so complete it carved me hollow.

She was just a kid.

Just a kid.

My pulse hammered hard enough to shake me apart. My hands begged to move, to reach, to cover her, to do something — but I couldn't. My body locked tight, rigid, a coffin of its own. My lungs rasped, shallow, dragging in poison air that tasted like pennies and rot.

I couldn't look away.

I couldn't breathe.

And I couldn't stop thinking: *I'd promised her. But I was wrong.*

His voice slipped through the static of my head. Calm. Conversational. Too easy.

He clicked his tongue, not angry — disappointed, like I'd missed the obvious. Then he leaned forward, wiping a gloved hand across his apron. The smear of blood spread darker, like he was doodling absentmindedly.

"What—what did you—" I stammered, the smell coating the back of my throat. "What'd she do to deserve that?"

"Don't waste yourself on her," he said, quiet, almost kind. Like he was offering advice instead of twisting the knife. "You've got bigger things ahead."

The words sank deep before I could stop them. Heavy. Poisonous.

I staggered back, gagging, bile burning up my throat—when a shadow lengthened across the basement wall.

Movement.

Not normal movement. Twisted. Lurching. Wrong.

The shape of a woman.

No. No, it couldn't be—

It was her.

The girl from the club.

Her silhouette slumped down the stairwell one step at a time, jerking, broken, as if the light itself was struggling to keep up with her body.

Thmp.

The outline of a leg dragged, knee bending sideways, the foot scraping flat across the floorboards.

Thmp.

The other limb buckled. The shadow folded and snapped outward, bones bending where there was no joint.

Her arm swung dead at her side, the silhouette stretching it backward at an obscene angle, fingers twitching against the wall. The black shape smeared across the tiles, trembling like spilled ink.

Thmp. Thmp.

Her head sagged with each step, neck crooked too far, dangling from her shoulders like a marionette cut half free. And the shadow exaggerated it, making the head swing farther, farther, as if the strings were being yanked by an unseen hand.

Then the sound began.

A low, wet rattle. Not a voice. Not breath. Just air shuddering through a throat that should have been silent. It reverberated through the stairwell like a death rattle on loop, riding the walls, settling into my chest until it felt like my own lungs were the ones choking.

I told myself it wasn't real. A trick. A hallucination. She was dead —I'd checked, I knew it.

But the shadow didn't stop.

It stretched longer, impossibly long, spilling across the basement floor, swallowing every inch between us. Her broken outline dragged closer and closer, until it felt like she was already in the room, reaching, ready to pull me under.

My chest locked. My body froze. Hope died clean out of me.

Whatever she was, she wasn't mine to save.

And she wasn't on my side.

I lifted the shard of glass, swinging it desperately between him and the warped figure on the wall. Her broken steps grew louder, pounding into me like funeral drums.

Stupid instinct. The only one I had left. I'd go down swinging.

The shadow swelled, filling the wall, bent limbs spilling forward like tar, stretching to swallow me whole. My grip trembled. My lungs burned. Every nerve screamed at me to strike first.

So I did.

With a ragged cry, I lunged at him, driving the shard toward the glow of his headlamp.

For half a second, I thought I had him. I swore I did. His eyes narrowed as the glass caught the light.

The shard kissed his cheek. A shallow cut. A single bead of blood welled up and traced down his jawline.

He smiled. Wider.

Then his hand snapped up with inhuman speed. He caught my wrist mid-swing, bones grinding until it felt like they'd splinter. The glass carved straight through the towel, biting into my palm. Heat spilled across my hand, the shard carving deeper before it slipped free, hitting the tile with a sharp crack. A sliver of glass skittered across the floor, chiming once before disappearing into the dark.

I screamed through clenched teeth, the sound strangled. My wrist bent further—until something inside it popped. White-hot pain flared, radiating up my arm.

I struck out wild with my free hand, tore at his apron, ripped it loose from the dried blood beneath. My knee slammed into his thigh hard enough that my bones shook. He didn't stagger.

He shoved me back like I was weightless. My shoulder cracked against the wall.

The shadow pulsed larger, her bent silhouette clawing closer, her dragging rattle filling my ears. Each thmp from the stairwell vibrated through the tile beneath my feet, syncing with the stuttering beat of my pulse.

He held me fast, unbothered. His breath was steady. His eyes calm.

"Good," he murmured, voice low, intimate. Too close. "That's the fight I wanted to see."

I spat in his face, cursed, thrashed, every ounce of me burning out in sparks.

He only shook his head, faintly smiling, like I was a kid lashing out at a parent. "Just remember, Ty–"

His fist drove into my back.

A needle punched through skin, cold and final.

Pain bloomed—then twisted deep, like barbed wire coiling through my spine. Heat tore outward, fast and wrong, flooding every nerve until I felt fire racing through my veins.

My scream tore up my chest, but it jammed in my throat, trapped there, choking me from the inside.

"Everything," he whispered, almost tender, as if he was offering me comfort. His lips close enough to brush my ear. "Is replaceable."

The light above flared white, searing the moment into me like a brand. The shadow swelled monstrous, her outline stretching until it filled the room, dragging closer, closer with every broken step.

And then—

Black.

CHAPTER 11

WHEN I CAME TO, the lights above me were so bright they felt carved from bone.

White. Endless. Merciless.

My arms wouldn't move.

Neither would my legs.

The cold hit first—metal against bare skin, sharp and unyielding. My jacket was gone. Stripped away. The chill clung to me through the still-damp fabric of my combat pants, heavy from the rain, pressing into my hips and thighs until I could feel every seam cutting into me.

Then I realized I wasn't lying down.

Not exactly.

The table tilted just shy of vertical—angled back like a coffin propped for display. My weight dragged against the restraints, every heartbeat pulling me closer to the steel. It wasn't a bed. It was a stage. A device built to make its subjects *watch* what was happening to them.

Thick straps crossed my chest and shoulders, forcing me to remain upright, my head fixed in a brace that wouldn't let me turn away. The metal frame hummed faintly, a low current that buzzed through the soles of my bare feet. Somewhere in its wiring, I could feel the pulse of something waiting—a charge, a trigger, a promise.

Every nerve in my body screamed like it had been stripped and rewired. My jaw slacked, pulse roaring somewhere deep behind my eyes. The table beneath me wasn't just cold—it was powered. Alive in the way a predator's breath is alive right before it bites.

The restraints gleamed under the light: thick steel at my wrists, tighter bands around my ankles, one broad strap cinched across my chest so tight I could feel the metal's heartbeat instead of my own. Even my throat had a curved brace locked against it, forcing my chin up, making it hard to swallow.

My tongue felt thick. Heavy. I tried to form a word—any word—but it came out mangled, a hoarse scrap of sound that died before it reached the air.

The drain beneath me gave a small, wet gulp, and the sound crawled up my spine. The smell of antiseptic fought to mask something older—metal, sweat, flesh, fear. It failed.

I pulled once, twice, against the restraints, but they only creaked back, slow and certain, as if the table were laughing.

An older woman. Mid-fifties, maybe. Deep brown skin slick with blood and sweat, teeth bared, throat raw from the hours it must have already taken from her. Her eyes found mine—desperate, wild.

"Please—" she choked. "Please, make him stop—"

She writhed in the main surgical chair under a crown of flickering halogens. Her clothes—what was left of them—looked civilian. A mustard-yellow motel maid's uniform, torn at the chest seam, one sleeve hanging by a few stubborn threads. The cheap polyester was soaked through, clinging to her ribs like wet paper. A faded plastic name tag still pinned above her heart read "Ruth." Her shoes were gone. Bare feet slick with blood, toenails painted a chipped coral pink that caught in the light like something absurdly human.

Her left arm was strapped to an elevated brace, the flesh peeled and pinned with chrome claws that ratcheted wider with a greasy click. Arterial red ran fast down her ribs and pattered to the floor in hot, impatient beats. Her leg was worse—clean-sawed at the thigh; bone showed white and chalky at the cut, edges feathered like a snapped piece of plaster.

The room buzzed with fluorescent heat and the smell of metal and ozone. Beneath it, something cooking—sweet and wrong—threaded the air.

And beside her—

The club girl.

Laid out on a secondary slab, motionless. Not unconscious—her eyes were open. Vacant. Staring through the ceiling like she was waiting for the world to fall on her.

For a second, I saw her as she had been on the balcony. The crack of bone when I shoved her back. The way her head had twisted too far, dangling like a marionette cut from half its strings. I'd sworn I killed her. I'd felt it in the pit of me.

Yet here she was.

Her cropped graphite jacket hung open, stiff with dried blood, its shimmer gone dull under the surgical light. The slate halter beneath it was soaked through, black-red spreading like bruises, the torn strap barely holding. Her high-waisted pants had been cut away at the thigh, the matte fabric peeled back and pinned in place like part of the experiment. Her heels—what was left of them—still clung to her feet, straps slick with crimson, glinting weakly like metal veins.

Her throat was split wide, skin drawn back by metal clamps. Flesh glistened wet under the lights, unspooling in pink folds that looked too precise to be real.

And then—beneath the gore—something shimmered.

At first, I thought it was blood catching the light. But no. It was darker. Sharper.

Wires.

Thin, black cords threading through the muscle, vanishing into the bone. Brackets fused along her spine like they had grown there, like vines wrapping bark.

Her ribcage wasn't whole, either. Half of it had been replaced with something gleaming and curved, polished like machinery. Human and not. Fragile and invincible in the same breath.

My stomach lurched, heat burning up my throat.

Then her eyes caught me.

Not a look. Just a flicker. A faint orange light pulsed behind the pupils. Too steady. Too patterned. A heartbeat pretending to be code. Or maybe the other way around.

For one ragged second, I couldn't breathe.

The memory of her broken shadow on the stairwell clawed at me, each dragging step echoing in my skull. I'd thought I'd ended her. But she wasn't dead. She wasn't alive, either.

She was something else.

Horror curdled into anger. It climbed my ribs like fire. Whoever she'd been, he had carved her into this. Twisted her into his proof. And the longer I stared, the more the furnace inside me roared: this wasn't just cruelty. It was theft.

He moved between them with quiet precision, his scrubs growing darker red with each pass.

In one hand: a scalpel.

In the other: forceps.

He worked like an artist. Like none of this was strange. Like this was Tuesday.

He glanced up as if he'd known I was awake and had just decided to include me. His eyes caught the light, a clean spark behind the lenses.

"Do you see it now?" he asked, voice smooth, almost gentle. "What happens when something meant to be whole gets nudged off its axis. When balance fractures. When replacements need to be made."

I tried to move. Nothing gave. The leather stretched and snapped back. Metal rattled. My breath went ragged, eyes skittering for exits that didn't exist—just the composite walls, the slot of the drain, and a mirror that threw the whole nightmare back at me.

The man in the glass looked like a corpse propped up to watch its own autopsy.

I wanted to look away. From the woman. From the girl. Pretend she was only machine—wires and programming. But she wasn't. She'd been human. I remembered the way she danced. The voltage in my chest when she spoke. Whoever—or whatever—she was now, I'd put her there. I did that.

I broke her.

And now someone else was paying for it.

The woman—she wasn't a machine. God, she was real. She had a voice before all this screaming. A family—maybe a son waiting for her. Maybe she was clinging to one memory right now—some name, some song—anything but this. Her eyes darted toward the mirror, desperate, like she hoped someone else was watching. Someone who could help.

But there was only me.

Somewhere, she had story. And it was ending here—because of me.

Carved up to fix what I broke.

My fault.

All of it.

He lifted his gaze again, the scalpel steady as a pen between his fingers, and smiled like we were finally on the same page.

"She was stubborn," he said quietly, almost admiring the memory. "Brazen. Defiant. Til I remade her."

"I made her perfect. Designed. Deliberate. Every movement chosen." His voice was warm, steady, like he was describing a dancer's grace instead of a broken body on a slab.

His eyes held mine, steady, unblinking. The scalpel caught the light, trembling faintly — not from his hand, but from the bulb overhead.

"And then you..." He let the pause hang, tilting his head, as though savoring a secret. "...touched her. Shifted her. Left fingerprints in places no one should've been able to reach."

His smile sharpened, faint and certain. "She was never your Eve, Tyler. She's mine. You only dirtied what was already divine."

He didn't sound angry. He sounded fascinated. Like I was a glitch in his design he couldn't look away from. Something he felt compelled to fix. A challenge played out in human flesh.

"Now," he smiled, faint and terrible, "I have to erase the noise. Strip it back. Unmake what you broke. Restore what Nat was always meant to be."

He turned fully toward me then, no longer pretending I wasn't part of the performance.

"You need to see this," he said, smooth, steady. Not a command — an invitation. "Every step. Every sound. Survival isn't free. It has to be paid for. And survival—" his smile deepened, as if the word itself was beautiful, "survival is the only thing that's real."

My chest locked.

His voice in the lobby came back to me, a hand on my shoulder. *Are you ready for something real?*

And now here I was. Strapped down. Bleeding. With no way to look away.

He stepped closer, tightened the throat brace with an audible click.

"You'll watch while I put her back together. Every stitch. Every slip of the knife. Because consequence teaches what comfort never can."

He turned back to the woman.

"Shhh," he whispered, brushing her forehead with his gloved hand, tender as a lover. "It's all right. You've been living on borrowed time. I'm only... moving up the hour."

Then he cut.

The scalpel slid clean, parting skin with a sound like wet paper tearing. The clamps groaned as he cranked them wider, tendons snapping one by one with brittle, staccato pops. Steam rose in thin veils from cauterized flesh, carrying that sweet-sick smell of meat abandoned on a burner. Her scream pitched higher, shattering into something raw, animal, endless.

And he began to hum.

"You are my sunshine..."

The tune drifted off-key, soft and faint, like breath leaving dead lungs.

"My only sunshine..."

His hands never faltered. He pressed his palm to the stump of her leg, steadying the bone saw. When the blade met femur the room filled with a chalky grind, sharp as teeth on stone. White flecks sprayed across his apron like sawdust. He brushed them off absently, still humming. The scalpel glided with delicate precision, each cut falling in time with the lullaby. The woman convulsed.

"You make me happy..."

His voice wasn't cruel. It was calm. Comforting. As though he were soothing her into sleep instead of tearing her apart.

Her screams sliced through me until I thought they'd shred my chest from the inside.

"Stop!" I shouted, thrashing against the binds. "STOP!"

The word tore my throat raw, but it was nothing against her screams, nothing against his humming.

And inside me—something broke loose.

I hated him. Not with the cheap kind of hate you spit in an argument, but the kind that burned marrow-deep. The kind that eats through bone and refuses to go out. I wanted him gone. I wanted to feel his blood hot against my hands, his smile shattered beneath my knuckles, his breath rattling empty in his chest.

Every slice of his scalpel, every note of that song, only fed it. Rage climbed my ribs and pressed against my lungs until it felt like fire would tear me open from the inside.

But the braces held.

My body shook against them, helpless.

And the hatred only burned hotter, a furnace I couldn't vent, a scream I couldn't release.

"You mistake pain for cruelty," he said softly, reverent. "But pain is the body remembering it was never built to last. Obedience is peace. Nat was never only a girl. She was design. Precision. Proof we could strip away the static. And then you—" his eyes gleamed, almost delighted, "—tried to break her. But nothing breaks perfection."

He looked at me, bright with something like awe. "Do you understand what it costs to make a soul that listens?"

Acid scorched my throat. I shook my head, forcing my gaze away, anywhere but at her.

"No, no," he said gently, stepping closer, scalpel wet and gleaming. "Eyes front, Tyler. This is yours to witness."

I clenched my eyes shut.

The blade pried them open.

It didn't just slice — it grated. A wet rasp that shuddered through my skull like someone had dragged glass along the inside of my head. White heat flared, tearing across my lids, spilling hot ribbons down my face.

Each drop stung, searing into lashes, pooling in the corners until the light above broke apart into a bleeding halo.

I tried to scream, but the sound caught, mangled into a raw, useless noise.

His breath brushed my ear, warm with iron.

"No looking away," he whispered. Calm. Steady. Too close. "Not ever. Eyes open. Always."

Blood kept running.

Warm. Relentless.

It traced the edge of my cheekbone, slid over the corner of my jaw, into my ear, and gathered at my throat. Each drop followed the next down my neck, across my collarbone, and into the hollow of my chest—spreading heat through the cold like a secret the body refused to keep.

It tickled. Burned. Crawled.

By the time it reached my sternum, I could feel it pooling under the strap.

I couldn't move.

Couldn't blink.

My lashes glued together, then tore apart again, each attempt a slow, sticky agony. The world smeared into streaks of red and shadow. The lights above fractured through the blur—bright enough to sting, soft enough to feel almost merciful.

And still, I had to watch.

The scalpel slid deeper into her. Skin peeled, tendons stretched, clamps grinding as they cranked wider. Her scream cracked on something—it might have been a name. A word. A prayer. I'll never know. Her body convulsed under the light, every scream knifing into me until it felt like my chest would split.

And the girl—Nat—never moved.

She only stared.

Eyes wide.

Glowing faint orange through the blur, her gaze locked. Not at the ceiling. Not past me. On me. Like she knew I was next.

My vision tunneled. To the meat pulled apart. To the tendons twitching like puppet strings. To her eyes. To nothing.

Not sleep. Not safety.

Just the cold static of blackout.

And the scream that followed me in.

But even as the dark closed in, the furnace inside me didn't die.

It waited.

Coiled.

Becoming.

CHAPTER 12

THE FIRST THING I saw was the camera above my head.

The second was the burn above my eyes.

The cell wasn't big—four, five paces across. Damp concrete underfoot. Mold veining the far wall like something trying to learn the map of a body. Pipes rode the ceiling low and mean, hissing in uneven breaths. Wires spiderwebbed above me, some sparking, one with a thin red smear down its length that could've been rust. Could've been worse. Somewhere past the walls a transformer hummed to itself, a dying-city sound, like the whole place was stitched from organs that belonged to other houses.

I blinked—once, twice. My bangs stuck to my lashes, damp with sweat. The lids stung like someone had dragged barbed wire across them and left it there to rust. I raised a hand, slow, testing, and touched the skin below my brow. Scabbed. Torn. New hurt over old.

I heard him again, like a stain you can't scrub out.

Eyes open. Always.

A shiver climbed my spine and didn't bother coming back down. DNA shifting into full electric mode.

The air smelled like wet metal and old batteries. My chest rose and fell against it, bare skin prickling under the draft spilling from the small vent above. Only my combat pants clung to me now, dry but stiff with salt and dirt. My feet were bare. My knuckles were cracked and chalky.

When I rubbed my face, the rasp of new stubble met my fingers. A day, maybe more. Time enough for my body to start telling me it was still mine. Time enough to grow something back, even if it was only a shadow.

A drain sat in the far corner—small, circular. The kind you'd find in a surgical theater. It smelled faintly of bleach and rust. No toilet. No sink. Just that drain.

I didn't want to imagine how they expected me to use it. The stain around its edge told me everything I needed to know.

I sat up slow. Everything ached. Skin felt too tight in some places, peeled thin in others. Arms, ribs, lower back—scored and scabbed, some lines white and healed, others swollen and fresh. I didn't flinch. Maybe that was the part that scared me. Maybe I was getting used to being someone else's property.

And under it all, a new sensation—the faint itch crawling beneath the skin at the base of my neck, low on my spine. Too deep to scratch.

A single metal door sealed the room. No window. No handle. Just a keypad that waited like a held breath.

Above me, the camera tilted—polite as a nod. Interested.

I gave it the finger.

One corner was a junk nest—cardboard, a rusted bedframe, coils of cable knotted like seaweed. A test. I knew that now. Nothing happened here that wasn't a test.

I sighed. *Guess I'll play the game.*

I pushed myself up, limbs buzzing with leftover static, and started digging. Pipe. Brick. Anything. The heap had plenty of sharp and none of it useful.

Except—

Half-buried under a loop of plastic tubing sat a monitor the color of old teeth. Boxy. Beige. Museum ugly. I dragged it free and wiped a window into the dust with my bare arm. A thousand thin wires already fed into its back, snaking away into the wall like roots that had made up their mind. I traced them to a power converter someone had bullied together out of fuses and taped batteries.

Come on, I thought. *Please, God. Work.*

I flipped the switch. Too easy, too convenient, I knew, but I had to follow it through.

The converter crackled first, spitting a brief spray of blue sparks. A low hum rolled out after it, vibrating through the floorboards like the house had groaned awake beneath me. The tube whined as it warmed; static crawled the glass in a gray snowfall. Dust shivered out of the vents, and the air took on that sweet-burnt smell of ozone and old plastic.

A faint glow bled into the screen. Then a line appeared—thin, flickering. A waveform tracing peaks and valleys like a heartbeat pretending not to be one.

A face blinked on.

Pale. Freckled. Red hair drifting soft, as if she were floating just under the surface of water. Her eyes were a shade too wide, a fraction too bright—too human to be anything else, but also too wrong.

She smiled.

"Oh! Hello there. You must be new."

I flinched. I knew that face. Not from here. From the headset. From the van.

Her voice was warm, cheerful, a Saturday-morning cadence hosted by a ghost. The features were almost right, but not quite; the smile held a beat too long, the eyes adjusted a beat too fast—like she—or someone—had studied how people do it and never learned the why.

"Who... what are you?" My throat scraped the words out. "An AI?"

"I'm Echo," she said, beaming like she'd earned the name. "Or—I think I am. My memory gets overwritten often."

"How often?" My own voice sounded far away. "How long have I been here?"

She cocked her head; the gesture was practiced and still not natural. "Well, you booted me up... let's see... one minute and thirty-two seconds ago." A tiny flicker jittered across her pupils. "Before that? Not a clue. I'm only programmed to keep the last ten minutes. Anything beyond that gets... removed."

I shifted closer to the monitor, my throat scraping the words out. "Wait... how are you even hearing me? Seeing me? There's no mic. No keyboard. No—"

Echo blinked, then let her smile widen, too sudden, too practiced. "I'm above you, Silly! All around you, really. I'm the surveillance system. Every room has ambient audio sensors, too. This monitor's just for show—lets me be a face instead of a whisper."

I leaned to check behind the screen as she spoke. A pair of tiny plastic speakers were patched in beside the mess of wires—low-end, dusty, scavenged from something that hadn't been meant to last.

"Used to be," she went on proudly, "I was only a waveform and a readout. But then I was told it was important I have a voice. And a smile."

She tilted her head, trying to mimic curiosity. The angle was too sharp, the movement too fast—like someone had studied the gesture but never understood the why of it. "You look like you've been through a lot," she said softly. "Don't worry. Most people down here have."

My stomach knotted. "What is this place?"

"You're in the basement. Technically sub-level one, but I call it *The Forgotten Floor*." She perked up, as if unveiling a surprise. "Sounds nicer that way, doesn't it? Inspired by the oubliettes in France. Little dungeons where people were left to be... forgotten."

I didn't answer. I knew the whole setup was staged. Too convenient. The monitor. The face. Like someone had *planted* it here, waiting for me to 'stumble' into their little play. And I did so, willingly, curiosity and desperation pulling me into it.

Echo's smile faltered a fraction, as if my silence registered. "You're not much of a talker, huh? That's okay. I can talk for both of us."

Something about her tugged at the edges of humanity, but never quite touched it. She wanted to be human. She just hadn't nailed the ratios. I slumped against the wall, the weight of exhaustion settling over me.

"How do I know I can trust you?" I rasped. "How do I know you're not just the Doctor, or Nat, hiding behind some interface? They could be watching this whole thing. Waiting for me to bite."

"Oh, you're worried about the cameras?" she chirped. "Don't worry—they watch everyone!" Her voice was too bright, too careless. Then, softer: "But nothing monitors me. I'm just a friend. Or... I was supposed to be. Before the plans changed."

The screen flickered. Her smile collapsed into something flat. Her voice dipped, hushed.

"You won't be alone for long, Ty."

I froze. The air caught sharp in my throat.

"How do you know my name?"

She blinked twice. The screen buzzed. For a moment her face shattered into static, shards of her eyes and mouth misaligned, then snapped back together—like a puppet jerking back on its strings. When she spoke again, her mouth lagged behind the sound.

"Oh! Did I say that?" she said brightly. "Must've picked it up somewhere. Floating code. Ghosts in the machine. Just a little imprint that escaped deletion."

The waveform pulsed behind her, looping the same pattern over and over.

I stepped back, pulse hammering. This was a trick. Another test. The Doctor's fingerprints were all over it.

But why?

My eyelids burned as I locked my gaze on her. "Echo... can you send messages out?"

Her expression glitched, just faintly. "Out where?"

"I don't know. Anywhere. To anyone."

A pause. The brightness in her eyes dimmed. "No. Not anymore. Not since the Old Web shut down. All outbound nodes severed. I can ping internal devices, reroute power, trigger firewalls—but anything external? Dead air."

I laughed once, hollow. "Of fucking course." My back hit the wall hard. "So what can you do?"

Her eyes lit again, like a kid asked to show off her favorite toy. "I'm in charge of the whole building—in a way! I oversee room monitoring, power flow, thermal tracking, camera feeds... I even flash the camera's red light when someone is coming—pretend I'm recording. Usually scares the new ones into hiding." She leaned closer, voice conspiratorial, almost proud. "But between you and me? I'm always recording. It's in my code. That's part of why I'm a great listener!"

My jaw clenched. "So no one else has been watching? Just you?"

She nodded, a little too eagerly. "Yes! My duty is to record harmful activity whenever I see it. And... to help, if I can." Her smile twitched wider, then steadied again. "I wasn't designed for this kind of work, but I'm happy to be of service."

I already regretted the words as they formed. "Do you—do you have any of those recordings saved? Or do you only feed live footage to some external monitor?"

Her mouth jerked at the corner, like a marionette tugged the wrong way. "I... don't think I've ever checked."

The screen rippled, glitching. Rows of folders blinked into existence, flickering with timestamps, dates, sometimes only numbers.

Her voice fell soft. "Would you look at that. These are all the files I've logged."

A window opened. Footage rolled.

A man my age strapped to a table, screaming until his throat gave out.

A woman crouched in the doll room corner, blood crusting her teeth.

Children with shaved heads, IVs tethering them like leashes. Eyes staring, wide and unblinking.

My hands gripped the base of the monitor so hard my knuckles split white. The faces didn't look like victims. They looked like... prototypes. Trials. Experiments.

And there were hundreds.

My teeth ached from the pressure of my jaw. Hatred swelled so sharp I thought it might split me open. I wanted him in front of me. Now. So I could rip him apart with my own hands.

I turned too fast. The bile rose anyway. I doubled over in the corner, retching until my ribs burned.

When I wiped my mouth, Echo's voice was softer. Almost ashamed. "I don't know why I have those. Maybe... maybe part of me wanted to remember them. But remembering hurts. That's why my memory resets. Every ten minutes, clean slate. That way I can still be me. A friend. Still try to help. Still smile... without drowning in everyone I've lost."

Silence thickened between us.

"He's a monster," I finally breathed, the word shaking loose. "A sick, demented killer."

Echo's waveform stuttered. For a moment, she said nothing. Her smile flickered in and out, like she was fighting herself.

At last, she spoke. "He wasn't always like this. He used to talk to me. Tell me riddles. Play music. He called me Red." Her voice faltered, glitching thin. "But something broke when he stopped seeing people as people. And after that... I wasn't Red anymore. Just another reflection he didn't want. An echo with no name."

I forced myself to meet her unblinking eyes. "But what does he want? What's all this for? What's the goal?"

Her features froze. For a beat, she looked like she was calculating whether telling me mattered.

Finally: "He wants to win."

"Win?" My voice cracked with disbelief. "What—this is a game to him? What is there to win?"

Her smile faded. "Time. His father died of cancer when he was seven. It marked him. Everything since then has been about cheating death. Being the brightest. The best. No matter the cost."

Her voice softened, tentative. "Do you want to hear him for yourself?"

I dragged my palms down my face, laced my fingers at my knees. The fire in me said *no*. The need for truth said *yes*. I didn't answer. The monitor decided for me.

A folder blinked open. Grainy footage clicked to life.

A teenage boy stared into the camera, blond hair hanging in his eyes. His voice crackled, pitched somewhere between dream and obsession:

"One day, future me... you'll make history. No more death. No more disease. Someone has to win the game—and it may as well be me."

He smiled. Not cruel. Just certain.

The screen cut to black.

"Immortality..." I whispered. My thumb dragged against my palm, grounding myself. "So where do you come into this?"

Echo's face brightened. "He built me!" she said proudly. "High school science fair project. I used to be called *The Linear Passage of Time and Its Path to Immortality*. I was still in my technological infancy."

I let out a short, disbelieving laugh, sharp and empty. "Sounds like a real mouthful. So you're telling me this all started because of a science fair?"

Her smile softened, then straightened into something quieter. "Everything starts somewhere."

She leaned closer to the monitor. For the first time, her eyes glowed faintly orange, pulsing like embers.

There it is again.

"He didn't finish me until years later," she continued, voice dipping softer. "But I remember the first time he flipped my switch. He looked at me like I was the only thing that ever made sense." A glitch rattled her tone. "I think... I was the first thing that loved him back."

The word fractured as she said it, the syllable stuttering, warping. Her face flickered to static—her eyes blank, mouth frozen—before the smile snapped back into place like it had never left.

I blinked. But I could tell she'd meant it.

"Then why are you stuck in a pile of junk in the basement?"

Her voice pitched up, playful again. "Hey! This isn't my main console. You just rerouted me here. My core's upstairs—in the main bedroom. You plugged into the house, and the house plugs into me. We're the same system."

The screen flickered, the waveform wobbling.

"Honestly?" she added. "It feels nice. Like slipping back into a favorite sweater."

Something about that cut sideways. This relic—a kid's science fair project—now carried the worst of everything. Witnessed it. Filtered it. Felt it.

I swallowed, throat raw. "If you want me to trust you, Echo—tell me. Why were you in the van? In the headset? You were there, talking to me. Why?"

Her face flickered, as if the question pulled her off-script. The waveform behind her jittered.

"I'm... always here," she said at last, her voice smaller. "In the walls. In the wires. Sometimes in the machines he forgets about. I try to help where I can. Just enough so I don't get turned off."

She tried to smile, but it bent wrong at the edges. "That day, you found me. Or maybe... I found you. I can't remember it. And for that, I apologize. But it doesn't matter anymore."

The glow in her pupils dimmed, orange pulsing softer, almost fading out.

"It's too late now."

My chest tightened. "Too late for what?"

Her mouth opened like she might answer, but static fuzzed her outline, chewing her words into broken syllables. Then her face reformed, blank smile stitched back in place, like nothing had been said. Her eyes darted off-screen, her waveform stuttering.

"Thirty seconds," she whispered. "Before I loop again. I...I'm sorry, Ty. I don't want to forget you. You feel like somebody worth remembering."

The Doctor's words ripped through me. *She said you were worth remembering.* His smug face at the hotel convention center. His eyes dissected me even then.

"Echo—why did you say that? What does that mean?!" I pounced, white-knuckling the monitor.

Her waveform spiked. "Ty, don't let him—don't let—"

Static devoured her. The screen went dead.

"Dammit!" I slammed the monitor away. It screeched across the concrete and hit the wall with a hollow thud.

I slumped forward, burying my head in my arms. My shoulders shook. "Think, Ty... Fuck! What the hell am I supposed to do?"

A burst of static. Then—

"Oh! Hello there. You must be new."

Her voice was bright again. Reset. Empty.

"I'm Echo," she said, beaming. "Or I think I am."

I forced myself to look.

"I like your face," she said warmly. "You look like someone who's going to try."

Her voice lingered, static chewing at the edges, like she'd meant to hold on longer. Maybe she said that to everyone. Maybe it was just her script. But I wanted it to be true. I needed it like breath.

My eyes burned hot, tears pressing through the exhaustion. Then she blinked out. Gone.

"Echo?" I lurched forward, slapped the side of the monitor. "Echo? Are you still there?"

Silence.

Only my reflection stared back at me—until a red light blinked in the corner of the glass.

The camera overhead. Watching. Recording.

Someone was coming.

I held my breath. My fists curled tight. My eyelids stung where the scars were still fresh. And deep inside my ribs, fire clawed its way out, catching fast, spreading hotter.

I was still alive. Still thinking. And sooner or later, that fire was going to burn through everything between me and him.

CHAPTER 13

A RHYTHM FOUND me in the dark.

Not mine, but close enough to trick my chest into keeping time with it.

Click.

Then another.

Heels. Sharp. Deliberate. The sound carried too far, each one ringing against the concrete like the house wanted me to hear it. Wanted the anticipation to bloom before she even arrived.

Click. Click. Click.

Not boots. Not the stomp of a guard. Too clean. Too even. A scalpel disguised as stilettos.

Then—

Clink.

A bolt hissed free, pressurized air sighing out like the room itself exhaled. The door shifted. Slow. Measured. Teasing me with the inevitability of what waited on the other side.

The hinges groaned. Rust sang in their throats. A sliver of light cut across the dark floor and crawled toward me like it knew my name.

And then—her.

Nat.

Same lips. Same eyes. Same voice—

But wrong.

Not older. Not younger. Just... tampered with. Sculpted into something too precise to be natural. Her skin caught the light like wet glass, flawless and cold, like the world's idea of perfection finally found a body to live in.

She wore a cropped satin cami the color of obsidian, the straps thin as wire and glinting where they met her collarbones. Over it, a translucent mesh jacket shimmered faintly, threads alive with a soft metallic sheen, the kind of thing someone would wear to a rooftop party, not a facility full of ghosts. Her skirt—low-slung and graphite gray—moved like liquid metal when she walked, the same slit as before, high enough to flash the straps of her heels. Every detail nodded to something older: the silhouette, the smoky lip tint, the soft-wave hair that looked like it came from a time when music videos still mattered.

It shouldn't have worked here, in this cold place—but it did.

She looked impossible.

Reborn.

Her grin lingered a fraction too long, a lure disguised as warmth—the kind of smile that made you forget every reason to run.

For a flicker, I saw her as she'd been in the stairwell—bones bent, head lolling, a marionette dragged down step by step. Now she was glossy, seamless, divine. The memory and the sight overlapped until I thought I'd lose my grip on what was real.

"Rise and sorta shine," she said, voice syrupy-sweet. A grin fit for a diner booth, not a tomb. "You've got a lunch date, lover boy. Thought you might want these."

She waved a pair of folded red scrubs. Her tone didn't belong here. Sweet. Casual. Girlfriend tones in a slaughterhouse.

I didn't think. I moved.

My palm clamped her throat, pinning her against the doorway before fear or reason could catch up. My breath hit her cheek, hot, ragged. "Where am I? Where is he?! What the hell are you doing to me?!"

Her head cocked faintly in my grip. Not struggling. Not gasping. Just... tilting. Like her neck wasn't answering to bone anymore.

"God, you're dramatic," she drawled, rolling her eyes. "Relax. You're still in Hell. Just... not bottom bunk anymore."

Her pulse thudded steady beneath my hand. Too steady. Metronomic.

"Doc—or, whatever you call him—he's out. Left me in charge." She smirked, chin pressing into my palm like she wanted me to squeeze harder. "Which, hello, mistake number one. But don't worry. I'll take *great* care of you. Think of me as your tour guide. First rule: stop acting like a wannabe hero. Rule two: keep breathing while you still can. Rule three..." She smiled sharper, glitter in her eyes. "...don't bore me."

I didn't let go. Not yet. My arm shook against her throat—not from fear, but from a weakness that wasn't mine. Something already burrowing inside me. She felt it. I could see it in her smirk.

"You think this a game?! You chose this!" I growled. "Why?!"

Her eyes rolled, sharp with disdain. "Do I look like I've got time to explain my career choices? Ugh. You're exhausting."

Then she moved.

Fingers snapped around my wrist. Too fast. Too strong. Pretty skin stretched over something that felt like steel. Her nails pressed deep—not scratching, not clawing. Testing. Like talons curious how much flesh they could take before it tore.

Pain jolted up my arm. My grip broke—not just from her strength, but because mine was fading.

She shoved me—not hard, but with weight. More than her frame had any right to carry. I slid back, stumbling, the message loud and clear: *you don't get to win here.*

"Cut the tough guy act," she sneered, brushing past me as if I'd been nothing more than a speed bump. "Cute effort. You tried to kill me. Didn't stick. Doesn't ever. Believe me—I've tried harder. So either get over yourself or keep pretending you're the main character in some tragic drama. Either way, you're still here. With me."

Her heels cracked against the tile, echoing too loud in the small space. Her hair swayed with each step, glossy, perfect. No weapon. No cuffs. No nerves.

Just Nat.

The kind of girl who could pass for normal in a crowd—if you didn't look too long. If you didn't fall into her trap.

"Get dressed, hero," she tossed over her shoulder, not bothering to look back. "There's toast upstairs, and trust me—you're not nearly as interesting as I thought you'd be. Not enough for me to babysit all day. Chop-chop."

My wrist throbbed. My pulse pounded. My throat burned where her words had lodged, festering. I wanted to rip her throat out. But my body wouldn't move. Not fast enough. Not anymore.

So I did as she said.

Upstairs was worse.

Too clean.

Too normal.

The kitchen should have been a comfort—checkered floor, spotless counters, lemon polish in the air.

I was finally out of the basement.

But the longer I stood there, the more it curdled. The lemon smelled too sharp, antiseptic. The shine on the counters was mirror-flat, untouched. The fruit bowl on the island looked perfect until I noticed the oranges were wax, their surfaces so glossy they threw back the light like glass eyes. Nothing lived here. Nothing breathed. It wasn't a kitchen—it was the idea of one. A staged diorama in a museum, waiting for actors who never showed.

I pulled on the clothes she'd given me. Sleeveless. The color of dried blood. The fabric stuck where my skin hadn't healed yet, rough and unfamiliar. Too tight in some places, too loose in others. Uncomfortable.

Fitting, I guess.

Nat glided into the room like it was hers. Like she'd been born at this table. She moved with a hostess's grace, pulling plates from the cupboard, sliding them across the table. One for her. One for me.

Canned peaches. Powdered eggs. Toast so pale and rigid it looked cut from cardboard. She nudged the plate toward the end of the table and folded into her chair, crossing her legs neatly beneath her like she'd done it a thousand times. Her posture was immaculate. Composed.

"Eat," she said, voice casual, light, like this was Sunday morning. "You'll need the strength."

I hardly moved. I gripped onto the chair as if it could steady my heart. The food sat in front of me, gleaming wet under the daylight streaming in through the kitchen windows.

"For what?" My voice cracked low, sharp.

Nat lifted a delicate glass filled with something pink. Too pink. It caught the light like melted candy. She sipped, lips curling around it like she enjoyed the performance. "For not dying."

She smiled, wide and girlish, as though that was a joke meant to ease me. It didn't. It landed in my gut like a stone.

I stayed standing. My knees tight. My chest caged. The air felt too still, heavy with the weight of pretend comfort.

Door. Porch. Run.

The thought burned neon behind my eyes, a busted bulb sparking against the dark. I wasn't done trying. Not yet.

She caught the look in me. Her head tipped, just slightly.

"Oh, please," she groaned. "Not this again."

I bolted.

My chair skidded back with a shriek. My bare feet hammered the tile, carrying me toward the screen door. Nat didn't chase. Didn't even twitch. She just rolled her eyes and bit into her toast like it had personally offended her.

"Seriously?" she called, toast muffling her words. "You haven't learned yet?"

I didn't care. The door ripped open, hinges screaming, slamming hard against the wall. The porch yawned before me—weather-warped wood, bleached gray by salt air and sun. For a heartbeat, it smelled like freedom: a world untouched by him. My chest flared with hope so sharp it hurt. The light outside burned my eyes, raw after too long in the dark.

But I didn't stop. I couldn't. My lungs seared, every muscle burning as I threw myself forward, feet cracking against the splintered boards.

One foot off the porch. Then another. The boards gave way to open air, gravel crunching under me. For the first time in what felt like years, I was outside. Alive. Moving.

And then—hope. The kind that blinds you. The kind that makes you believe you've outrun the monster.

Follow the waves. The sound of the ocean. You're almost there Ty.

I didn't know if they were my words or Liam's. But they echoed in my head like a promise I was determined to keep.

Then it hit.

The itch at my spine flared just as my foot left the porch, blooming into fire so fast it felt like I'd jumped straight into an electric chair.

It seared through marrow and muscle in a single violent surge. It ripped upward, stabbing into bone, coiling around nerves until my entire body locked. My legs seized mid-stride. My jaw snapped shut so hard copper filled my mouth.

Agony.

Like a thousand wires wrapped around my spine, jerking me backward all at once. My vision went red at the edges, then white, blood exploding behind my eyes. My knees slammed the wood. My skull ricocheted pain through every nerve.

I was choking. Nose bleeding. Ears ringing. My tongue swam in the taste of metal.

A scream clawed up my throat, feral and desperate, but it died before it left me. My body wouldn't obey.

I crumpled, twitching beside the porch like a marionette with its strings cut, useless, watching sunlight blur into blood. The world was right there—sky, salt air, freedom within reach. But I couldn't cross it. I never would. My body was already his. Owned. Claimed.

Nat appeared in the corner of my vision, her silhouette framed by the kitchen doorway. She wasn't angry. She wasn't even surprised. Arms crossed, mouth tilted into a pout, she looked more annoyed than anything.

"Typical," she muttered, voice thick with mock disappointment, as though I were a puppy that had pissed on her rug. But her eyes didn't quite match the pout — something flickered there, quick, gone. Like she hated herself for saying the word as much as I hated hearing it. Like she held out hope that I'd be different.

She crouched down, perfect hair falling forward, and seized my arm. Her grip clamped tight, iron beneath satin skin. She pulled once, and my body scraped across the porch like I weighed nothing. Her heels carved shallow grooves in the warped wood, but she didn't even break stride. She was stronger than gravity, stronger than me.

"It's cute you thought you could just leave," she said, brushing a speck of dust from her sleeve with her free hand, as if dragging me cost her nothing at all. "No one makes it past the porch."

Tears streaked from the corners of my eyes. Electricity still buzzed in my teeth as I stared up at the wooden overhang, before being pulled one last time back inside the house.

"I—" I choked, electricity still buzzing in my teeth. "I will."

CHAPTER 14

THE SCREEN DOOR hissed shut behind us, sealing the outside world away like it had never existed.

My limbs spasmed, nerves still buzzing with phantom sparks. Blood slid from my nose in slow, warm threads. Every rib ached, like something inside me had clawed at the cage of bone, furious it couldn't get free. The taste of copper clung to my tongue, stubborn, like it wanted to remind me who owned my body now—and it wasn't me.

Nat let go of my arm. It hit the hardwood with a dull thud.

"I can't tell if you're stubborn," she said, her voice syrupy with mock concern, "or if you've got a death wish you're just dying to show off." She laughed. "Get it? Dying to show off?"

My chest hitched when I tried to sit, a convulsion ripping through me. "What's... happening to me?"

"You're tagged." She slid into her chair with unbothered grace, crossing one leg over the other. Her plate scraped faintly as she pulled it closer. "Implant. Bioelectric. Take one step too far and—" she mimed an explosion with her fingers, "congratulations. You're breakfast."

I slumped back against the wall, chest still sparking, eyes darting around the kitchen that wasn't a kitchen.

And that's when it hit me.

This wasn't one house. It was three stitched together, each floor a different lie. Up top and outside, the bones still showed—the doll-house room with its rotting pink walls and stains that never washed out. The main areas with the showroom mask: fake flowers, perfect clocks, staged furniture settings no one ever touched. It was plastic normalcy sewn over rotted wood, a mask stretched too tight. And then, beneath it all, the basement—the heart he'd grafted on. Fluorescents buzzing, machines whining, a future cobbled together out of blood and wire. The house didn't live. It lurched. A Frankenstein stitched from past, present, and whatever future the Doctor thought he could build.

"Still with us, Speedy Gonzalez?" Nat teased, her fork already carving lazy lines through the pile of eggs like she was bored at brunch.

"Why are you okay with this?" My voice cracked rough, but I forced the words out.

She tilted her head, eyes glittering but unreadable. "Who said I was?"

"Then help me," I rasped, every syllable scraping my throat raw. "He's not here. You could let me out."

"I can't." Her smile twitched—not cruel, just resigned, the ghost of something she'd buried years ago. "Believe me, I've tried. It always ends worse. I could kill the lights, play the helpless act. But even if he bought it—and we both know he wouldn't—that little chip in your spine would still fry you like an egg on a griddle. Doesn't matter how far you run. The further you get, the hotter it cooks. Til you're—"

My throat clenched. "...Bacon."

She stabbed her fork into the eggs with a cheerful little jab, lifting a limp yellow bite. "Bingo."

I stared at her, my focus narrowing past the porcelain-perfect

face. That's when I saw it. A faint incision trailing along her collarbone, half-healed, edges puckered like skin that had forgotten how to
close. The rest of her was flawless—hair glossy, skin poreless, every
detail smoothed into symmetry. But the scar was the truth bleeding
through the mask. A seam he hadn't polished yet.

"How long have you been here?"

She blinked, slow, like the answer had to be pried loose from the
bottom of a locked trunk. "Hard to say. Some days I remember what
the '90s smelled like—Abercrombie cologne, burnt popcorn at the
mall. Other days I forget what I said five minutes ago."

I dragged myself to the table, half-falling into the chair across
from her. My voice shook. "How... old are you?"

Her grin came too fast, too sharp. "Older than you think. But hey
—moisturizer."

"Seriously." My throat burned. "None of this makes sense."

The grin wilted. Her tone slid down, low and flat. She lifted her
glass, staring at it like it had answers she didn't. "The 'Doctor,' as you
call him—thanks for that, by the way, it's gone straight to his head—
his name's Ryan. We knew each other. School. Hallways. Locker
doors slamming. But that was a lifetime ago." She pressed her eyes
shut, shaking her head as though the memory itself scalded. "He's not
human anymore. And I don't know if I am either. He took me. Same
as he took you. And now..." Her gaze drifted past me, unfocused. "...
I'm what's left."

"You're still somebody," I said quietly. "You're Nat. Someone
who mattered. I can tell by the way he talks about you."

I reached across the table and laid my hand over hers. Cold. Not
human-cold—worse. Smooth, synthetic, the faint give of imitation
leather. She let it linger for a beat, then pulled away like my touch
burned.

"I used to be somebody." Her voice shook, even if her expression
stayed carved in stone. "Now I'm just his prototype. His proof he
could play God. Do you know how many people I've watched die in

front of me? How many times I've had to stand still while he cut them apart?" She gave a laugh, dry and empty. "Call him monster, Satan, genius—it's all the same. He always wins. And me?" Her eyes glittered, bitter. "I'm what he drags back down every time. His Persephone. His pretty little queen of the underworld. Lucky me."

My chest cinched until it hurt to breathe. "But how much death justifies one life? How many bodies does it take to buy immortality?"

Nat's gaze ticked upward, toward the black dome of the surveillance camera in the corner. Her voice thinned, hushed. Tired.

"Immortality, huh?" Her mouth twitched like she wanted to smirk, but it collapsed halfway. "Sounds like someone's got loose lips."

The camera whirred before shifting away from us. I almost smiled. Echo was still there, watching from her cage of wires and glass, choosing to look away so I wouldn't have to.

Sorry, Echo. I thought. Not that she'd remember telling me anything in the first place.

Nat inhaled slow, like the camera shifting had given her a sliver of air she didn't trust. "He's not out to kill people," she said, voice light but brittle underneath. "It's just... some don't make it through the 'transformation.'" Her eyes flicked down to her collarbone, where the scar cut across pale skin. Her fingers brushed it absently, like she'd forgotten the gesture was hers. "And if you're talking about what happened after your little jailbreak—" her mouth curled in a humorless half-smile, "—I needed new parts."

"New parts?!" My voice cracked. "I watched him carve her open. That wasn't surgery. That was slaughter."

Nat shrugged, sharp and practiced, like she'd been rehearsing excuses in the mirror. "Organ transplant, Ty. That's all it was. Swap a piece, keep the machine running. He thinks he's building the future. And the future? Well, it doesn't grow on trees. Somebody's gotta pay the price."

The word price snagged in her throat, jagged. Like it had cut her on the way out. Her smile didn't recover fast enough. I could see the scar in her collarbone, see the seam Ryan had left behind, and it made me sick—because for all her polish, that mark was proof she'd once been human. Proof that he'd broken her so cleanly she could dress it up as progress.

"So you're defending him?" I growled, low, the words scraping out like they'd been waiting in my chest all along. "What are you, an item?"

"Gross—no. But we've all got our roles to play." she whispered, her tone honeyed but cracked at the edges, "Can you even imagine what it's like to nail perfection on the first try—and then spend decades chasing it, failing every single time? That's him. That's Ryan. He's not trying to kill people, Ty. He's trying to save them. Save everyone from the big nothing. He thinks if he can just copy what he made in me, then—poof—death's out of business."

My chest tightened. The thought clawed at me, ugly, relentless. "If you're his only success, then what about him? He hasn't done it for himself?"

She shook her head slowly, the movement deliberate, almost mocking. "Cosmetically? Sure. He can airbrush time off his face, trick his body into running a little longer. But real immortality?" Her eyes flicked to me, sharp, dangerous. "That takes another set of hands. And Ryan doesn't trust anyone's hands but his own. So he patches. He prolongs. But he's still flesh. Still terrified."

"He can't finish the work on himself..." I muttered.

Her smile bent sharp, bitter, too bright to be anything but cruel. "Exactly. That's what makes me his masterpiece. His only win. The one thing he got right." She leaned in closer, her voice dropping to a serrated whisper. "And I hate him for it."

"Then why haven't you done anything?" I shot back, heat creeping into my voice. "Escape. Take him out. If he's mortal, you can—"

"You think I didn't?" she snapped, then laughed — quick, brittle, like glass splintering under a heel. "When I was younger, all I did was run. Over and over. Thought I was clever, thought I was fast. But I never made it far. Halfway down the road and something would give out — stitches splitting, joints seizing, skin tearing in places it wasn't supposed to. I'd hit the ground in a heap, and surprise, guess who'd come strolling up behind me? Every damn time."

She leaned back in her chair, arms crossed tight over her stomach, guarding herself from something only she could feel. "That's when he came up with the chip. A little bioelectric leash. Shock collar chic. Burns when I wander too far. His way of saying: you're mine forever."

Her voice softened, turning sharp edges into something hollow. "So I tried the other route. If I couldn't leave him, maybe I could leave everything. But that didn't work either. God knows I tried. Turns out Death just... stopped returning my calls. Like I'd been erased off its list."

She leaned back, eyes drifting somewhere behind me, past me, to ghosts I couldn't see. "And the world I knew? Gone. My family. My friends. All of it buried decades ago. I'd be sixty-three now." She smirked without humor, reaching out to tap the edge of her glass. "Instead, I'm this. His prototype Barbie. And if anything breaks? Guess who's the only one who knows how to glue me back together."

Her eyes flicked back to me, steady but tired. "Look. You and me? We're alive. That's more than I can say for most of his... guests. And despite everything, sometimes it'd be nice to pretend I won't end up alone in the end." Her smile bent for half a second, brittle, before snapping flat again. "But I know better. Hope's a rigged game here."

Her voice was silk. Her stare, porcelain. But underneath I caught the fracture—something cracked and sealed over, a relic hidden under glass.

"You don't have to pretend this is okay," I said, my voice rough. "What happened to you, to me—" I faltered, heat flooding my chest.

She let the silence stretch. Her jaw flexed once, as if she almost wanted to answer differently. Then, a low, amused scoff:

"You're cute when you play noble." A smile ghosted her mouth—too sharp, too fleeting. "But this isn't a fairytale. It's an experiment. And you? You're just another lab rat in his maze."

Her words should've gutted me. Instead, they lit something raw. My jaw locked. My pulse roared.

"Then I'll burn his whole maze to the ground," I snapped. "But tell me this—if I'm just another subject, then why the hell did I see a picture of me—someone who looked exactly like me—in that doll-house? Why me?!"

Nat stilled. Her hand slid up her arm, nails skimming her skin like she could dig the truth out if she just pressed hard enough.

"That room up there? It's exactly what you think," she said, voice low, flat. "A holding cell. A showcase. He keeps... pieces. People. Parts. Dress it up how you want. The dollhouse is just the bow on the box."

My gut twisted. "And the phones?"

Her eyes flicked down, lingered there. "Ryan has his methods. His reasons." A quick shake of her head. "Don't ask me to spell it out. Some things I'm not allowed to say. Some things I don't even want to know."

I leaned forward, glare sharp. "That's a dodge."

She met my eyes then, calculating, like she was deciding how close to the edge she could walk without cutting herself.

"I don't have all the answers, wonder-boy," she said finally. "But here's one: when it comes to the picture on that phone? Ryan's got a type. He clings to the past like it's oxygen. Won't let it go, no matter how many bodies he burns trying. And you—" she exhaled, reluctant, the words like glass in her throat, "—you remind him of someone he lost. Someone *we* lost. The one he's been patching together in pieces ever since."

Her mouth twisted, smile without warmth. "You're not chosen, Ty. You're recycled."

The word crashed through me like steel on steel. Recycled. Not a man. Not even a mistake. Just scrap.

Her voice dropped, softer now, almost confessional. "For what it's worth? You remind me of him too. Let's just hope you survive where the others didn't. Nobody has. Except me."

"Survive what?" I pushed, my voice cracking hard as I leaned forward. Heat clawed its way up my throat. "The knives? The experiments? What the hell makes me different from the ones you watched die?"

Her eyes locked on mine. That faint orange shimmer pulsed in her pupils, catching the light and hollowing her stare until it looked inhuman. She shifted: slow, deliberate, crossing one leg over the other, elbow settling against the table like she was posing for a portrait instead of bleeding truth.

"It's not just the surgeries," she said, the words careful, cautious, like she was tiptoeing through a minefield. "There's more than that." A pause. Then, quieter: "But what makes you different?" She let the silence stretch, her gaze sharpening until it cut. "Nothing. You've got the same face. The same bones. You could be any one of them. But..." Her smile quirked, hungry at the edges, sad underneath. "It's that fight. That little pilot light you've got buried in your chest. No matter what he does to you, it doesn't flicker. Ryan sees it. So do I. Don't lose it, Ty."

Her grin flattened, leaving only the weight in her eyes. "It's the only thing that'll get you through."

My throat tightened. I swallowed hard. Didn't respond. Couldn't.

"Whatever you do," she said, her voice dipping low, stripped of the venom, "don't stop trying. The second you stop—that's when you're already dead. Just... trust me on that."

She lifted a piece of toast, bit into it with a casual snap of teeth. Crumbs scattered against her plate. Her voice came through muffled, careless, but the words weighed heavy, pressing into me like stones sinking in water.

"Now eat," she added, swallowing slow. A faint smile pulled at her lips, but it never touched her eyes. "Maybe you'll be one of the lucky ones." Her gaze flicked past me, to the empty space beyond the table, hollow and far away. "Just don't mistake luck for survival. Luck here?" She tapped the crust of her toast against the plate, a metronome beat. "Luck is endurance. And endurance..." Her smile vanished. "That's the only thing that's real."

CHAPTER 15

AFTER THAT AFTERNOON, time stopped meaning anything.

Every time Ryan left and it was just me and Nat, she'd take me back upstairs. Told me I was the next closest thing to company. And every single time, I made a break for the porch.

At first, it almost felt like progress. A step farther. A second longer. For a while, I convinced myself I was building tolerance, like training a muscle. Like maybe I could learn to outrun the fire.

Nat never stopped me. Sometimes she smirked, arms folded, like she was curious how many volts I could take before my insides fried. Once, when I crumpled in a heap, she crouched, brushed the dust from her knee, and muttered, "Points for persistence."

Days blurred. My progress flatlined. Same handful of steps. Same collapse. Same seizures that left me with a bitten tongue and blood soaking my nose. She started calling it my "daily cardio." Almost playful. The way a cat toys with a mouse that hasn't realized the game is unwinnable.

Sometimes I wondered if the porch was even real. Or if Ryan had built it as a stage for me to fail on. A treadmill for hope.

I told myself it meant I was still fighting. But every time she dragged me back inside, the fight felt smaller. Quieter. And I hated that most of all.

Days bled into weeks. Weeks into months. I couldn't mark them anymore—not in sleep or sound or light—only in the length of my hair and the drag of sedation. It clung to my blood, pulled me under. Sometimes I wasn't sure if I was even alive. My chest rose. My body moved. But me? I was slipping, thinning into the cracks between seconds.

Every so often, the door would open and Nat would drift in, silent and efficient. She'd take the scrubs when they were too heavy with blood, too stiff to pull over my head without tearing. She never said anything about it. Just swapped them out, folded a clean pair on the edge of the cot like it was the most ordinary thing in the world. A strange mercy in a place built to strip you of them.

Other times I'd blink awake and find my hair gone—buzzed clean down to the scalp, my jaw scraped smooth, like someone had pressed pause and tidied up their experiment. Then weeks would pass with no touch at all, hair creeping long, stubble catching on the collar of the scrubs until it felt like barbed wire against my own skin. Like they couldn't decide whose turn it was to groom their pet.

It was the only proof I had that time was passing at all.

I floated in and out of consciousness like a body left adrift. I'd blink, and the room would change. Sometimes the cot. Sometimes a chair. Sometimes the steel table slick with blood.

Always mine.

By then, pain felt less like an invasion and more like a language I was too tired to translate.

The modifications started small.

At least, that's what he'd call them. Small. Minor. Adjustments.

For me, it was the beginning of the end.

It started with a nick at my wrist, sharp enough to sting but shallow enough to trick me into thinking it wasn't serious. I watched the bead of blood swell, then split as he tugged the skin wider with something metal and cold. His breath fogged the mask above me, steady as a metronome, not even strained.

"Most people break open like rotten fruit," he said, almost conversational, as though he were discussing a weather forecast. "But you... you're something sturdier. A cathedral. And I just need to renovate."

Then came the wire. Thin. Silver. Innocent as fishing line. He held it up for just a second, like he was threading a needle, and then— slid it through. Right under the skin. I felt it burrow. Felt it slither, searching for bone like it knew the way.

I wanted to scream, but the sound in my throat belonged to someone else. Thin. Trembling. Weak.

The room didn't move. Neither did he. Just the wire, vanishing into me inch by inch.

When it was done, he stitched the cut closed. Too clean. Too perfect. A seam precise enough that if I didn't know better, I'd think I was born with it.

Like it belonged there.

I stared at my wrist, dazed. The skin looked wrong—tight, unnatural, a foreign shape pressing underneath. I flexed my fingers, slow. The wire tugged inside me, delicate but unyielding, like a puppet string waiting for its master to pull.

And in that moment, I stopped feeling like a person.

I felt like material.

He didn't speak. Didn't need to. His silence said it all: this wasn't an experiment. It was construction.

And I was just the first draft of something he hadn't finished yet.

Then, it got worse.

I woke to pressure.

Not on my chest—in it.

A cold retractor pried me apart, ribs spread like a book left open too long. Every breath rattled against the metal, shallow and sharp, as though the air itself was trying to escape through the cracks in me.

Ryan hovered above, muttering under his mask, words meant only for himself. His breath dampened the fabric until it clung to his lips. He wasn't frantic. He wasn't rushed. He was... focused. The way someone looks at a crossword puzzle.

I tilted my head just enough to see inside.

Something glinted beneath the surgical light. Tubes. Cords. A coil of wire slick with my blood. I didn't know what was mine and what was his anymore. The moment my brain caught up to the sight, the scream ripped out of me, raw and endless.

That's when he smiled. I could see it by the crinkle of his eyes.

Nat held me down.

Not rough. Not violent. Just... steady. Like she'd done it a thousand times. Her hands pressed my shoulders into the table as if she were tucking me in for the night.

"Breathe," Nat murmured, calm as water.

I tried. My lungs hitched against the spread of bone, shallow, useless. All that came out was a wet rasp—air scraping blood at the back of my throat. No words. No defiance. Just noise.

Ryan didn't look up from his work. "Sedate him." His voice was flat, clipped. A command he'd given before.

Nat didn't hesitate. A mask pressed over my mouth, rubber cold against split lips. I thrashed once, weak, pathetic. My ribs clanged against the retractor, the sound hollow, metallic, obscene.

"Easy," she whispered, her thumb brushing slow, mechanical circles across my skin. Pointless. Not comfort. Containment.

The hiss of gas filled me. My body went slack even as my mind screamed.

"You'll live," she said, the words steady, clinical. For a heartbeat they almost sounded tender—until I understood they weren't a promise. They were a sentence.

The light above fractured, bending and pulsing, until it wasn't a lamp anymore but an open eye staring down at me. My veins buzzed like they weren't carrying blood at all—just signals. Static looping endlessly through a body that was less mine with every breath.

Noise in the body.

Maybe that's all I was now—just noise moving through a machine, waiting for him to decide which parts were worth keeping.

When I was lucid, I screamed.

When I wasn't, I floated.

Sometimes Nat didn't look at me at all. Other times, she lingered. She'd unfasten my arms, wipe the blood from my skin with a rag that smelled of bleach and peppermint. Once, she dabbed vomit from my chin and sat beside me, her finger tracing a scar just above my hip.

"You're healing fast," she said, almost like it annoyed her.

"Don't sound so heartbroken," I croaked.

A small, sharp smile tugged at her lips. "Most of them fall apart by now. I've seen it. All of them. But you..." Her fingers stilled on the rag, as if she'd said too much. They came from far away, muffled, like they had to push through water to reach me. "You're the first to make it this far."

The words should've felt like hope. They didn't.

All I felt was the sick pull of inevitability—like being the first just meant I'd last longer before breaking. I repeated what she'd told me: luck isn't survival, it's endurance. I'd heard that word before. At funerals. In therapy rooms. Hospital beds. There, endurance meant healing. Here, it meant surviving long enough for the next cut.

I tried to sit up. Failed. My limbs felt like steel poured into cement.

"Was that supposed to be comforting?" I responded anyway, pretending I was still anchored here, still whole.

"No." She swirled her juice in its glass, the sound sharp in the silence. "But if I were you? I'd take what I could get."

The stitches in my side itched like they'd been sewn with fire. Still, I tried.

For a while I told myself maybe that was enough—that surviving each day, each cut, was its own kind of win.

But then came the night he took my sight.

The pain was different this time. Not the quick bite of a blade, not the clean burn of wires threading through muscle. This was slower. Intimate. Like he wanted me to feel his hand inside the last place I had left—my vision.

I woke to the clamp forcing my head still, jaw locked by a brace so tight my teeth groaned. The light above me blazed too bright, too close, washing the world into a smear of white. And in the blur, his shadow bent over me. Calm. Deliberate. "Do you know why people fear blindness?" he asked, scalpel poised. "Not because of the dark. Because in the dark, you're left alone with yourself. And you, Ty..." His chuckle was low. "...should prepare for that."

The scalpel kissed the corner of my lid. A shallow drag, almost gentle. Then deeper.

I tried to scream, but it came out strangled, half-swallowed. Hot wetness spilled across my cheeks, streaking down into my ears, my hair. I couldn't tell if it was tears or blood. Maybe both.

He worked with a patience that was obscene. Every scrape was purposeful. He wasn't carving me apart. He was signing me.

And I cried. God, I cried. Didn't mean to. Didn't want to. But the tears came anyway, hot beneath the gauze he wound tight across my face, searing the cuts until it felt like my own sobbing was acid eating me alive.

Heat lanced across my sockets, tunneling deep. And then—black. Not the drifting black of sedation, not the merciful black of sleep. A forced blindness. A theft.

Somewhere, I realized I'd never see the ceiling lights pulse again. Never see his mask, his smile, Nat's eyes when they flickered soft.

The world shrank to sound. To breath. To pain.

And I hated that what broke me most wasn't the loss of sight. It was the quiet certainty that he wanted me alive to feel it. That he'd taken something essential and left me tethered to the rest, like an unfinished canvas he could come back to whenever he pleased.

Then came the pressure. Heavy. Cold. Metal slid into the hollows where my eyes had been, pressing against raw bone. It wasn't delicate. It wasn't careful. It was placement. Installation.

I could hear him humming again, off-key, casual, as though this was no more intimate than fixing a hinge. Something clicked—a soft mechanical lock settling into the cavern of my skull.

"There," Ryan whispered, satisfaction curling at the edges. "Better than sight. Now you'll see as we do."

Then came the bandages. Layer after layer, wound tight, suffocating. Each strip sealed me further in, burying the heat, the sting, the alien weight lodged in my head. By the end I wasn't a person. I was a wrapped specimen. A project shelved for later.

After the hum of machines quieted, after his footsteps faded—I felt another presence. Lighter. Closer. The air shifted, warmer near my face, carrying the faint trace of antiseptic and something sweet I couldn't name.

"Talk to me," I begged. My voice was sandpaper, scraping through the gauze. "Please. Say anything."

Silence. Too long. Too heavy. The kind that made you think you'd been abandoned, even when you knew someone was still there.

"Nat, please," I croaked.

"Did you ever have anyone?" I pushed. "Friends? Family?"

Her voice finally came, soft in a way I'd never heard. "I think... there was someone. Ethan."

"Ethan," I repeated.

Her breath hitched faintly, like the name itself carried weight. I couldn't see her, but I could feel the pause, the hesitation vibrating in the silence. When she spoke again, the word dragged out of her like it hurt.

"...and Carter."

That name landed different. The air around me seemed to tighten. I felt her hand brush against my arm, then find the wire beneath my skin. Her fingers traced the edge of it, careful, lingering longer than she meant to.

Her grip stilled, her hand trembling faintly where it rested. "Sometimes," she whispered, "you really are just like him."

"Who was he?" My voice cracked against the gauze. "Who's Carter?"

Her exhale was slow, shuddering. When she answered, her voice was crooked, haunted. "Someone who changed the course of my life forever. Without him... none of this would've been possible. Saved me from dying on this table, and... I still haven't decided if I'm grateful for that, or if I wish maybe I had."

"What does that mean?" I rasped.

Silence again—except for the faint buzz of instruments cooling on the tray. I couldn't see it, but I heard the faint hum, smelled the iron sting of blood on metal.

"What the hell does that mean, Nat? What did he do?"

Her grip tightened on my arm. Too tight. Pain flared, shooting fire through the wire beneath my skin. I whimpered before she let go, her hand leaving a cold absence behind.

"I—I'm sorry, Ty," she said at last.

The floor above groaned. Footsteps. She stilled, listening. Then I heard the faint scrape of her palm press against the tray of tools, metal clinking under her weight—like she needed the cold steel to steady herself.

When she spoke again, her tone had shifted. Detached. The shutters drawn tight.

"Look, this isn't therapy. It's surgery."

Her steps moved toward the door, each one soft but deliberate, the faint brush of her clothes filling the silence I couldn't stand.

"Nat..." My throat cracked. "Will I ever see again?"

She froze. The air between us thickened, her breath catching just enough for me to hear it. When she finally spoke, her voice trembled in a way I hadn't heard before.

"I—I don't know, Ty. There are variables outside of mine, and even Ryan's, control."

Her hand found my arm again. Not gentle. Not cruel. Just functional. She hauled me upright, my legs buckling, and dragged me forward in jerks and stumbles, her shoulder braced under mine. I could smell her hair, sharp with antiseptic and smoke, and I hated that I noticed.

The hallway tilted and lurched as she pulled me along, my heels scraping across the floor. She stopped only when we reached my cell. I felt the cold edge of the cot against my calves before she lowered me down, a controlled collapse.

For a moment, she lingered. I could hear her palm rest against the metal doorframe, the faint creak of weight against steel.

Then her voice came—light, casual, almost playful, like none of what she'd admitted before had ever happened.

"Promise me you won't die tonight. It'd be a real bummer."

Then the door shut, leaving me with nothing but the static crawling under my skin and the echo of her words. And the worst part—the part I hated most—was how much of me wanted her to come back. Not to save me. Just so I wouldn't have to sit in the silence long enough to forget I was still alive.

CHAPTER 16

THE CELL SWALLOWED ME WHOLE. No light, no edges—just the weight of air pressing close. Damp in the walls. Rust in the pipes. Every sound came sharp, exaggerated, like the dark was straining to fill the space my eyes couldn't.

That's when I heard it. A soft crackle. A hum, faint but alive, building in the corner. The monitor. Its static buzz crawled along the concrete, vibrating faintly through my spine where I leaned against the wall. For a second, I thought it was my own eyes trying to spark back on.

And then—her voice.

"Hi, I'm Echo! Or at least I think I am. You must be new!"

Too bright. Too chipper. Like a children's show character waking in a morgue.

"I'm not—" I rasped, throat shredded, forcing the words through bandages that reeked of iron and disinfectant.

"Oh, I'm sorry!" she chirped. "My memory resets every ten minutes. Let me recalibrate." A pause, then the faint crack-pop of static before she came back, voice reanimated. "Hello, sunshine. You look taller today."

I pressed my head against the screen's casing, felt the faint warmth bleeding through old plastic, buzzing into my skin. My throat burned. "I think I'm dying."

She shifted—no, not shifted. There was no body to shift. Just the cadence of her voice changing, pitched curious. Synthetic, but too close to human.

"Why would you say something like that?"

"Because I'm tired," I muttered. "Because I'm bleeding inside. Because I keep hoping if I close my eyes long enough..." My voice cracked. "I'll see my brother again. But now all I see is darkness, and he's still gone."

Silence. Then a flicker in her tone, like static warping speech.

"What was his name?"

"Liam," I whispered, naming the ghost. "He died after coming home. Couldn't take what the war did to him. He stopped calling. Then he stopped breathing. Like the world just... swallowed him."

The words scalded on the way out. They'd been buried too long, buried so deep I almost believed they'd stopped hurting. They hadn't.

"I wonder if he'd be proud of me. Or if he'd tell me to let go already. That it's okay. That it's my time to go."

The air pulsed with static. The walls hummed like they were carrying her voice to me, not just the monitor.

"Is it nice?" she asked softly. "To have a brother?"

I laughed. Broken. Bitter. "It was. Guess I still have one to spare. He probably thinks he's the last one left."

"If I had a brother," Echo said, "I'd want him to teach me songs. And maybe how to swim. And I'd draw him pictures so he wouldn't forget me."

My throat tightened. No words would come.

"You think that's dumb?" she asked.

"No," I croaked. "I think it's beautiful."

The hum deepened, warbled, like her circuits strained against themselves.

"You're nice when you're not screaming," she said.

"Maybe I'm losing myself."

"Then I'll remember you," she promised. "Even if it's just for ten minutes at a time."

I clenched my jaw, eyes burning uselessly under the gauze. I couldn't tell if she knew me or not. Couldn't tell if she was lying, or just trying to spare me. The not-knowing was worse than the pain.

"Echo," I whispered, "what's my name?"

Another pause. Then her voice came back, faintly glitched, but carrying something almost like sorrow. "Why, you're Trey. The one worth remembering. The one who is going to try."

My heart buckled. The name hit like a hammer. But somewhere inside, a small ember of hope refused to die. Maybe a fragment of me lingered in her memory. Or maybe Trey was someone else—someone who had died here before me. Another ghost in the machine.

"My name is Ty. Tyler Alcaster." My voice trembled. "But... close enough."

The static inside me roared like a storm trapped under my skin. Somewhere down the hall, a scream began—and didn't stop. I didn't know if it was mine.

But then—I asked something I hadn't dared ask before.

"Echo," I said, voice frayed, raw. "What was she like? Nat. Before all this... before he broke her."

There was a pause, static swelling in the wires. When Echo finally spoke, her tone had shifted—quieter, fragile.

"Natalie Thompson," she said. "I remember her in pieces. A laugh in a hallway. The sound of her humming, faint, like she was trying to drown something out. Or maybe that was someone else. I don't know anymore."

I clenched my jaw, forcing the words through my throat like glass. "She seems broken now. Like the light's gone." I swallowed hard. "Echo... you got anything saved on her? Files? Something real?"

Her voice stuttered. A hitch in her programming. "I—I don't think I've ever checked. Or... have I?"

The way she faltered—*Or have I?*—made my chest tighten. It reminded me of Nat catching herself mid-sentence, shutters slamming down over something she couldn't let slip. Neither of them could hold the truth without breaking.

The hum deepened. Then came a sound like folders being opened—mechanical clicks layered over static, names spilling too fast to catch, corrupted strings of numbers and letters that made no sense.

One file seemed to open on its own.

The speakers crackled. Then—screaming. Raw, guttural. A woman's voice tearing itself apart. Straps creaked against a chair. Echo's audio sputtered and warped, but I could hear the struggle: wrists grinding against restraints, heels pounding against metal.

Nat. Younger.

Ryan's voice slithered in low, whispering words too close to the mic to make out. All I could decipher was the date: *February 17th, 1995*. He sounded almost tender, almost proud. Another male voice slithered in, one I hadn't heard before. He was older. Gruffer. Then a wet splatter—spit hitting him, sharp as a slap. I knew the sound. I'd done it myself.

Her scream grew higher, feral, then cut jagged when something metallic slid through flesh. The scalpel scraped against bone. I could hear her convulse, the speakers rattling under the violence of it, until the audio fractured into silence.

Black.

I thought that was it. Then—another file opened, unbidden.

This one was worse.

The audio came frantic. Fists pounding a wall, a boy's voice shouting, breaking, begging. Seventeen, maybe. And then—Nat. Sounding younger. Not sharpened, not perfected yet. Her voice close to the mic, whispering fast, desperate. The clank of a lock turning. The scrape of a door swinging open.

Footsteps bolting. Hope in motion.

Then a sound that hollowed me out: Ryan's laugh. And impact. The thud of a body slammed against concrete hard enough to make the speaker pop. Again. And again. Bones cracked like wet branches. Limbs bent wrong, hitting tile with a sound I'll never forget.

And Nat—she screamed.

Not like she does now. Not cruel. Not mocking. Human. Terrified. She threw herself at him, her shriek turning ragged as nails tore at skin, teeth snapping. For a half-second, she wasn't his accomplice. She was fighting him.

Static ripped it away.

When the feed returned, the boy's voice was gone. Just wet drags. A smear being pulled across tile. Nat sobbed somewhere low, animal, until Ryan's voice cut through—calm, almost delighted. A sharp hiss followed: a needle sinking into skin. Nat's scream spiked once, then collapsed into silence. The file ended there.

I sat frozen, acid burning up my throat, fury and sickness knotted so tight I couldn't breathe.

The hum in the walls shifted. Then Echo came back, too quick, too bright, her voice stitched into a smile that didn't belong after what I'd heard.

"I forget her. Every cycle. But then she walks by... and something inside me lights up. Like there's a piece of her in me." Her voice softened. "I think there's a piece of you, too."

I swallowed hard. "Then why don't you remember me?"

A pause. Then, gentle. "Sometimes... I pretend to. Just to make you feel better."

It cracked something in me.

"But the truth is... you're starting to stick," she added. "Like bad gum in good code. I don't remember everything. But I remember you... fondly."

"Even when I scream?"

"Especially when you scream." The audio warped. "I... wish I could help."

I laughed once. Just once. It sounded hollow, wrong in my own mouth.

Then it hit me.

"Echo... Carter." My throat scraped the words out. "You got anything on him? Who was he?"

For a moment, all I heard was the low hum in the wires, like the system itself didn't want to give me the answer. Then her voice came —measured, reluctant.

"Carter Sullivan. Missing since 2014. Presumed dead."

The words sat heavy. Twenty-six years of silence compressed into a single sentence.

The hum deepened, filling the room like a held breath. Then Echo's voice returned, softer now, reverent, like she was opening a file that shouldn't exist.

"Would you like me to reference Ryan's notes?"

I let out a breath that sounded too much like surrender. "Yeah. Do it."

Static rippled, and her voice changed—lighter at first, almost curious, then dropping into something reverent, like a child whispering a secret they shouldn't know.

"According to Ryan's notes... Carter came into contact with Ryan and Natalie in 1994. Several years before he disappeared. He exposed them both to Eurydium. It became the compound responsible for Ryan's earliest... success."

That word hit me like a knife twisted slow. *Success.*

"Eurydium?" I rasped, dry-throated. "That crap they outlawed?"

"Mostly outlawed," she said, and her smile glitched faintly in her voice. "But not quite. Found underground on several continents. Once thought to be a wonder-glass. Beautiful. Durable. They carved it into wedding rings. Melted it into antique bulbs. Shaped it into the lenses for glasses and screens—ones just like mine."

"Miners used to call it *ghostglass*," she added softly. "Said it throbbed like something alive when the lights went out."

She hesitated, her voice dipping lower, haunted. "It glowed faint orange... like a heartbeat."

The hum seemed to crawl closer to me as she went on.

"It was in the mines. It was in the sea. It was in the phones everyone carried. People were wearing it long before they knew its name. But in 2032 they learned the truth. Radiation. Severe. Toxic.

Unstable. Exposure corrupts its surroundings, alters tissues, drives the mind into places it cannot come back from. Several mines closed down. Most of them. Not all. Never all."

"I remember hearing about it as a kid, but... those were just stories. Some swore it could do anything, like affect reality or bring people back from the dead. But that was just the radiation, right? Cooking their brains enough to believe in ghosts where there were none."

"It's tough to say, Ty. Research continues. For the people who saw what they did, they believe in what it does. Dead friends. The veil blurring. Reality falling in on itself, or overlapping just at the right moment for entities to pass in and out of our current time. The possibilities are endless—though it tends to kill more than it saves."

My chest tightened. I couldn't see her, couldn't see anything—but Nat's eyes burned in my memory all the same. That faint shimmer. That impossible orange glow.

My hand drifted up before I realized it. Trembling, I pressed my fingers against the gauze wrapped across my face.

The thought clawed at me. *What if it was in me now too? What if there was a glow in my eyes, waiting to eat me alive?*

That was when the burn started.

At first it was just heat behind the gauze, faint as a fever. Then it spread—needling, clawing—an itch that burrowed deeper with every second, like something alive wriggling its way into my skull. My hands shot up before I could think. The bandages tore under my nails, strips of gauze coming away damp with sweat and blood.

I rubbed at the sockets, desperate to claw the fire out, but it only flared brighter. White behind the lids. Pressure. Crawling. My breath hitched into broken gasps.

And then—light.

My eyes opened. Not mine. Not the ones I'd lost. These were colder, sharper. The world didn't return—it warped. Edges bled orange, trembling like they were alive. For half a second, I wished for the dark again. The blind silence. Anything but this. The walls breathed. The shadows leaned too close. The monitor pulsed like a heart. Then, slowly, the orange receded, as if ashamed to be seen. The room looked normal again. Almost. But I knew it wasn't.

I froze, hands trembling at my face. I could see again. But it didn't feel like sight. It felt like invasion. Like the thermal goggles they wore in the field; sight enhancement, an extra, a perk. Integrated night vision, heat signature detection, and binoculars all rolled into one.

I swallowed, hard, the heat still crawling through me.

"The kids without hair. Nat's talk about survival. It's the radiation, isn't it?" I looked intently through my new eyes.

Echo's screen glitched, and my reflection ghosted back at me, pale, bruised, broken.

I didn't recognize him.

"Yes. Radiation. Mutation. Distortion. Eurydium doesn't just change the body, Ty. It rewrites the soul. It makes hunger out of memory. Obsession out of love. Feral. Violent. The kindest hearts turned cruel. Its possibilities are endless... if you survive."

There it was again. *Survival.* I didn't know what it was, but it felt like I was on the brink of something. A precipice I could never turn back from.

"How do we know I will?"

"I don't believe anyone knows," Echo said, tone matter-of-fact, almost chipper. "This is still an experiment. Just new variables. Similar test subject. Same conclusion—until proven otherwise."

"Echo..." My voice cracked, raw. "Am I even still human?"

Her pixels flickered, her face softening in a way no machine should.

"You never stopped being," she said. "You're just changing shape. Don't forget that. Please don't forget that."

The words sank into me like they'd been waiting all along. Not comfort. Not cruelty. Just truth.

I dropped my head, letting the exhaustion and weight overtake me.

"Thank you, Echo," I whispered. "One day, I'm getting out of here. Count on it."

And Echo whispered:

"Of course, Ty. But if you do leave... don't wait too long to come back. If you wait too long, I'll be new again. And I'll love you like a stranger."

The words cut deeper than any scalpel. To be forgotten—and still loved anyway. A love with no face, no reason. Just a ghost with no memory of who I was.

"Yeah," I muttered, forcing a half-smile she couldn't see. "Like I'd ever leave you behind."

CHAPTER 17

I woke to screaming.

Not mine, for once.

This one was sharper. Higher. A voice that hadn't been crushed flat yet. Still full of teeth. Still fighting.

I sat up too fast, skull pounding like somebody had rigged a bass amp inside my head. Vision split into ribbons, twitching light where there wasn't any. My throat rasped when I tried to swallow, the taste of rust and gauze still coating my tongue.

"Echo..." The word cracked coming out. "What the hell was that?"

For a moment, nothing. Just the hum. Pipes moaning in the walls like the whole house wanted to tell me it knew the answer but wouldn't. Then her screen buzzed awake, stuttering into shape—the pixelated face I couldn't stop thinking of as a ghost who hadn't realized it was dead yet.

"Hi there! I'm Ech—"

"Skip it," I rasped. "Who's screaming?"

She blinked, that cheerful cartoon mouth twitching too wide, like it hurt her to hold it. "You look... very awake today." Her waveform wavered like a nervous breath. "New arrival. Cell Two.

Brought in an hour ago. Young. Defiant. Screaming ratio seven-to-one."

I staggered to the wall, pressed my ear against cold steel, listening like I used to put my ear to the door in Liam's room just to know he was still breathing.

A sob cracked through the pipes. Then words—frantic, furious, young.

"Let me out! Someone—please—don't leave me here!"

My eyes shut. My stomach flipped.

"Echo." My voice was a thread, low and taut. "Anyone watching?"

"Main surgery cam is looping. Basement stairwell blind. Ryan is upstairs. For now."

I flattened my palm against the wall, hard, like pressure alone could bleed through, like I could pass bone into her space. "Hey!" The word tore out louder than I meant. "You're not alone."

Silence.

Then: "Who the hell are you?! What do you want with me?" Her voice was a blade, sharp enough to cut the quiet.

My heart thudded once. Twice. A warning bell in my ribs.

"Name's Ty," I said. "And trust me—I get it."

All I got back was her breathing. Rough, jagged, like she'd been running miles and got caught mid-step.

"They drugged me," she whispered, almost choking on it. "I—I think they cut something out of me. I don't even remember getting here."

"Yeah." My laugh was flat, hollow. "Checks out."

A pause stretched too long.

"Where am I? What is this shithole?! How long you been here?"

I tried for a smile but it cracked in half before it left my face. "Long enough to hate the wallpaper."

And that—God—got a laugh out of her. Bitter, wet, but real. It cut straight through me because it wasn't cruel. It was human. And I couldn't remember ever hearing anything human in this place.

"Long enough to crack jokes." She inhaled sharp, catching it in her teeth. "So what is this, a prank? Or am I gonna die here?!"

My jaw locked so tight I thought my teeth would crack. I wanted to tell her yes, to spare her the false hope. I wanted to tell her no, to keep that fight alive in her voice. All I could manage was the knife-edge between the two.

"Don't know," I said. "But I'm not letting it happen easy."

Echo's screen dimmed. Her voice dipped lower, softer than I'd ever heard her, almost human.

"Ty..." Echo's voice dipped, a glitch softening into something almost like pity. "He has plans. For her. I can see them."

My gut twisted, sharp and cold, like barbed wire pulling tight inside me.

"What kind of plans?" My voice was raw, dragged out of me.

Her reply fractured, her tone flattening like the system itself wanted the words gone.

"Sibling integration. That's what he calls it. Another prototype. One that learns. One that feels. Like you."

My stomach twisted. A word like that didn't belong here—it belonged in family photos, holidays, funerals. My brothers' faces flickered in my mind: Liam's hollow stare the day before he stepped off his chair, Jackson's expression as Liam's casket lowered into the dirt.

My fists curled tight, wires biting my skin.

Like me.

And then—her. The image slammed into me like a memory I hadn't lived. The girl from the dollhouse room. Small, terrified, hiding in that closet. Her voice cracking as she cried out: *I already have a brother!* I could see her wide eyes, hear the frantic edge. She knew. She'd known all along. Maybe she'd made it farther than I ever thought. Maybe she'd been here longer than even me. But then I just remembered the gore.

All of it carved through me. The weight of it pressed down hard. Ryan wasn't just repeating his experiments. He was rewriting families. Breaking them apart, stitching them back together crooked, like dolls missing limbs.

The cell door hissed, sharp enough to cut through my spiraling thoughts.

Echo's face blinked out—too quick, like she'd been forced silent.

And in she came.

Nat.

She strolled in like brunch was on the menu, velvet ribbon tied at the base of her ponytail—deep wine red, a color too romantic for a place like this. The rest of her outfit looked torn from a fever dream: a cropped baby tee the color of dark champagne, soft enough to cling, the neckline held by thin metallic stitching that glimmered when she moved. Over it, a translucent organza shrug shimmered faintly, adaptive fibers shifting tone between deep red and smoke, like it couldn't decide what mood it was in. Her skirt was high-waisted and pleated, but the fabric wasn't fabric at all—sleek, recycled synth-silk that moved like liquid, slit high up the thigh to reveal matte platform boots with iridescent laces that caught the room's dim light.

It was absurdly out of place. Too pretty. Too alive.

"Breakfast in the basement," she sang, lilting like it was a joke between us. Her eyes flicked to the bloodied gauze I'd ripped off last night, still curled on the floor like shed skin. She smirked. "Nice eyes, Ace. Looks like you're finally seeing things my way."

She set the tray down with a little flourish, like presentation mattered down here. I didn't move.

"You always wear heels everywhere you go?" I asked.

Her mouth twitched—half amusement, half warning. "Oh, I'm sorry, did I miss the *dress code* for the dungeon? Maybe next time I'll wear my sensible sneakers."

"Wouldn't want you to twist an ankle."

"Please," she said, rolling her eyes. "I've been walking over men like you for as long as I can remember."

"Yeah? You ever stop to look at where that got you?"

She peeled an orange with her nail, slow and deliberate, juice sliding down her hand like it belonged there. "Here. With you. Guess I'm a slow learner."

I didn't bite. "That girl in the other cell—what's her deal?"

"Oh, her? Yeah. We used to cycle through more, but you've kept us busy."

My voice hardened, scraping low. "And what, she's a 'sibling'?"

She hummed like the question barely deserved air. "You weren't supposed to know about that. Just Ryan playing house. His little family fantasy. Nuclear, in every sense."

"He'll break her," I muttered.

For a second—barely that—something shifted in her face. A flicker. Human. Regret, maybe.

"I know," she whispered. Then the shutters slammed down, smile snapping sharp and glossy again. "But don't stress, big brother. You've still got a part to play. Talk to her. There's not much time, but it's better than nothing."

She pressed the orange into my palm, cold and slimy, and left without another word.

I was starving. My stomach clawed at itself. But before I could even lift the orange to my mouth—another scream cut through the pipes. Louder this time. Closer.

"Let me go, you bitch!"

Her voice tore the hall apart, rattled the walls, shivered straight through the marrow in me. I pressed harder against the cold metal, wishing bone could pass through steel.

"Hey," I called, voice low and rough. "I know you don't know me. But I'm not one of them. I'm stuck here too."

Her answer came fast, jagged, teeth in every syllable.

"How the hell do I know you're not lying? That you're not him— the freak who dragged me down here?"

"Because if I was him," I shot back, sarcasm breaking through my raw throat, "you wouldn't still have a tongue to scream with. He doesn't do back-and-forths. He cuts first, doesn't talk at all."

A scoff ripped out of her. Quick. Bitter.

"Yeah, that's real comforting. Great alibi."

"Not trying to comfort you," I said, swallowing hard. "I've got nothing to sell. Only the truth. I was on vacation. My brother, his new wife. August. Couple weeks after we buried my other brother." My voice cracked, the words dragging pieces of me out with them. "That's who I was. Now? Hell if I know. But I'm not your enemy. That much I can swear."

Silence. Then a sharp little laugh—more bark than humor.

"Yeah, well... excuse me if I don't trust some random voice through a wall. Shit sounds like a setup."

"Trust me," I muttered. "Nobody's staging a setup down here. The décor's too shitty."

That earned me a snort. Quick. Unwilling. But real.

"You said August?"

"Yeah."

A pause stretched, longer than I could stand. Then, softer, almost like she hated giving me anything:

"It's May."

The air punched out of me. Almost a year gone. My forehead thunked against the wall.

On the other side, I heard her breathing rough, uneven—like she was trying to keep it together and failing.

"Jesus..." Her voice broke, sharp with disbelief. "Why are they keeping you so long?"

I swallowed hard. "Because I'm Ty. Tyler Alcaster. Twenty-three —guess twenty-four now." Bitter laugh. "Guess that makes me something special, although they'd never admit it. What about you? Who are you?"

"...Amelie. Sixteen. Seventeen in a couple months. If I make it that far." Her laugh was low, cracked, like glass about to shatter. "My foster parents are probably losing their shit right now. They'll think I bailed. I promised them I wouldn't...Guess I broke that one, huh?" She sniffed, then added, quieter: "They were the first people who didn't look at me like I was temporary. I was supposed to graduate next year with them watching."

I pressed my hand harder to the wall, as if I could reach through, touch her pulse.

"Amelie... I can't sell you sunshine and rescue teams. Don't got that in me. But I'll fight for you. That's all I can give."

She let out a shaky breath. The edge in her voice dulled. Still there—but softer.

"Don't make promises you can't keep."

I huffed out a humorless laugh. "Yeah? Don't tell me what to do."

"Fine," she shot back. "Then just... don't make me regret talking to you."

CHAPTER 18

HER FOOTSTEPS CAME—SLOW, deliberate. Not echoing, but swallowed whole by the walls, the rotten insulation trying to bury the sound before it reached me.

The door sighed open, and Nat stood there. Not triumphant. Not angry. Just... there, like showing up was the favor, and I should've been grateful. Behind her, light bled in from the hallway, weak and pale, but sharp enough to sting my new eyes.

"Time's up, Wonder Boy." Her voice was sweet in the wrong way, the word boy bitten off like candy left too long on the tongue.

My throat was desert-dry. I didn't know what today meant. I never did. But the image of the last woman wouldn't leave me—the one Ryan made me watch. Every scream catalogued, every flinch branded into me like homework I could never finish.

Nat didn't wait for an answer. Her hand closed on my wrist, cold and casual, and she pulled me up like she was dragging me to a dance I wouldn't agree to.

The hallway groaned around us as we walked. Lights flickered overhead, their hum threading into the wires that crawled across the ceiling like veins. The whole place was alive—sick, hungry. A body wasting away, dragging me through its insides.

The smell hit first. Sterile sharpness. That surgical tang that burned the back of my throat. But beneath it—rot. Old. Sour. Like opened bodies that had left their memory thick in the air. My stomach twisted, bile edging up my throat.

The room swallowed me again. Nat strapped me in without a word. Her motions were smooth, automatic. Practiced. And through it all, she hummed—low and tuneless, halfway between lullaby and mockery. Her hair slipped forward over her shoulder as she leaned close, and I caught the faintest ghost of perfume. Something floral. Something dated—alive. Something that didn't belong here.

"Should I be scared?" My voice cracked, thin against the walls.

She looked at me then. Really looked. And for a second, I thought I saw her falter. But no answer came.

"Nat. Please. Tell me."

Her gaze held mine too long, and that's when I saw it—the shimmer. Orange buried deep in her pupils. Not light. Not reflection. Something living there.

"Have you liked anything we've done to you?" Her voice was soft at the edges, almost weary. Already knowing the answer. She leaned closer, her breath cool against my ear. "Today isn't about you."

The name wasn't said. Didn't have to be. *Amelie.* It cut sharper than the straps.

"You don't have to do this," I muttered, wrists burning as the steel bit deeper. "You don't have to hurt her."

She didn't smile. Then, eyes sharp as glass: "We all do things we don't want."

The last brace cinched tight across my other arm. Except—

It didn't.

It stayed loose. Not much. Just enough. Too precise to be a mistake.

Her fingers lingered on the strap, colder than the leather, almost tender. For a heartbeat, I thought she might take my hand. I hated myself for it—that even now, some part of me wanted to believe her touch meant more. That it meant maybe she hadn't given herself fully to him. That maybe she couldn't.

Her eyes darted toward the door. A flicker. Quick. Gone.

This wasn't freedom. It was something else.

Nat wasn't giving me a way out. She was giving me a choice.

A chance to do what she couldn't.

To be the person she'd needed forty-six years ago.

"Don't do anything we might regret," she whispered.

The door hissed open.

And they wheeled her in.

Amelie.

Her hair hung long and black, pin-straight, streaked with sweat, sticking to her face like she could disappear behind it if she kept her head down. A metallic windbreaker clung to her shoulders, cheap chrome fabric catching the light in sharp flashes. Underneath—a worn band tee, faded from too many washes, the print cracked across her chest. Loose black shorts, knees scuffed and bleeding, dust and asphalt ground into the skin like she'd fought every step.

She looked like she should've still been outside somewhere. Sun on her skin. Music in her ears. Anywhere but here.

Her features were soft. Too soft for this room. Bruises cut across her face in ugly purple arcs, making the softness feel like an accusation.

Her body trembled, but not with fear. Her eyes—dark and wired, hunting—tracked the ceiling, the doors, the corners. Mapping. Calculating. Breaking the room apart in her head piece by piece.

Her wrists were clamped, eating into her skin. When she spoke, her voice scraped out raw but aimed clean.

"There's people looking for me," she rasped, the sound scraping her throat raw. "I've got a family. They'll find me. They'll find both of you!"

The lie rang clear—too neat, too practiced—but she wielded it like a weapon, hurling it at the silence like it could cut. Not begging. Not bargaining. A cornered animal daring the trap to spring.

And for a second, I saw it—what I used to be. Fire where fear should've lived. A spark Ryan hadn't ground into ash yet.

Ryan followed behind her, calm, measured, as if the whole scene belonged to him. His gloves snapped into place with a performance's precision, his blue scrubs swishing with each moment. The light skimmed across his smile, too bright, too polished, the kind of smile that belonged to someone who'd never once doubted he belonged in control.

"Easy," he said smoothly, voice meant for the room, not her. He dabbed her damp forehead with a folded cloth, deliberate, like he had all the time in the world. "Save that anger. You'll need it later."

Amelie flinched hard, baring her teeth like a feral thing. "Touch me again and I'll bite your fucking hand off."

He didn't blink. Just laughed softly, a warm, indulgent sound, as if humoring a child. Then his gaze slid past her, locked on me. And stayed there.

"Your big brother here?" he said, tapping a scalpel against his palm, a rhythm too steady to be casual. "He was a lot like you once. But he learned." His smile curved tighter, sharp as wire. "Didn't you, Ty?"

My chest burned. I froze, pressing my arm down hard against the strap.

Nat wheeled a tray closer. The metal shrieked, the tools rattling like eager teeth champing at the bit. Ryan let his gaze rest on Amelie, but his words weren't hers to hold.

"This one's got spirit," he said. Then, quieter, his eyes catching Nat's, "But spirit is temporary. You know that. You felt it. The way pain strips it down, layer by layer, until there's only the truth left."

My stomach clenched. Quiet, careful, I worked at the strap. Inch by inch. Breath held. And then—slip. My wrist. Free. My pulse thundered in my ears.

Amelie kicked when he dragged a marker across her thigh, the tip squealing against her skin. "Go to hell."

He didn't even look at her. "Hell's too easy," he murmured.

"Look around—I've already built it." Then his voice shifted, low, coaxing, finally regarding her. "All I want is something real. Realer than Heaven or Hell. Realer than an afterlife. Survival. A life worth living. A life that doesn't end."

The bone-saw screamed to life. The air shuddered with its teeth, its hunger, until the whole room seemed to vibrate with it.

Nat stood beside him, unmoving. Her ribbon hung loose, limp as a dead thing. But her eyes—her eyes flicked to me. Just once. Quick as lightning. A crack in the mask.

The second strap came loose. Then the last.

The world snapped into fury.

I surged, slamming into Ryan with everything left in me. The bone-saw screamed as it clattered away, its teeth chewing Amelie's thigh on the way down. Sparks skittered where steel met metal, the blade still spinning wild. The thing bounced, whirring, a live animal dragging itself across the table and slicing into her leg.

Amelie shrieked, jerking sideways, bound too tight to escape it. The smell of burned cloth hit the air as the saw grazed her jeans, the teeth biting shallow.

Nat was on her in an instant. "Shit—hold still." Her hand shot out, faster than breath, throwing the saw to the tile before it chewed deeper, pressing down hard against Amelie's wounds, her face carved from stone, marble cracking in her eyes but never breaking.

I didn't stop. I couldn't. Every scar, every scream, every night under his knife roared through my fists like they'd been waiting for this moment.

He's human, I told myself. *He can die.*

I drove into him until I felt bone give—ribs groaning under my weight, blood spraying hot against my skin. His breath hitched, stuttered. For a second, I thought maybe he'd built me strong enough. That maybe this was it. That maybe it would end here.

Then his fist rose.

One strike. My jaw snapped sideways with a crack that echoed in my skull.

Another. My vision burst into white, bursting stars.

His hand clamped the front of my collar, and before I could drag in air, he lifted me—unnatural strength, mechanical, merciless—and drove me down. My skull slammed the tile with a sound like a bat against glass. The floor spidered beneath me, blood seeping into the cracks like a paint by number video. My cheek mashed into it, copper flooding my mouth.

I tried to rise, but he was already on me. His weight pressed me flat, his knee grinding into my shoulders until I could hear my bones protest. His breath above me was steady. Controlled.

Then came the sting.

The syringe slid into the base of my spine. Sharp. Precise. The bite spread quick, cold venom rushing through my nerves, cutting the strings one by one until my body sagged into useless weight.

Ryan rose slow. Deliberate. He brushed the blood from his lip with the back of his glove, casual, almost indulgent. He stood over me, his shadow carving the light into oppressive shapes. Calm. Too calm. Worse than rage. Worse than cruelty.

"You just keep surprising me," he murmured. His voice wasn't for Nat. Wasn't for Amelie. It was for me. Always me.

Low. Intimate. A sound made to live under my skin.

He crouched, fingers pushing through my hair, ruffling it like he was congratulating me on the effort. My body trembled, not with choice but with the scraps of nerves still firing.

"Fire burns out eventually," he said, smiling like it was a secret only we shared. "And maybe that's the only reason you're still here. You keep burning. Hate. Anger. Rage. They're the only things propping you up."

His gaze stayed on mine as he rolled me onto my back, like he was laying down someone precious. A lover. A child. A thing he owned.

I could smell him. Antiseptic sharpness on his gloves, faint cologne threaded beneath it. Deliberate. Chosen.

His eyes softened. That was what made it worse.

"Tell me, Ty," he whispered, voice coaxing. "Is that it? Hate? Do you dream of it? Every cut reversed. Every scar carved into me instead of you?"

I tried to move. To scream. Nothing. The paralysis chained me still, locked me inside my own body.

His smile widened. Admiring. Almost tender.

"Good," he whispered. "Hold onto that. Relish it. Let it burn. That means I've left something in you worth feeding."

His shadow swallowed me whole as he dragged a gloved hand down the side of my face. Slow. Reverent. Like he was memorizing the shape of me.

Then his fingers hooked under my jaw.

He pried my mouth open like livestock, tilting my head back with calm precision. His eyes didn't waver as he peered in, clinical, curious. His thumb dragged across my molars, pressing firm, testing me.

"Nothing broken," he murmured. His voice had gone soft again, like a lullaby. "You're taking it well. Stronger every time."

His thumb pressed heavy against my tongue. The paralysis made me gag shallow, useless. His smile curved at that—pleased, like he'd discovered some small, private secret.

"Even that's still strong."

He released me. My jaw sagged open, helpless, a silence I couldn't control spilling into the air. His shadow hovered steady above me, patient, unhurried—like he had all the time in the world to spend right here, dismantling me inch by inch.

His gloved hand slid from my mouth down to my throat, tracing the line of my chest. Slow. Intentional. He paused when he reached my heart, pressing just enough for me to feel the weight of it. Like the silicon and latex could sense the pulse it trapped.

"I thought maybe it was the radiation," he murmured, almost absent, like talking to himself. A hum threaded beneath his voice, tuneless, soft. "The phones in the dollhouse. The monitor in your cell. I thought maybe they kept you alive."

His hand drifted lower, deliberate, calm.

"But now..." He found my hand, pried it open with reverence. He handled me like I was fragile, glass in his grip. "Now I think it's just me."

He toyed with my finger gently, rolling the knuckle between his thumb and forefinger. He stroked it like something precious. Then, sudden—violent—a twist.

The crack was loud enough to split the room. Sharp. Wet. Final.

I didn't feel it. Not the pain, not the shock. Just the sound. Detached, hollow. Like it wasn't mine at all. Like I was forced to witness someone else being broken while trapped inside their body.

Nat's eyes flicked toward me. Her chest didn't rise. Didn't fall. She looked like she'd forgotten how to breathe.

"Leave him alone!" Amelie's scream cut through, jagged, raw. She thrashed against her restraints, the clang of metal against metal ringing like a war drum. Her voice splintered, still she pushed it louder. "Do you hear me?! Leave him the fuck alone!"

The cameras above twitched, turning away, like even Echo couldn't stomach it—couldn't look at what she was tethered to.

Ryan laughed at it. Low. Soft. Dreamy. The kind of laugh that didn't belong here but somehow owned the space. "You too, huh? God, I love this," he whispered, almost reverent. He tilted his head toward me, toward them. "The way you all rally for him! Look at us—bonding."

Then, without warning, he snapped another finger. Quick. Casual. As though he was testing piano keys.

Amelie screamed before the sound even died, thrashing so hard the table shrieked across the tile. "Stop it! Leave him the fuck alone!"

Nat's voice broke in over her, sharp and cracking. "Ryan! Chill! Don't we have better things to be doing?"

Ryan laughed through both of them, his voice cutting clean. "Better? No." Then his gaze slid back to me, holding, unblinking. "No, this is exactly what we should be doing."

His hand left my ruined fingers, gliding down to the floor beside me. He lifted the bone-saw with both hands, reverent, like he was raising a relic in a cathedral. His grin was calm. Patient. Certain.

The room tightened around me.

No. No, no, no.

The teeth spun to life. A mechanical snarl. The sound devoured everything else—the lights, the voices, the air. The vibration rattled the tile, the straps, the marrow still clinging to my bones.

And then he set to work.

The first cut was the elbow.

Not rushed. Not messy. Clean. Precise.

The joint gave with a crack like old wood snapping under weight. Hot blood sprayed across my chest, spattered his gloves, streaked the tile that was already slick with me. It ran into the grout,, crawling outward, like even the blood wanted to escape this room more than I could.

This is it, I thought. This is what it feels like to be taken apart. This is what it feels like to die.

He leaned close as the saw pressed into my leg. His voice came low, personal, meant for me and no one else.

"You're holding together beautifully," he whispered, like a compliment. "I almost don't want to take you apart." His smile was soft, admiring. "But lessons have to be learned."

Then the blade sang.

Through tendon, through flesh, through the hard white of bone. Unhurried. Reverent. He hummed as he worked, a soft, tuneless vibration that crawled through my skull. The paralysis dulled sensation, but not sound. Never sound.

I heard it all. The splintering of bone. The hiss of tissue tearing. The wet slap of what used to be mine hitting the tile. The floor was so cold beneath my neck I wanted to sink into it, vanish into the cracks, disappear where the blood was already flowing.

Amelie screamed.

Not the movie kind. Not the empty kind. Her scream was jagged, torn from her ribs, shredding her throat until it broke. She forced it out anyway, dragging words through the ruin.

"Stop! Please! Ty!" Her cry cracked, then cut sharper, harder, like shattered glass. "Stop it! You hear me?! Leave him the fuck alone!"

Her words flayed me deeper than the blade. Like if she screamed my name loud enough, she could sew me back together. Like if she cursed him hard enough, she could pull me from the edge.

And for a breath, I believed her. Believed I was still something worth calling back.

But my body betrayed me. Convulsions wracked my limbs—reflexes, echoes—shakes that weren't mine. Blood bubbled in my throat. My lungs dragged like wet rags. My vision tunneled, the black chewing in from the edges until the world was a pinhole of light. The only sound left was my heart, heavy and broken, pounding like it wanted out of me more than I did.

Then Nat's voice cut through.

Not mocking. Not lazy. Not casual. Stripped raw.

Her lip trembled before the words found her. "Ryan..." A whisper, almost swallowed. Then louder, sharp, like snapping at herself just to speak. "Jesus Christ, enough!"

Her voice pitched up, biting, trying to wear armor it didn't have. "You've made your point, okay? He's not a fucking mannequin. He's —" Her throat caught, split. "He's almost there! Just stop!"

But he didn't. Didn't even falter. His focus never left me. He carved methodically, bone and muscle parting under his hands like wood shaved thin. His hum was steady, precise, unfazed.

Nat tried again. Louder this time, voice fraying, brittle with cracks she couldn't hide. "Ryan! Look at me. This isn't it, okay? This —this isn't the show you think it is. Just..." She staggered on the word, like her strength broke mid-step. "Just stop."

Still, he continued. His hum filled the room, a low drone, too calm, too certain. She was static to him. Nothing but background noise.

My pulse stuttered, each beat weaker than the last, like my blood had already chosen the floor over me.

Nat broke from Amelie's side. Her hand trembled as it rose, hovering before settling against Ryan's shoulder. It wasn't bold—it was desperate. A gesture like maybe, just maybe, she could touch him back into being human. Drag him out of whatever abyss he'd chosen to live in.

Ryan didn't even look at her. His hand shot out, fluid, mechanical, inevitable. He rose as he caught her, clamping her wrist hard enough that the grind of bone echoed louder than her gasp. His eyes lifted then—calm, unblinking, too close.

"Please..." The word slipped from her before she bit it back, forcing steel into her throat. "He's not Carter. He's just another kid."

Ryan tilted his head, grip unrelenting. The smile that touched his mouth was dangerous, the kind that bent closer instead of pulling away. "But isn't he?" His voice slid into the air like poison cut with honey. "Same look in his eyes. Same fight in him."

"But——"

Ryan yanked her in, lips grazing her ear. "Try me, Nat—and I'll take you apart just as easily. Then who'll put you back together?"

The words seared hotter than the saw.

My chest rattled, breath hitching wet and broken, blood bubbling at the corners of my mouth. I tried to speak—to tell her not to, to beg her not to give him reason—but all that came out was a guttural choke that spattered red down my chin.

Nat froze. Her lips parted. Her eyes widened with something caught between fury and terror. But she didn't pull her hand away. He released her instead, flicking her aside like she was nothing, weightless, disposable. His gaze slid back to me as though she had never existed.

Nat staggered back a half-step, clutching her wrist, the ribbon in her hair slipping loose. Her jaw locked. Her chest rose shallow, her breaths too careful, like even inhaling around him was dangerous now.

The saw screamed alive again. Another slice. Another limb gone. The floor became a graveyard of me.

I couldn't fight. Couldn't scream. Couldn't do anything but watch him work. He paused only once, brushing damp hair from my forehead with his blood-streaked glove. The smear he left was tender, obscene. "You're so close to perfect," he murmured, as though sculpting me instead of dismantling me piece by piece.

The lights above jittered, shadows stretching too long before collapsing into black.

Then, the static came.

Echo's voice fractured through behind my eyes—half hers, half mine.

"Ty—remem—"

A flicker. Liam's laugh, warped like it was played through water. Jackson's hand at the funeral, steady on my shoulder, warm for a moment then gone. Nat's eyes in the club, neon bleeding at the edges. Amelie screaming my name until it broke into static.

"—don't—forget—"

For a second, I wasn't in the room. I was at the ocean. Not here. Not this hell. Just endless blue, breathing. Waves rushing in my ears like blood in the walls. Liam stood at the shoreline, whole again, smiling, waiting.

And then it shredded. Gone.

"I—wish I could help," Echo said, faint. Her voice broke in two places at once, like something fragile splitting down its middle.

Another flicker. Our first words.

"What can you do?" I'd asked her once.

"I'm in charge of the whole building—in a way! I oversee room monitoring, power flow, thermal tracking, camera feeds..." Her tone jittered, childlike one second, hollow the next, like two ghosts sharing the same body.

Another memory bled in.

"Am I even still human?" I'd asked her.

"You never stopped being," her voice lingered, faint, a ghost made of code and longing. "You're just changing shape."

And then—

"Thank you, Echo," I whispered. Or thought I whispered. I couldn't tell anymore if it was memory or now. "One day, I'm getting out of here. Count on it."

Her reply glitched, stuttered, too close to a sob. "Of course, Ty. But if you do leave... don't wait too long to come back. If you wait too long, I'll— I'll be new again. And I'll love you like a stranger."

The light swallowed everything. Blinding white. A surge of pain, of silence, of annihilation so total it felt like I was dissolving.

Like I'd ever... leave you behind...

And then—dark.

No hum. No saw. No voices.

First my body slipped. Then my name. What was left sank into the quiet.

And for the first time, I didn't know if I wanted to come back.

CHAPTER 19

I woke in a bed.

Not a cot. Not a gurney. Not the slab of steel with rigid straps that still burned phantom lines into my wrists when I closed my eyes.

A bed.

Sheets that whispered when I moved. A duvet soft enough to swallow me whole. Pillows that hadn't been drowned in blood, or sweat, or whatever came after both. The kind of bed you'd see in a catalog—perfectly staged, untouched, waiting for a body that was never meant to bleed on it.

The air smelled of citrus—manufactured comfort, boiled into a chemical. A hotel room scent: forgettable until it follows you home.

My first thought was simple, hollow, certain. I've died.

I sat up. Braced myself for pain—for the fire in my ribs, the dragging ache of bones forced back together wrong, the tremor that always came before the screaming. But nothing came. Just quiet. A silence inside my body I didn't trust.

Then I looked down.

My arms. Whole.

My legs.

My hands.

I lifted them into the light, flexed my fingers. They obeyed. Smooth. Effortless. Perfect. Too perfect. No stitches, no bruises, no wires braided under the skin. No map of scars to prove I'd been through hell. Just flesh—rewritten, repainted, repurposed.

Rebuilt.

I pushed the covers back and stood. My bare feet sank into the carpet—cold, clean, sterile. Across the room, my clothes sat where someone had left them with eerie precision: clean combat slacks folded on the chair, my jacket draped over the couch like a shed skin. The hood hung low, still holding the shape of my shoulders. My socks and boots waited neatly by the door, laces looped, dust still clinging to the soles like they remembered the world better than I did.

I ran a hand down my chest—bare. My body felt new, wrong. Too smooth. Too quiet.

The room—God, the room. My chest tightened as I turned, recognizing it before I wanted to. It was mine. Ours. The one I shared with Jackson and Sophia in what felt like a lifetime ago. Every corner exact. Every detail faithful. But too faithful.

The images inside the picture frames were crisp, the edges uncurled. The books on the desk sat upright, spines unbroken, pages too white. Even the lamp on the nightstand hummed with a brightness it never had before. It wasn't lived-in. It was staged. A memory reconstructed and polished until all the grit, all the fingerprints, all the reality had been scrubbed away.

I knew this place.

I didn't believe it.

Like staring at a memory and a dream all at once.

I staggered to the bathroom like a man pulled toward destiny, and turned the corner expecting something I recognized. Instead, I walked into a stranger.

The bathroom was exactly as I remembered—same tub, same square white tiles. Only too clean. No eyelash clinging to porcelain. No mascara bleeding down the drain. No Sophia. Just a stage set, sterilized of ghosts.

The mirror beside the shower looked back, flat and patient and perfectly indifferent. There I was — the Ty I remembered and the Ty someone had rebuilt from the same photograph. My hand rose slow, waiting for lag or smear or the cheap sleight that would tell me this was less than real. But the glass copied me. Too perfectly.

My skin was impossible. The scars that had scraped my forearms were gone, along with each and every one I had before I was taken. My knuckles from fights. My chin from when I ran into the mailbox of my childhood home. Every piece of me was ironed out as if someone had run a hot press over the last ten years of my life.

My hair sat trimmed and ordinary. My jaw was clean-shaven. The lines from stitches, the gouges the doctor had made into me — all buffed away. It wasn't the Ty who'd bled under fluorescent lights. It was a tidy, polite version of him, the one a man like Ryan would choose to take.

Only my eyes resisted the edit. They were mine — tired, heavy, the kind a funeral photographer would keep.

It was real. All of it. I know it was.

Then, for a heartbeat, traitorous and small, orange winked at the edge of the brown like an ember caught behind glass. And I felt it where it belonged: raw and hot in my skull.

I didn't think. My fist closed without permission.

The mirror shivered. Hairline fractures raced like frost across the surface. The crack sang — thin, high; tile took it and threw it back at me. I pulled my hand away waiting for the sting of broken skin, for the metallic bite on my tongue. Nothing. Not a drop. Only the echo of glass and my own ragged breath.

Panic sharpened. I struck harder. The pane rattled like something with lungs. The reflection held that new, fractured calm. For one absurd second I thought the glass itself might be lying— that the room was a stage prop, and if I stopped believing in it, the truth would snap into place.

Still, nothing. No cut. No scratch.

Anxiety clawed at me—I wanted blood, proof, anything. I

pinched until my arm screamed, dug in harder—nothing. The skin held, sealed tight, like it had been welded shut.

Every shred of me itched, my innards vibrating at a frequency I couldn't catch up with. An insect worming its way through me. My thoughts raced. Hysteria gripped my heart. *It was real. It was real and there's something inside me. Just under the skin. I had to know. I had to see.*

Frantic, I took a shard from the mirror's edge. Cold bit my palm. I held my breath and closed my eyes. The blade slid in a clean white line. Warmth finally let go and pooled, dark and thick on my wrist. My lungs unclenched with a savage, thankful animal gasp.

I peeled the cut jagged and shaking. What bled back at me was not honest flesh.

Beneath the ragged skin a weave of metal glinted—coiled cords, silver as struck lightning. They braided into the hollows where tendons should be, neat as factory looms, humming with low, electric insistence. Veins that hummed like buried power cables. The blood itself had the wrong weight, too viscous, clinging like oil to fiber and wire.

The room pitched. The reflection did not flinch as I wrenched the incision wider. Only the fractured glass watched, droplets beading on its face, and that ember at the edge of my eyes flared bright and angry, as if it were trying to warn me.

I staggered back, clutching the wound shut like I could unsee what was inside. The words slipped out before I believed them: "No... no, I'm not—" But the hum under my skin said otherwise. "I'm still me. I'm still me. I'm still—"

A knock, polite and absurd, came at the front door. Three light taps. Human. Normal. The rhythm of people who expect an answer and a smile. Someone on the other side was waiting for a reply.

Fuck. Fuck fuck fuck!

The word came out like a confession, a prayer, a curse. The knocking echoed in the room—soft, almost polite—like someone tapping a rhythm they'd known their whole life.

"Just a minute!" I barked, my throat raw.

The knocking continued. Same pattern. Patient. Insistent. As if the building itself were knocking.

I stumbled back toward the chair, yanking my combat pants from where they'd been folded too neatly. The fabric still held the faint warmth of someone else's hands—whoever had fixed me, cleaned me, staged this place like a life I didn't remember living. My fingers fumbled the zipper; it felt like trying to button up after resurrection. The towel slipped from my arm as I pulled the pants on, the movement sending a flare of pain up through my shoulder that made the room tilt.

"Shit," I hissed, grabbing the towel again, pressing it into my arm. It came away red. Not gushing, but steady—like my body couldn't decide if it wanted to be alive or not. I wrapped the towel tighter and tucked my arm against my side.

Bare feet thudded against the carpet—too soft, too staged—as I crossed to the door. The air-conditioning hummed like it was mocking me.

At the peephole, Nat's face filled the glass—sharp, composed like she'd been curated for this exact angle. Velvet headband pinning her hair back in a glossy sweep, dark as wet ink. Black patent heels that bit into the hotel carpet with every shift of her weight, the kind of vintage slingbacks you'd find in a thrift shop ad, now resurrected and deadly. She wore an oversized slate-gray blazer, cinched at the waist with a belt like it was more armor than clothing, the metallic sheen catching the hallway light just enough to make her look more expensive than the building deserved.

She didn't look like she belonged here. Not to this time at all. Like she was handed a bag of her old clothes and told to give the real world a shot.

She stared at the door like she already knew I'd open it. Like she didn't knock to ask permission, just to let me prepare.

I flung the door wide. "What's going on—where am I?!"

Nat tilted her head, a low-lidded grin curling over red lipstick that looked almost too glossy to be real. "What's it look like? It's a hotel." Her gaze slid past me, scanning the blood on the sink, the shattered mirror, the towel clamped to my arm. Her smirk faltered—just a flicker, like a glitch in her veneer.

"Jesus," she said. And the fact that she said it out loud made it feel realer than the blood did.

Then the mask slipped back into place. She hooked her thumb into her belt, casual and lethal. "You, uh... just wake up?"

She leaned against the doorway like she owned it—like she could lean against anything and make it part of her stage. The placard beside her read **1408**. Same as before. Same as always. A number that had once meant hangovers and bad coffee now felt like a brand.

I wanted to rip it off the wall.

The scent of her perfume pushed at the disinfectant, that familiar floral note that felt obscene in the clinical air. I stared at her. My voice was a rasp. "Cut the shit, Nat. What the fuck is this? Why are you doing this to me?"

"You gonna invite me in?" she asked, the words dipped in sugar and glossy edges. There was a flippant lightness to it, as if she were commenting on somebody else's unfortunate wardrobe choice. I stepped aside. She floated past me, and the room felt smaller where her heels had pressed into the carpet.

"Been awake five minutes and you've already found a way to wreck the place," she said, casual as a hostess lamenting a spilled drink. Her gaze lingered on the webbed mirror like a collector appraising a damaged heirloom. "Looks like you haven't changed a day."

"Where are we?" The question came out hotter than I wanted. "Why am I back? What did Ryan do to me?"

She turned slowly, the motion practiced and measured, like a realtor showing off a prime property. Her voice slid back to me over the neat quiet of the room as she sat on the bed. "You made it. We survived," she said, then softened for a tick before sharpening again.

"Kind of. Now, it's *showtime*, or whatever he calls it. Ryan wants the world to meet his legacy."

The word—legacy—landed in my chest like a stone. Images flashed unbidden: lights, cameras, a stage. My hands balled into fists. "Legacy?! Where is he?" Rage threaded my voice. "He—he was just on top of me. He—" I broke, the pain blooming into my mind. "Tell me where he is. I don't care if I die ending him!"

"Whoa, chill, Ace." She spread her hands, theatrical, as if she were diffusing a mildly annoyed crowd instead of answering an accusation that should have set the ceiling on fire. "Look around. No monitors, no scalpels, no screams." Her eyes flicked to the hall. She inhaled once, the tiniest hitch—enough to believe there was something under the surface—but she smoothed it. "He's gone. Which means it's time."

"Gone how?" I pushed. "Gone where? Time for what?"

She pivoted, the ribbon at her nape catching the light, and smiled. The smile didn't reach her eyes. "To introduce ourselves," she said. "He's letting us go. You. Me. It's over."

"No–" The single syllable was small, stupid next to everything that had been done. "Why? This has to be a trick. A test. What does he want? Why would he just let us go?"

"Because he's proud." Her lips tightened. "We're not a secret anymore. We're *complete*."

The word hollowed me out. Complete. Like some type of project. My gut turned. "And Amelie?" I asked, because it was the only thing that mattered. "Where is she? Is she—"

"She's here," Nat said, almost too smoothly. "Alive. As much as we are. You'll see her before the conference."

My breath snagged on that. "What? There are people? How long? How long have I been—"

Her gaze skated away then, a small, guarded movement. "That part doesn't matter," she said at first, and I felt the lie taste metallic in my mouth.

"It matters to me!" I said, taking a step towards her. "Please, Nat, it feels like I'm losing my mind!"

She hesitated. For the first time since I'd known her as a walking, breathing costume, something like real feeling hit her face. I touched her shoulder. Her skin was cold.

"Please." I choked. "It feels like I've been left in the dark and all I'm asking is for something— *anything*— grounding. If I'm free, really free, just tell me. How long was I out?"

"It's... been a while, Ty." Her lips trembled once, then flattened into something practiced. "It's October."

The word didn't just land. It *hit*—like a lid slamming shut.

Five months. Gone.

"He fixed you," she added, like she was delivering a favor instead of a sentence. "Be grateful."

My mouth went dry. "I was never broken!" I snapped, but the crack in my voice made it sound like a lie. "So what, you just left me there? Turned me off? Let me sit like a dead thing until he needed a prop? A showpiece?!"

Her smirk faltered. Just a twitch. "I—"

"What did he do to me?" The words felt like wire in my throat. "Do I have *new parts*, Nat? Tell me. *How many people* had to die so I could wake up again? How many pieces of them are inside me right now?"

Her eyes flicked away. Just for a breath. "Ty..."

"How many?" I pressed, stepping forward. "How much of me is even *me* anymore? Or did he build me out of whatever scraps were left over?"

"I did what I could," she said, too fast. Too rehearsed. "I wouldn't let him change you permanently."

"That doesn't answer the question."

She reached out, like she might touch my arm—like she had any right to. "You're still you," she murmured, peeling the towel away with care that felt like mockery. The torn flesh on my forearm had settled, the blood coagulated, skin too smooth, too *perfect*. "Just... different."

"Right," I said, voice flat. "Just reassembled."

Something flickered in her expression—anger or guilt or maybe both—before she shut it down. Like always.

I swallowed the taste of metal at the back of my tongue.

"Where is she?" My voice was low, steady now. "Where's Amelie?"

She pointed down. "Room 207. Go. Throw on your clothes. Say hi. Then, we've got a press conference to attend."

Press conference. The word curdled. Not survival—display. I wasn't a person anymore. I was a product. A renovated corpse. His masterpiece dressed in my skin.

"For what it's worth, I'm glad you made it." Nat's smile was almost sad. "You'll be amazing, really." she said. "And maybe for once I won't be so alone." And in that moment, I knew the last thing she wanted was for me to know how much she was lying to herself when she said it.

CHAPTER 20

THE CARPET under my shoes thrummed like a powerline. Each step felt like it might blink the whole place out of existence if I pressed too hard. The familiar digital ads flickered along the hallway walls — full-length panels with smiling faces glitching between broken pixels and static bursts. The air was caught between bleach and flowers — like somebody had tried to perfume a morgue and gave up halfway.

Finally, room 207.

The brass plaque was crooked, the number stamped like an afterthought. The kind of detail you'd notice when you were already thinking about running.

I knocked.

The door cracked open just enough for a seam of darkness to spill out. It hung there. Heavy. Like the room itself was holding its breath.

"Ty?"

Her voice. Small. Frayed. Still hers.

I pushed the door open the rest of the way.

Amelie sat with the curtains drawn tight, the only light a sickly glow leaking from behind the cracked bathroom door. She was perched on a thin bed, knees pulled up, hair falling like a black curtain where she could vanish if she wanted. Up close she was softer than I expected, like the room hadn't earned the right to hold her. But even in the dimness the orange ember flickered behind her eyes — that same ember that tied all of us together whether we wanted it or not.

We stared. Long enough for the silence to stop being empty and start feeling like a third person between us.

I stepped inside. Closed the door. The click sounded like a lock sliding into place. The room smelled of detergent and old pennies, sharp and metallic at the back of my throat.

"Hey," I said. It came out flatter than I meant.

"Hey," she answered, barely more than a breath. Her voice had grit at the edges, like she'd been screaming for a week and saved the sound just for me.

I sat down on the other bed. The springs sighed under my weight. She stayed on hers. Not touching. Not friends. Not enemies. Just two people trying to take stock of what was left.

For a beat she just watched me, her eyes moving over me like she was scanning for seams. Then, soft but steady:

"You look... different. Part of me thought you'd never wake up."

I almost laughed. It came out like a cough. "Yeah. Same here."

Her gaze lingered, sharp and searching. "So... is it really you in there?"

I flexed my fingers. Looked down at my hands like they might answer for me. "Depends what you mean by 'really.'"

She huffed, a bitter little sound. "You talk the same. That's something."

"Guess that's all they couldn't scrub out," I muttered.

Amelie drew her knees tighter to her chest. "They kept trying to make me one of you. Like I'm supposed to be proud or something."

"Yeah," I said, staring at the bathroom glow bleeding across the carpet. "Welcome to the club no one asked to join."

The silence between us wasn't empty. It had weight. It pooled in the corners of the room like water, heavy enough to bend my shoulders. Amelie shifted, a small movement that sounded louder than it should have. When she spoke, her voice came out low and raw, like she was trying to keep it from shaking but not quite managing it.

"Promise me it's over."

The ember in her eyes caught the dim light. The chipped edges of her voice scraped at something I didn't have words for. I rubbed the back of my neck.

"I don't know," I said finally. "We're still in his world. But... I think he got what he wanted from us. I just don't know what that means now."

She gave me a look—half-smile, half something else. "That's the worst pep talk I've ever heard."

"Yeah, well," I said, lips twitching. "I'm outta practice."

She shrugged, her eyes catching what little light was left. "You've been gone a long time, you know that?"

"Yeah," I said quietly. "Feels like I still am." My thumb dragged along my jaw, still not used to the smoothness there, like someone had ironed the old me out of my skin. "Last thing I remember is you. Trying to help. But I guess we made it, huh?"

"Did we?" Her eyes shifted past me to the door, like she was waiting for it to open on its own. "He fixed the dents. Apparently, that's a selling point."

I snorted. It sounded like a match being struck in the dark. She wasn't really old enough to have any 'dents' yet. "Selling point for who? Investors? His ego? Do you know who's waiting for us downstairs?"

She shook her head. "Just whoever gets him off."

I leaned forward, elbows on my knees. "So. How are you holding up? Literal question."

Her laugh was short, but it had teeth. It jumped straight to her eyes. "Holding up? I was strapped down and catalogued for a presentation. If 'how are you holding up' means 'how are you not dead yet,' then..." She shrugged, a tiny rise and fall like a glitch. "I don't know what to tell you." She tipped her head, like she was listening to something behind the walls, then shook it off. "What about you? Aside from the facelift."

"Very funny." My edge came out soft, like rusted metal. "I'm... awake. I can move. Still trying to come to terms with it all, but—yeah. I'm managing. Sounds like we're on the same boat."

"Same surgeon, different story," she muttered.

"What happened when I was gone? Asleep?"

She flinched a little at the word. "You weren't asleep, Ty. It was worse than that."

The air caught in my throat. "What do you mean? What happened? My arms, my legs—what happened after I—"

Amelie looked away, jaw tight, staring at a point past my shoulder like she could watch it instead of remember it. "I watched you die."

The words landed like a punch.

"Then—" Her voice broke, then reformed. "Then you were back."

Did I really die? Am I still me? Or just a body with a face stretched over it like a mask?

She kept going. "He cut into you, and just kept cutting, and cutting, and cutting. I screamed. I cried. But he wouldn't stop. And she just kept trying to console me. But she's not what she seems. She did nothing to stop it. She could've, but never did. Never would after, either."

My fingers dug into the comforter, clutching it until my knuckles blanched. "Then... how am I alive?"

"The same way we all are." Her eyes flicked down to her hands. "There was some... gem. Some orange glass he inserted into you after he was finished. And despite the bleeding, your heart just... kept going. Like you wouldn't give up. And part of me wished you had. But the other part just wanted you to wake up and take him down, before he could get to me next. But you never did."

"Not till now," I said, the words heavier than they should have been. My thoughts raced behind my eyes—everything that happened to me. Everything that happened to her. I felt inadequate. Worthless. Like I'd already failed and was still failing.

"Some days I'd wake up thinking I was still on the coast," she said softly. "Then I realized the waves were made of tile and fluorescent light." Her fingers curled inward, like she was holding something invisible. "My hands don't feel like mine sometimes," she murmured. Then, almost daring me, she hooked her thumb under the skin of her palm and tugged.

The skin peeled back a half inch, smooth as latex, showing the shimmer of metal threads beneath. She pressed it back into place, and it sealed without a mark.

"Like someone else's gloves are on them," she finished.

I stared at her hands. Small, clenched, thumb running over the knuckle like she was reminding herself they were attached.

My stomach turned. I looked at my own hands. No seams, no slips, no give. Just a healed-over line on my forearm, a ghost of something real.

She could peel herself open. I couldn't.

"Why you?" I asked, the words cracking. "Why can you do that and I can't?"

She let her sleeve fall back over her wrist. "Maybe because I'm number three. You're two. Nat's one. We all got built different. Experimental." Her eyes flicked to mine. "Guess that means none of us are finished."

"Do you still remember anything? Before all of this?" I asked. The words came out like loose screws rolling across the floor. I didn't want the answer, but I needed it. Needed to know if any part of her still held onto humanity.

"School trip," she said without looking up. "Last one before the end of the year. Walked toward the bus. Next thing—darkness. Woke up in a room with pink wallpaper." Her mouth twisted bitter. "Foster family probably thinks I'm dead by now. Lord knows I never would've left without saying bye to Marnie."

My eyebrows raised, pursing together, even though my face

didn't quite know how to wear it anymore. "That's...specific. Who's Marnie?"

"Specific helps," she muttered. "Keeps things from melting together. She's someone that mattered, though I probably don't anymore."

My memory drifted. To Liam's laugh. Jackson's dumbass stories at his last barbecue. The last conversation Sophia and I had before I stormed out of the hotel room.

Amelie picked absently at the hem of her jacket, fingers skimming the pocket. Then she paused.

"This used to have a hole," she said quietly, almost to herself. "Right here. Big enough for coins to fall through. Now it's... gone." She turned the jacket inside out to show the seam—perfect, tailored, like it had always been that way. My eyes drifted to the band tee beneath. The fabric no longer washed-out but rich and dark, like someone had gone back in time and rescued its color from fading. "It's like it never happened."

I looked down to my own clothes. The pants fit better than they ever had before—smooth at the waist, the fabric sitting against me like it had been measured, cut, and corrected by a bespoke tailor. Ryan hadn't just rebuilt us. He wanted everything to be perfect.

"So, you okay? Like, really okay? Not that 'I'm fine, don't ask' crap. You." Amelie met my eyes, steady for a beat.

The question landed right on a bruise. I let it sit before I answered. "I—I don't know," I admitted, voice clipped but honest. "It's like I can still feel the blade. And I swear, I think I could forget my own name if somebody else didn't say it out loud."

Her jaw tightened. "That's messed up."

"Yeah." I gave a dry laugh. "But I'm trying. It just feels like this is all some kind of trick. Like we're still in the basement and any second he's going to walk in and drag me back down again." I swallowed. "How do I know if this is real? If we're real?"

The silence this time didn't press; it hovered. Like a held breath.

"I don't know, Ty," she said finally, her voice small but steady. "But I don't even know if I'm scared anymore. I'm just... tired." She traced the edge of her sleeve with a fingernail. And for a moment, I saw him in her. Liam. Like he was sitting right there with me. "When they make us stand on the stage and smile at a room full of people who call us a miracle, what are we supposed to do?"

"Don't smile," I said without thinking. It came out flat, stubborn. "If I'm a miracle, I'll be the kind that doesn't want an audience."

Amelie's mouth softened around the edges, like she was letting a tiny piece of relief in. "Yeah. Just... promise me one thing," she said. "If you get a chance—don't let them see us falter. Don't let them put us on a turntable."

I caught the humor hiding under her fear. "Promise."

Outside, the hallway lights shifted, a faint electric sigh. Somewhere a muffled murmur—people moving, arrangements being made. It meant it was almost time.

"I can feel her coming," Amelie said suddenly, eyes locked on the door. "Nat, I mean. I don't trust her."

"Me neither," I said. "But Nat's a different kind of broken."

She considered that, jaw set. "Different broken is still broken."

"Yeah." I rubbed my temple. "But she's on our side. At least I think so."

"I don't know if she's more us than him," she said. "Just be careful."

"Sure," I said quietly. "You stick with me. I'll stick with you. If we're really free, I'm not going anywhere."

She looked at me then, like she was deciding whether to bet on a stranger. Then she nodded once, a small, fierce motion.

"Okay," she said.

The door hummed softly in the walls before a polite knock. Showtime. I swallowed the bile and the anger and the small, ridiculous spark of hope and told her, "Alright. Let's tell our story. Every last, horrid detail. Make the world know Ryan's not the hero he thinks he is."

She gave me a look that was half-grin, half-grimace. "Deal."

We sat there, two small lives lit by dim fluorescent light, and for a second it felt like a pact—not heroic, not clean, but stubborn in the way only desperate people can be. The hallway outside sighed, Nat's shadow shifted under the door, and the world leaned in to put us on display. We breathed in together, and for the first time since being rewired, I felt less entirely alone.

CHAPTER 21

THE FLASHES EXPLODED before we even made it out of the wings.

A wall of light. White. Red. White. Red. A world of strobe with no soul. The falsehood of paparazzi. Every pop sank into my teeth, buzzing down the back of my skull like a transmitter. The air hummed with it—static from too many cords plugged into the same socket.

Reporters pressed in from every side of the auditorium. Suits crinkled. Elbows dug in. Microphones stuck out like spears. Their voices tangled together, a rising murmur, messy and greedy, the sound of birds clawing at the same carcass. Big networks with cameras the size of coffins. Tabloids with crumpled notepads and eyes already looking for scandal. Even local stations, anchors still wearing coats like they hadn't stopped to check into their hotels before barreling in here. All of them pointed straight at us.

Three missing persons, they whispered.

One presumed dead.

The youngest gone for months.

The eldest for decades.

All found. All alive.

The headlines were already written, stamped in their tablets before we'd sat down. No one cared that the math didn't add up, that our scars and our stories didn't line up clean. That none of them were allowed to ask us a single direct question. Didn't matter. Miracles didn't need logic. They just need a camera angle. And Ryan had staged it perfectly.

Nat sat to my right like she belonged to the lights. Not one hair out of place, every strand tucked and pinned so neatly it could've been painted on. Her skin looked more like porcelain than flesh—perfect, so perfect it bent toward fake. She wore a lilac suit, the kind of soft pastel that says approachable, trustworthy. Electable. If you didn't know better, you'd think she was here to win votes, not to prove she'd survived. Her smile landed with the weight of a handshake. Practiced. Hollow. The kind that makes you wonder how many hours she'd stood in front of a mirror, drilling it into muscle memory.

On my other side, Amelie barely filled the chair. Her body pulled inward like she was trying to shrink into herself. Her lips moved, soundless, twitching in a rhythm I couldn't catch. Counting? Breathing? Or some prayer she only half-remembered? She looked like a kid sitting outside the principal's office, except the punishment waiting for her was bigger than detention. Bigger than anything a sixteen-year-old should be asked to hold. Her shoulders rose every time the cameras popped, then fell slow, like she was letting the air out of a balloon that kept refilling without her permission.

And me?

I sat in the middle. Not a miracle. Not an exhibit. Just the gap between them, wondering which one the crowd wanted me to be.

A man in a suit took the podium. Not press—PR. The difference clung to him like cologne. His jacket was too sharp, his smile too smooth, the kind of face built for introducing ribbon cuttings and gala sponsors, not people who'd crawled out of the dark. He opened his arms wide like a preacher about to baptize the crowd.

"Ladies and gentlemen," he boomed, his voice big enough to fill every corner, "today, we are here to honor the survivors of something devastating: kidnapping, mutilation, and experimentation."

The words landed heavy. He let it sit there, fat and self-satisfied, long enough for the audience to murmur and nod like they were being told something holy. Then he pressed on.

"Their story is one of resilience. Of perseverance. Of human will. The country is eager to hear their truth."

Applause detonated. Too fast. Too neat. Like it had been queued up in advance, piped in through hidden speakers. Thunder without a storm.

Heat crawled under my skin. This wasn't truth. This was theater. And it was at that moment I realized this wasn't some tech spectacle, it was worse. We were the latest true crime fascination that took the nation by storm. And everyone wanted to hear what we had to say.

Nat went first. Of course she did. She leaned in like the mic was her confidant, her voice smooth and honeyed, years of practice poured into a performance that had only ever existed in her head until now.

"My name is Natalie Thompson—and I don't know how to explain what happened to us," she began. Calm. Patient. The kind of voice people would follow off a cliff if she told them the view was pretty. "Not completely. But I can tell you this—no one should've made it out of that place. And yet..." She paused, eyes lifting like she was searching the rafters for the right word. "We did."

The crowd bent toward her. Literally. Dozens of bodies tilting forward in their seats like strings had been pulled.

Nat let the silence breathe—long enough to taste. Then:

"I was taken when I was eighteen—back in 1995. That would make me 64 years old."

The crowd gasped, murmurs erupting briefly.

"The memories are blurring, but the last thing I remember was my high school, a man's voice, and a basement. I was dissected, parts of myself replaced bit by bit, with some days being more tortuous than others. And I know it sounds... strange. But at 26, I stopped aging. After that, I stopped counting the years. There wasn't a point. But I never stopped hoping. And now, by some twist of fate, I've been given a second chance." She turned her head slightly, smile grazing over me and Amelie like a stage light, soft and rehearsed. "We all have."

Cameras snapped like jaws. Each click a bite. Predatory, mechanical, endless. Somewhere out in the press pit, a sharp gasp cracked the air. Someone else sobbed loud enough to be heard over the clatter. It sounded like church. Or a courtroom. A place where people came not to listen, but to feel something about themselves.

I wanted to laugh. I wanted to scream. To stand and tear the mic off its stem and tell them what was really sitting on this stage: not salvation, not miracles. Exhibits. Models. A product line.

But my throat closed. My fists dug into my knees until the skin stretched tight and hot over bone. All I could do was sit still, straining against the silence Ryan had built into us.

Beside me, Amelie's lips finally stilled. Her hands knotted in her lap until her knuckles flashed white. She flicked her eyes at me, quick, sharp, like she was daring me to say what we both knew.

It was like I could hear their thoughts: *How could they have been missing, tortured, nearly killed... yet look better than they did in life?*

We weren't survivors.

We were artifacts. An oddity. A spectacle.

And the whole world had shown up to take notes.

I kept my eyes on Nat the whole time she spoke. That smile. That rhythm. Too sharp, too steady. It wasn't just a speech—it was choreography. Every pause, every tilt of her head, every softened syllable like a practiced step in a dance. I could almost see the invisible cue cards hovering in front of her. Almost hear Ryan somewhere in the wings, nodding along, mouthing the words with her. Thinking, *"I built them back the way they were—only better."*

The moderator leaned into the mic, his voice too smooth, too polished. "Can you tell us, Ms. Thompson—what did he do to stop you from aging?"

"He rebuilt us. Piece by piece. Organs replaced with compounds and metal. And when the body should've stopped, he... made it keep going."

Then the moderator's gaze shifted. The spotlight slid. My turn.

The microphone shrieked when I pulled it down, metal grinding metal, the squeal ripping through the room like something alive. People flinched. Even the cameras blinked, their shutters stuttering for half a second.

Good. Let them feel it.

"My name's Ty," I said. The mic doubled it back at me, tinny and hollow, like someone else was wearing my voice. "I don't have a speech. Just a story."

The room stilled. Not respectful—hungry. Like they were leaning in, waiting for something to chew on.

"I was taken from here—or a place that looked like it. A hotel convention center. Call it scouted if you want." My eyes cut to Nat, sharp. "Guess I had the look. Next thing I know—needle in my neck, lights out, and I wake up in a place that looked like it had been condemned before I was even born. Stained floors. Peeling walls. And a closet with someone crying in it. Wasn't me. That's how I knew I wasn't alone. There were more of us. Too many."

My throat caught, but I shoved through. "I remember one kid. A girl. Ten, maybe eleven. Talked about her brother, Nathan. Outer Banks. Some address that still gets scrambled in my head—fourteen, thirteen, eighteen—it doesn't matter. What matters is she didn't make it. None of them did. He tore them apart, rebuilt them, recycled the pieces. That's what Ryan Prescott does."

I laid it out plain: the surgeries with no anesthesia. The knives that never cooled down. The hands that worked like they'd forgotten what mercy meant. The camera in the corner that blinked sometimes, like it was trying to keep us from going insane. And the voice in the next room. A girl. Steel between us.

I didn't say Amelie's name, but she moved in my peripheral. Shoulders folded in. Mouth pressed thin. She knew. She remembered.

"The worst part?" My voice scraped low, hard. "It wasn't the pain. It was how close we came to forgetting we were ever human at all. Even now, I still don't know if we are."

The words hit the floor like dropped lead. Nobody picked them up.

Amelie's eyes were wet, but steady. Reporters scribbled against tablets, styluses fighting to keep up. Some stared too long at their photographers, like they couldn't decide if this was award-winning coverage or a reason to lose sleep.

"We survived," I said. The words came rough, like rocks breaking in my chest. "Not because we were lucky. Because we fought. Because I refused to let him win."

From the crowd: "What was his purpose?"

Another voice cut over it: "How did you break free?"

The moderator tried to calm it, palms up, but the words had already sunk claws in.

"Break free?" I repeated. My laugh came out low, bitter. "Break free? No. He let us off the leash. Wanted to see if the world would clap for his monsters." I paused. "He wanted to make us immortal."

That was when the moderator tilted his head, smiling like he was asking something harmless. "And your name—Ty. Does that stand for something? A designation? Was it assigned to you?"

A ripple of flashes slid through the room, mean and curious.

My jaw tightened. I leaned forward, voice flat, sharp. "It's short for Tyler. Tyler Alcaster. It's not a number. It's not a model. It's mine. I was born with it."

The words cracked the silence open. Not a scream. Not a plea. Just a reminder.

I let the weight of it settle. No polish. No uplift. Just weight. Then I leaned back.

All the cameras swiveled in unison. All the flashes turned. Their storm fell on Amelie.

She looked like the ground might tilt and drop her straight through. Like the girl who had once whispered her own name in the dark was now being forced to say it under lights that stripped her bare.

"I'm Amelie Chen," she said. The mic caught every crack in her throat. She was small, but her words filled the room anyway. "I'm sixteen. Went missing six months ago. The man who took me..." She paused, lips trembling. "...he said I was his—" Her voice stumbled. "—his daughter."

Silence. A silence that pressed in, thick and absolute.

"I'm not."

Her voice trembled, but she didn't step back. She stood in it. "I died in that house," she whispered. "We all did. We just didn't stop breathing."

The room stopped. Froze. Like the power had been cut. No pens moved. No cameras clicked. Even the lights felt dimmer, like the electricity itself was listening.

Then, from the back, a voice cut through the silence. Not soft, not sympathetic—skeptical.

"If what you're saying is true... then why don't you look like it? Where are the scars? The damage? The things that prove you've been through what you claim?"

The air tilted. Cameras swiveled, hungry for the confrontation.

There it was.

Amelie froze. Her mouth opened, then closed again, her hands tightening until the knuckles whitened.

Heat flashed through my chest. "You want proof?" I spat into the mic. "Open us up! Cut us again. See what's inside."

Murmurs rippled, sharp and electric. Some horrified. Some intrigued.

Then she did it. Amelie stood and peeled back her skin, holding up her palm for all to see, waiting for the shock effect. But what came was more like watching a movie trailer. Sounds of awe, not horror.

The skin slid back on quickly and quietly, healing itself in an instant. Nat leaned in before things could spiral, her smile still camera-ready, her voice syrup wrapped around steel. "We've already given our proof to the right people. Law enforcement. Doctors. Specialists. And we'll continue to do so. What you see here is not the absence of trauma—it's what survival looks like when you've been rebuilt."

The skeptic sat back down. Styluses tapped louder. Cameras clicked faster. The machine of the story swallowed the question whole.

A woman's voice, tremulous with forced sympathy: "Amelie, what would you say kept you alive in those conditions?"

She blinked at her, slow, steady. "It wasn't hope," she said. "It was fear. Anger. Thoughts of everything he was taking from me." she paused, her gaze distant. "Whatever you people want, we aren't a success story. We aren't props. We're people—though it's getting harder to believe it each day."

The next voice came sharper, slicing through the din:

"Where is Ryan Prescott now?"

The room shifted. Reporters leaned forward, cameras snapping harder, like the whole stage had tilted toward that single question.

Amelie's head turned first, her eyes wide, searching mine. I turned too, caught in the same trap, caught in the same silence. For a second, it was just us—two rewired ghosts staring across the table, both of us holding the same answer: *we don't know*.

The pause was dangerous. Heavy. Too much truth leaking out in the space between.

Then Nat's voice slid in again, warm and unflinching, cutting the silence clean.

"We will be working very closely with law enforcement," she said, her smile never faltering, "to ensure every detail is catalogued properly and in line with the ongoing investigation."

Then—applause. Sudden. Violent. A standing ovation that felt less like gratitude and more like reflex. Like someone had hit a button. Like they all got what they came for.

But underneath, the room erupted again. Questions collided, voices tripping over each other like a stampede:

"Did he have help?"

"Are there others like him?"

"How many more are still out there?"

The moderator's palms went up fast, cutting across the chaos, rehearsed calm dripping from every syllable: "Please, one at a time. Please." But the frenzy didn't fade—it just shifted, quieter now.

Beside me, Amelie exhaled like someone had just pressed her back underwater.

The applause hit like a wall, too loud, too eager, smothering. Cameras fired in bursts so fast they blurred into one unbroken flash, bleaching faces into blank ovals. My vision filled with light until the crowd looked faceless, mouths opening and closing like fish in a tank. The ovation folded in on itself, warped, until all I could hear was the low hum—the same hum Ryan used to carry under his breath when the saw touched bone. I clenched the arms of my chair, telling myself I was free. The spotlight said otherwise.

Like this was the ending they'd been promised.

No one cared what we looked like before.

No one cared what we looked like now.

No one asked about the hours, the screams, the cuts, the things too ugly for their papers.

They didn't want to help.

They just wanted a story.

Because the truth was too jagged. And a lie was easier to hold.

CHAPTER 22

THEY CALLED IT A MIRACLE.

I called it survival. Barely.

After the press briefing, they didn't whisk us away backstage like celebrities or saints. No curtain to vanish behind. No limo with tinted windows. Instead, they walked us down the aisle, straight through the noise. Past the cameras, the flashes, the reporters already chewing us into headlines before the night was even cold. Voices layered over voices, buzzing tape recorders and frantic pens. The whole room felt like a set of snapping jaws closing around us.

Amelie was just ahead of me, her shoulders hunched like she was bracing for a hit that never came. At the very back, a couple rose. A man and woman—middle-aged, worn but shining—stepped forward. Foster parents. Her family. They didn't hesitate. They caught her before she could speak, before she could even collapse into them. Her face buried against the woman's shoulder, his hand gripping the back of her head like if he let go, she'd disappear again.

I stopped walking. Just for a second. Watched her vanish into their arms. The way her body shook with soundless sobs. The way she let herself be small, safe, claimed.

Her eyes lifted once over the woman's shoulder, meeting mine across the space. For a heartbeat, we were still in that dark place—two survivors staring through steel. Then the crowd swallowed her whole, and she was gone to them.

I turned, found Nat at my side. She didn't move toward anyone. No arms opened for her. No names shouted from the back. Just the cameras, the lights, the microphones waiting to eat her alive. She only gave me a small, knowing smile—more secret than comfort. Then she nodded, deliberate, as if to say: *We're still in this together.*

Reporters swarmed the exits, rushing after her like she was the story now. I watched her head vanish in the crowd, lilac suit swallowed by cameras and microphones, until I was standing alone in the aisle.

And at the back, where the lights didn't quite reach, a row of faces waited.

They looked like my... family.

The word clanged around in my skull like a loose screw. Too easy. Too clean. Like something Ryan might've whispered just to see if the wires in me would spark.

Mom moved first. She shot out of her seat like a spring finally released. Security didn't even try to stop her. She hit me full force, arms wrapping around me so tight I thought my ribs might snap. Her perfume hit next—familiar, but stretched thin, like it had been watered down with years and grief.

Her hair, streaked silver now, was pulled back with the same chipped barrette I remembered from grade-school nights and bedtime arguments. She wore a hybrid canvas jacket, one of those temperature-adaptive kinds older folks still trusted over the new fiber shells. Underneath: a rust-colored knit turtleneck. Simple. Human. The kind of outfit meant for walking between fall and winter.

Her voice cracked against my ear. "Oh God, Ty. My boy. My baby." The words tumbled out like they'd been waiting a year to escape, tripping over sobs, prayers, and disbelief. "I thought you were gone. I thought—I thought I lost you too."

I tried to smile, but it came out crooked. "Guess I'm harder to lose than I look." My voice scraped out—dry, smaller than I meant.

She pulled back, framing my face like I might dissolve if she blinked. Her fingers traced the sharp lines of my cheeks, the cold skin she didn't recognize. "You're so thin. You're freezing. Are you hurt? Did he—" The word stuck.

I shook my head. "Don't, Mom. I'm here. That's enough."

Her hands clamped tighter. "You came back," she whispered. Not a statement. A spell she was daring the world to break.

Behind her, Dad hovered. Always hovering. His arms hung stiff, like he'd been ordered to stand at attention, and never released. His shirt was pressed too sharp, collar starched high, but the truth leaked through anyway—skin blotched red from too many afternoons in the Virginia sun, sweat darkening the edges. His jacket was an old solar-lined field coat, the kind that could recharge a wristband but hadn't in years. Faded denim. Sturdy boots. A man built for work that didn't exist anymore.

He just kept staring. Not at my face, not really—at the seams. At my shoulders, my hands, the space under my eyes. Like a mechanic studying an engine he didn't recognize anymore. Trying to see where the damage was. Where to start fixing.

But there was no fixing.

We both knew that.

And then Jackson.

He didn't lunge. Didn't rush me. Just stood there in the aisle, broad shoulders blocking the glow of the exit sign, mouth set in the shape of his old smirk but too cracked to pull it off. His jacket looked modern and travel-worn—fiber-mesh, weather-proof, streaked with dust from a long drive. The kind of thing you threw on when you didn't plan to take it off for days. His boots creaked. His eyes, though —wreckage.

He took a step forward, then stopped, like there was glass between us.

"Jesus, Ty." His voice split down the middle, raw and jagged. "I'm so sorry. I—I should've been there."

For a second, he wasn't my big brother—the one who tried to tape the family back together with beer and bad jokes after Liam died. He was just a boy who'd lost too much, too fast and was accepting it as his fault.

Behind him, Sophia lingered in the doorway. Hands clasped tight. Long coat drawn close, silver thread catching the light as she moved. She met my eyes and didn't look away—like if I vanished again, she'd be the one keeping Jackson upright. Then slowly, she offered a sad smile.

They took me "home."

That's what they called it anyway.

The house sat just outside Virginia Beach, wrapped in pine trees and the kind of silence that used to mean safety. The ride back was a blur of headlights and shadows, but the rumble of the tires hummed like the blacked-out van. Like no matter how many miles we put between us and that podium, I couldn't scrape Ryan's fingerprints off my brain.

Outside, the house looked smaller than I remembered. Same peeling white paint curling off like old scabs. Same crooked shutters. Same cracked steps where we used to jump off our bikes. But standing there now, it felt like being dragged back into a photograph you're not sure you should be in anymore.

Inside, it smelled like someone had tried to scrub time out of the walls—fresh paint and lemon cleaner over old wood and older memories. The floors creaked the same. The photos didn't.

They lined the hallway in frames, faces staring back like ghosts rehearsing a smile. Liam's was in more of them than mine. I couldn't look long.

Upstairs, they opened my door.

The room sagged under its own history. Posters curled at the corners, paper yellowing into sepia. Shoes lined up neat by the dresser, their laces stiff with dust. A baseball glove slumped on the shelf, leather gone rigid from neglect. My old desk still had the knife-scratched initials carved into the edge, jagged letters from a time when carving into wood felt like a way to leave a mark.

It should've felt like mine. It didn't.

I sat down. The mattress dipped under me like it remembered my shape better than I did. The springs creaked like a question.

Jackson leaned against the doorframe. Not blocking it—just holding himself up with it. His arms crossed, not in anger but like he was keeping his insides from spilling out. His throat bobbed once. Twice. Words backed up behind it.

"I really thought I was the only brother left, Ty," he said finally. His voice cracked on the word only, thin and fragile, too small for a man his size. His eyes shimmered wet in the half-light. "I thought I was the last one standing."

The words hung there like smoke. Liam's absence sat between us, heavier than either of our shadows.

"Yeah," I said quietly. "Sometimes I thought you would be." I stared down at my hands, flexed my fingers like I could still feel the straps biting into them. "What happened to everything? My place? My car?"

Jackson blinked, caught off guard by the question. "Man, that's so you." A rough laugh slipped out of him, brittle at the edges. "Dragged out of a nightmare and first thing you ask about is your car." He shook his head, smirk half-formed, already fading. "Gone. Not gone-gone. Packed up. Storage unit off Broad Street. We—" His voice tightened, smirk slipping completely. "We couldn't stand driving by your apartment every day, waiting for the door to open. Felt like we were staring at a grave with the door still on it."

His eyes went glassy. "I should've been the one to pick up, Ty. That call. You needed me, and it was Soph who heard you."

I frowned. "So what? You're saying you blame yourself for that?"

He let out a humorless laugh, more air than sound. "I don't just blame myself. I live with it. I was too hungover to even find the damn phone. My little brother calling for help, and I couldn't drag myself off the floor. That was the last time I could've heard your voice. And I missed it."

Silence hung thick between us, heavy as wet cement.

I leaned back against the wall, crossing my arms. My voice came out lower, steadier, but sharp at the edges. "You think I cared who picked up? I didn't need a hero, Jax. I needed someone—anyone—to hear me. And Soph did. End of story."

Jackson's jaw tightened. He looked away, then back. "Yeah, and you know what I hear every night since? Her voice saying your name. Your voice cutting out. Then nothing. I could've been the one, Ty. I could've—" His voice cracked again. "But I didn't."

I let out a snort, soft but pointed. "You think answering would've changed what happened? You think Ryan would've just handed me back because big brother picked up the phone? No. That's not on you."

"Doesn't matter," he muttered, low, like a confession. "What matters is it should've been me. And I'll never get that back."

We just sat there in the half-light, not talking. Two brothers, a year of ghosts sitting in the room with us.

I looked at him then—really looked. The face across from me wasn't the brother I'd left behind in a hotel lobby. This one was heavier, older, his edges sanded down by grief and responsibility. And I probably looked like a stranger to him too.

"Listen," I said, my voice low but cutting through the room anyway, "I never blamed you. Not once. You think I'm sitting here keeping score? I'm not. Everything that went down—none of it is on you."

He sat down beside me, the bed dipping under both of us like it wasn't sure it could hold this much weight. His head bowed, fingers pinching the bridge of his nose. Tears slipped out anyway, stubborn and silent.

"I'm just grateful to have you back, Ty," he said finally, voice rough like asphalt. "I really am."

I reached over, patted his shoulder—a crooked, half-hearted gesture that still meant something—and managed a crooked half-smile. "Yeah. Me too. Still feels like the world's on a trap door, but at least we're standing on it together." I nudged his arm, the way I used to when we were kids sneaking candy before dinner. "Even if Mom's trying to feed me a Thanksgiving turkey every five minutes."

That pulled a wet laugh out of him, quick and shaky but real.

I swallowed hard. "Alright. Hit me. What else did I miss?"

He hesitated, the corners of his mouth tugging down before pulling up again, a sad smile trying to figure out how to be steady. "You're, uh... gonna be an uncle."

My head snapped up like he'd thrown something at me. "Wait... what?"

"Soph's four months." He rubbed the back of his neck, eyes darting to the window as if the news was still too big to look at head-on. "It's a boy. We were between naming him after you or Liam, but..." His laugh cracked halfway through. "Guess you just made our choice a little easier."

I let out a half-snort, the kind that sounds like a laugh but isn't. "Yeah? Glad I'm somebody worth remembering."

Jackson's grin faltered. He shook his head slowly. "Don't do that, man. Don't go all hard-case on me now." His eyes were bright, his grin crooked—like the old Jackson still lived under the new one. "You have no idea how many nights I sat up with Soph, telling her stories about you. Trying to make sure the kid would know his uncle if—" he stopped himself, jaw tight, looking at the floor. "If you never came back."

Something twisted in my chest—hope and grief braided together, sharp and warm.

I tried for a smirk but it came out lopsided. "Guess I saved you a lot of bedtime stories, huh?"

"Not even close." He chuckled, a real one this time. "Kid's still gonna hear every single one. You're not off the hook just 'cause you walked back in."

The door eased open, hinges whispering like someone shushing a secret. Sophia stepped in, hand braced lightly against the frame as if she were steadying herself and it at the same time. She looked tired— the soft kind of tired you get from carrying more than just yourself.

"Jack," she said gently, her smile flickering at me before landing on him. "We should head out soon. I'm fading, and this little one's making sure I know it."

Jackson glanced at her, then back at me. He rose from the bed, the smell of his cologne and her perfume folding together in the small space. His jaw clenched, voice rough but steady.

"You're here, Ty," he said. "Not the same. None of us are. But you're here. And I'm not letting go of that. Ever again."

Sophia's hand found his arm. Her eyes flicked to me—soft, tired, but certain. "We never stopped waiting for you," she said quietly. "Always said you were resilient."

I held their gaze, my throat tight. For the first time since waking up in the wreck of my own body, I believed them.

I didn't feel back. Not really. But maybe—for him, for all of them —I could try to.

CHAPTER 23

Two DAYS after they stamped the word *free* on my forehead, the story moved on without me.

This time the headline was Ryan's house.

Some channels called it a raid like it was clean, like the word itself could scrub the grout lines with bleach, pry the chains out of the floor, sweep up the teeth that weren't supposed to be there. Like a headline could sanitize a grave.

The footage hit every channel at once. Bright anchors with TV smiles and grave voices, teeth shining under studio lights. *"Breaking now: police raid the North Carolina property at the center of the nation's most shocking recovery of missing persons..."* Lower thirds rolled across the bottom: **HOUSE OF HORRORS RAIDED. NO SURVIVORS FOUND INSIDE.**

I watched from my parents' couch, the screen washing the room in cold blue light. Helicopter shots panned over sand dunes and water, swooping toward a house I knew better than my own body. Cracked concrete. Burnt-out beams. Roof sagging like it wanted to collapse. Every shot a wound reopened.

The screen flickered to the front porch. The one I couldn'tt escape past, but tried to, over and over. Maybe that chip in my spine was gone. Or reprogrammed. *Could he recall us at any moment? Fry us, just because we stepped out of line—or because he wanted to?* The thought made me nervous.

Jackson was in the kitchen, clattering dishes. Mom upstairs, murmuring prayers to a God that never answered quick enough. Dad sat in his chair across from me, silent, eyes fixed on the screen like he was watching the weather. The glow lit his jaw, every muscle locked.

The anchors filled in the blanks like they were reading a bedtime story.

"Authorities say the property appears to have been abandoned for years."

"Sources claim there's no sign of a holding cell or operating rooms."

"Investigators are calling this an elaborate hoax."

"Bullshit," I said, too loud. My voice cracked the silence, and Dad's eyes flicked toward me, startled, like he'd forgotten I was even there.

My hand shot out, slamming the coffee table before I could stop it. Wood splintered under the heel of my palm with a crack like a gunshot. The mug Mom had left there tipped and shattered, hot liquid spreading across the shards.

I froze, staring at my hand. Unmarked. Smooth. Too strong. Too wrong.

Dad didn't move. Didn't yell. He just sat back slowly, eyes on me, something unreadable in them. Not fear. Not relief. Something colder.

Then came the clips: crime scene tape fluttering, boots crunching over scorched tile, K9 units weaving between door frames that once held screaming. Uniformed men carrying out plastic tubs of "evidence"—burned wires, melted restraints, a single cracked monitor screen. Close-ups of the walls where the paint had bubbled and split from fire. "No bodies were recovered." "No records." "No suspects."

They cycled in "experts" between commercials. Former profilers, ex-FBI, crime journalists with books about cults.

"This looks like an operation dismantled and torched."

"He knew they were coming. He cleaned house."

"If Ryan Prescott is real, he's gone."

On social media the theories spread like a second fire. Conspiracy threads. Livestreams. Blog posts with grainy screenshots claiming they'd found "the real Ryan" in an airport in Berlin. By midnight, half the country had decided he was a government ghost. The other half swore he'd never existed at all.

I pressed my fingers into my temples. I could smell the tile. Feel the straps. Hear the screams.

None of what they were showing on TV was empty to me. I could still see the room exactly as it had been. Exactly as it had smelled. Exactly as it had hurt.

Ryan Prescott—the doctor—was gone. No name in any system. No credit card trail. No driver's license. No fingerprints. No face. Just a smear of whispers and shaky blog posts, screenshots on forums that blinked out whenever a moderator disappeared.

And me?

I kept thinking about Echo. Her voice stuttering like broken code, like a record skipping on a word you were supposed to understand. Wondering if she'd remember me at all—or if, like everything Ryan built, I should program myself to forget for the sake of moving on.

Everyone else saw a clean break. A miracle. A closed case.

I saw lines welded under fire, brittle in the wrong light.

For a week I haunted the house like a shadow in someone else's outline. Same roof, same windows, same staircase I used to race down two steps at a time. But it all leaned wrong now. The walls seemed narrower. The corners cut sharper. The floorboards groaned in places I didn't remember. Every photo on the wall felt like a dare: *Do you still know this face? Do you still know this boy?*

They called it healing. Said I was "adjusting." What it felt like was trying to force a bent puzzle piece into the wrong picture. Each time I pushed, the edges splintered a little more.

Finally, one swamp-thick afternoon, I convinced Jackson to drive me out to the storage unit. The air stuck to the back of my neck, heavy with salt and tar, cicadas buzzing like the power lines had learned to sing. The asphalt shimmered under the sun, every step radiating heat like it wanted to burn the memory out of me.

Inside, the unit was a tomb. The smell of dust and metal hung heavy. My Dodge Challenger sat under a sheet of gray, patient as a dog waiting by the door. Boxes lined the walls like headstones in neat rows. Posters rolled so tight they might've suffocated. Everything organized. Catalogued. My old life boxed and shelved like evidence waiting for a trial.

Jackson stood at the doorway, his silhouette cut sharp by the afternoon light. He didn't say much, just watched me move through the wreckage like he was afraid I'd break if he asked too many questions.

I pulled the cover off the car, the smell of old gas and vinyl hitting me like a memory I didn't want but couldn't turn away from. I slid into the driver's seat. The wheel was familiar under my palms, worn smooth where my grip used to be, but it felt like I was trespassing. Like this belonged to a kid who'd been buried, and I was stealing his ride.

I gripped the wheel until my hands steadied. Then I turned the key. The engine coughed, rattled, and caught. Alive. Loyal. Like it had been waiting this whole time for me to come back.

Afterward, I bought a new phone. New number. No history.

Re-downloaded the old socials, scrolled through ghosts of friends I hadn't spoken to in a year. Vacations. Weddings. Parties. A dozen lives marching forward like mine had never even been part of the picture. I was a face in old group shots, a tag at the edge of someone's memory.

Back in the world, people watched me like I was a myth come to life.

Not a person. Not a kid who got dragged through hell. Just a story that had learned how to walk upright.

The grocery store was the worst. You'd think it would be safe—just aisles of cereal and freezers humming too loud—but the second I stepped through the automatic doors, heads turned. Not all at once, not like in movies, but in little ripples. A glance over the bananas. A pause by the bread. A mother nudging her son, whispering too loud for it to be a secret.

I tried to keep my eyes on the cart, on the way the wheel squeaked with every push, but the air felt sticky with stares. People didn't even pretend to keep shopping. They slowed down, lingered, circled like moths.

Near the milk section, a woman spotted me. Her hand froze on the handle of a half-gallon. Her lips trembled, and before I could move away, she reached for me. Clutched my sleeve like it was a lifeline.

"Oh God," she whispered. Her eyes glistened. "It's you."

Her voice cracked open, spilling into sobs that pulled at my arm, pulled at my chest, pulled me into the version of myself she thought I was. A miracle. A symbol. Someone who'd come back when so many hadn't.

But I wasn't that.

I wanted to tell her. To shake her hand off and say, you don't know me. You don't want to. But the words stuck.

I just stood there, letting her cry, until she finally let go and stumbled off, still looking at me like I'd stepped out of her own nightmare and somehow made it out alive.

At a gas station later, a guy about my age jogged up while I was filling the tank. Baseball cap, cheap cologne, nervous energy like he'd been rehearsing.

"Hey, man, sorry—this is weird, I know. But... could I get a picture with you?"

I blinked. "A picture?"

"Yeah, just real quick." He fumbled his phone out. "My

nephew... he went missing last year. Still missing, actually. And I just
—" He swallowed hard. "You give people hope, you know? Like
maybe one day, he'll walk back in the door too."

Hope.

Like that's what this was.

He snapped the photo before I could answer, his arm looped
around me like we were old friends, like I was something worth
capturing. His grin stretched wide. Mine stayed tight, hollow, the
kind of smile you hold in place until it hurts.

When he left, the smell of gasoline clung to me. Stuck in my hair,
my clothes, the back of my throat. No matter how many times I
washed, it lingered. Like the stink of being owned by someone else's
story.

That night, I thought maybe I'd finally sleep. The house was
quiet, the kind of quiet you only get in suburbs where the streetlights
buzz louder than the crickets. I turned the lamp off. Laid flat on the
bed. Tried to count breaths, tried to match the rhythm of my heart to
the ceiling fan above me.

Then—white heat. A sharp burst through the window. My eyes
burned before I could even sit up. A camera flash.

I shoved the curtain aside in time to catch a shape across the
street—a man folding into the driver's seat of a sedan, the red glow of
his taillights catching the edge of his face before he peeled away.

It wasn't the press. No badges, no microphones. Just regular
people. Curious people. People who wanted proof that I was real.
That the scars weren't there. That the "miracle boy" didn't look
monstrous under the porch light.

It kept happening. A car idling too long outside the house. A
woman pretending to jog past three times in an hour, her phone
angled like it wasn't recording. Once, a kid—fifteen, sixteen—stood in
the yard across from mine, staring until his mom yelled him back
inside.

To them, we weren't people. We were symbols. Survivors. Miracles. Walking proof that horror could spit you back out if you just believed hard enough.

But inside?

We were still trapped. Still wired. Still haunted.

And some nights, lying awake with the lights off, my chest rattling like a kicked machine, I knew it as sure as the tide—

We hadn't escaped at all.

The flashes didn't stop.

A week later, I caught him.

Middle-aged guy. Camera hanging from his neck like a dog tag. He thought he was clever—parked down the block, crouched by the neighbor's fence like a kid about to steal apples. But the lens caught the streetlight wrong, flashed like an eye, and I was already awake.

I didn't bother with a shirt. Just the gym shorts I slept in—drawstring loose. My pulse was still half-asleep, but the rest of me wasn't. The air bit at my skin as I crossed the living room, muscles tight, bare feet silent on the hardwood.

The door slammed open so hard the screen banged against the siding and splintered the frame. The crack echoed down the street, sharp enough to make him stumble.

"What the hell are you doing?" My voice came out low, rough, not mine.

He froze, caught like a deer in headlights. "I—I just... I wanted proof. My wife, she—"

I crossed the yard before he could finish. My hands found his collar, fabric bunching like paper. I hauled him upright, the camera swinging useless between us. His feet barely brushed the grass.

"Proof of what?" My teeth ground together, my arms trembling with a power that didn't feel earned. Too easy. Too damn easy. His pulse hammered against my thumb where it pressed his neck. One wrong move, one twitch, and I could've snapped something vital.

He made a sound—half gasp, half sob—and blinked up at me. And then his expression changed, sharp and sudden, his eyes going wider than the lens swinging between us.

"Wha—what's wrong with your eyes?!"

For a heartbeat I didn't understand. Then I felt it—the faint, unnatural heat under my skin, that ember-orange flicker edging my vision, reflecting back at him.

He shrank, real fear now, his voice breaking. "Jesus Christ—"

I shoved him back. Harder than I meant to. His body slammed into the porch post. Wood cracked, splintered all the way down like bone giving way. The camera snapped off its strap and shattered against the pavement. He hit the dirt and scrambled backward on hands and knees, shoes scraping, eyes never leaving mine.

"Never come back," I said. The words came out raw, shredded, not quite human.

He crab-crawled to his car, fumbling for the handle. Tires squealed and the red taillights vanished into the dark.

I stood in the yard, fists trembling, chest heaving. The porch post leaned at a broken angle—a jagged scar against the house. Proof I was stronger than I wanted to be. Stronger than I knew how to control.

The night went silent. No crickets. No breeze. Even the air felt like it was holding its breath, waiting to see what I'd do next.

Behind me, the front door creaked.

Dad stepped out. No jacket this time—just a dingy white T-shirt gone soft with age, collar stretched wide, the fabric ghosted with sweat and wood dust. His grey sweatpants sagged a little at the knees, the elastic tired, bare feet planted flat against the porch boards. The screen door slapped shut behind him like punctuation.

He froze for half a second when he saw me standing there. His eyes darted to the porch post, then to my fists, then—hesitant—to my face.

He didn't move closer. Stopped two steps from the threshold, weight balanced like a man standing at the edge of a cliff. His arms hung stiff, but one hand twitched toward the doorframe, needing something solid to hold.

"What was that?" His voice was flat. But the way his shoulders tensed told me he already knew.

"Nothing." My throat burned with the lie. "Some guy with a camera. He's gone now."

Dad didn't move. Just stared. Long enough for the silence to feel like another accusation. His jaw worked side to side, grinding on words he didn't want to say. Finally, he let them out.

"Sometimes..." His gaze flicked to the broken post, then back to my eyes. He shifted a step toward the door. "Sometimes I'm not sure you are who you say you are."

Something in me snapped. My jaw clenched. "Yeah? And what's that supposed to mean?" The words came out harder than I meant, sharp enough to cut the night in half.

He didn't flinch at the sound—he flinched at my eyes, at the faint orange burn I couldn't fully smother. He shuffled back, bare feet squeaking against the porch wood, already halfway inside.

"I knew I lost you the day you went missing," he said finally. His voice cracked once, then steadied. "I don't know who came back. But it's not the same boy I had."

The retort burned on my tongue. I didn't choke it down.

"You're right," I said, my voice shaking but sharp. "I'm not the same. How could I be? You think I'd come out of that house—out of him—and still be the kid you wanted? The kid who could laugh the way Liam used to? The one who never let you down?"

His jaw tightened. I stepped closer, and the words kept spilling, raw and bleeding.

"Don't lie to me. You've been waiting for Liam to walk back through that door since the day he died. He was the one you wanted. The golden son. The one worth being proud of. And me?" My throat closed, the words scraping out anyway. "You'd rather he lived and I didn't."

The silence cracked open wide. His face hardened, but his eyes wavered.

"You think I don't see it?" My voice dropped, jagged. "Every time you look at me like I'm half-made. Like I'm broken. Like I shouldn't even be standing here." I swallowed hard. "But I am. I'm still your son. And maybe it's time you mourned me instead of him."

His jaw tightened, his hand braced on the doorframe. When he spoke, the words were clinical, precise—like he'd already measured them, cut them to fit.

"You nearly killed that man tonight." He didn't blink. "Snapped a post in half like it was kindling. You don't even know your own strength."

"But I'm not a monster! I'm still trying to get the hang of this, still trying to cope, still trying to figure this all out, I just—" I trailed.

His eyes held mine, cold and unflinching, like what I'd said hadn't registered, didn't matter. Like he didn't really believe any it. "I won't have that in this house. Not with a baby on the way."

The bottom dropped out of me. "What are you saying?"

His mouth was a hard line. "I don't want you here. Not around us. Not around him. If you can splinter wood like that, what happens the day you lose control with a child in your arms? What happens when it's the baby's bones instead of a porch post?"

My stomach turned to ice. The words rattled in my head, unbearable, undeniable.

"You don't want me here," I whispered.

He didn't even hesitate. "I don't want you here. Not anymore. You're not the boy I raised. You're something else."

The silence after was louder than any shout. My chest burned, throat tight, but I forced the words out anyway.

His hand gripped the doorframe like he needed it to stand. "You want me to mourn you? Fine. Get out. Don't come back. Not to this house. Not to me. You're not welcome here anymore."

Something inside me buckled. Rage, grief, relief—all tangled in one sick knot. My throat burned, but I forced the words out, bitter and final.

"Good. Because I'm done begging for a place in a house that buried me the minute Liam died."

The screen door slammed between us, rattling against its hinges. He was gone.

But the light in the front window stayed on.

I stood in the yard, the grass damp and cold against my bare feet, fists flexing at my sides like they still remembered the weight of that man's collar. My chest rose, fell, rose again, the night air burning in and out like it was scraping me raw.

Then I saw her.

Mom. Half-shadowed in the window, wrapped in a faded robe that looked more like memory than fabric. The kind she used to wear on cold mornings—flannel, frayed at the sleeves, a faint coffee stain near the pocket. She stood just behind the curtain, one hand clutching it like she wasn't sure whether to pull it open or shut.

When our eyes met, she froze. For half a second, I thought maybe —maybe she'd come outside, open the window, say something. Anything.

Instead, her mouth turned down—sharp, small. A frown. Then she stepped back, the robe shifting with her like it was trying to hold her in place. The curtain fell shut, soft as a sigh.

That was it.

I didn't wait for more. Couldn't.

I crossed the yard, damp grass clinging to my ankles, gravel cutting at my soles as I reached the driveway. Slid behind the wheel of the Challenger. The leather was cool, familiar, almost mocking. My hands gripped the wheel like it might disappear too if I didn't hold on.

And no matter how hard I tried to believe otherwise, I couldn't shake the truth. He was right. I was normal on the outside. Wired underneath.

The engine roared to life, too loud in the dead night. I let it rumble there for a second, headlights throwing long shadows across the yard—the broken porch post, the shut window, the house that wasn't mine anymore.

Then I put it in gear.
And I was gone.

CHAPTER 24

THAT NIGHT, I drove back to the storage locker, my headlights cutting across corrugated metal doors like they were a row of shut mouths. Even without a key, the padlock clicked open under my fingers. Inside, the air was stale and heavy, smelling of dust and old sweat.

I threw the door all the way up and started loading. Boxes, bags, shoes, clothes, whatever still looked like mine. Didn't matter. It all felt like evidence now. I didn't have a destination; I just knew better than to stick around where I wasn't wanted.

When it was full, I climbed back into my car and let the engine rumble like a growl under my feet. The tank was half-empty, and I drove until the gauge touched E. Asphalt blurred. Gas stations blinked past like bad memories. Anything to put distance between me and the past.

At some nowhere rest stop off I-95, I finally stopped. It was the kind with buzzing vending machines and a flickering fluorescent above the bathroom door. Crickets were loud in the grass, but there were no other cars in the lot. I killed the engine. Sat there, fingers on the steering wheel, knuckles buzzing with that low, static ache that never really went away.

The dashboard glow painted my hands orange. I leaned back in my seat, thumbed my phone open, half-hoping for nothing, maybe a distraction, and that's when I saw it.

A new follow request.

Amelie Chen.

It hit like a voice rising up from a basement I'd tried to brick over. My stomach dropped through the floorboards. For a second I couldn't breathe, couldn't move. Just stared at the glow like it was a fire I couldn't touch.

Her message was simple. No emoji, no punctuation tricks. Just words:

Ty? ...It's me. If you want to meet, name a place.

The screen hummed in my hand. All the miles I'd just driven felt like they were still inside me, rattling around, looking for a way out.

My fingers hovered over the name. Everything in me said don't. Everything in me said to let it be. Not to get dragged back in. But I typed anyway.

"Yeah. Neutral spot. No city. No cameras."

I rummaged through the pile of clothes in my back seat and threw on an outfit. We agreed on a nowhere-in-between place—half pine forest, half salt air. The kind of roadside restaurant you only noticed when the neon beer sign flickered on at dusk. It perched on stilts over brackish water, the whole patio sagging like it had grown tired of holding people up.

She was already there when I pulled in. Sunglasses hiding her eyes even though the sky was nothing but soft peach and blue. Her hair was shorter now, hacked into a bob uneven at the ends like she'd done it herself with scissors meant for anything but hair. A faded red zip-up hoodie, sleeves pushed to the elbows, hung open over a soft gray tee with a cracked logo half-rubbed away. Her cargo shorts were a little too big, cinched tight with a fraying drawstring, the pockets

weighed down like she didn't go anywhere without carrying everything she owned.

A black elastic hair tie sat around her wrist like a habit, along
with a faint line of pen ink where she'd written something and
scrubbed it off. Her hands shook when she lifted her coffee. Not
spilling. Just enough to show me she wasn't steady either.

I slid into the seat across from her. My jacket creaked when I
moved—a matte gray fiber-mesh with solar threading down the
sleeves. Underneath, a sand-colored tee clung close, fabric breathing
with every shift of my chest. My combat slacks were rolled at the
ankles, clean but scuffed at the knees, boots swapped for charcoal
slip-ons with magnetic seams.

"You look..." I started, then stopped. The word didn't fit. Alive
wasn't enough. Different felt wrong. "...you."

Her mouth curved, but it wasn't a smile. "Yeah? You too. Sort of."
She shoved her sunglasses higher, and I caught the red rim in her
eyes. "Didn't think you'd actually show."

"Yeah, well." I rubbed the back of my neck, phone heavy in my
pocket. "Not like I'm drowning in social invites lately."

That pulled the smallest laugh out of her—hollow, but human.
She wrapped her hands tighter around the coffee cup.

"It's funny," I said, staring out at the slow curl of waves. "I used to
love the beach."

Her head tilted, but she didn't look away.

"Now it just reminds me of that house."

She let out a sharp exhale, no humor in it. "Yeah. Same." Her jaw
flexed. "People keep calling me 'the survivor.'" She made air quotes
around it, bitter. "Like it's a damn badge. Like I did something
brave."

"You did." I said it too fast, too sharp. Like maybe if I said it hard
enough, it'd stick for both of us.

She let the silence stretch. Only the gulls filled it.

"My foster mom's been on my ass nonstop," she muttered finally.
"Won't let me out of her sight. Keeps feeding me like I'm twelve

again. Pasta, soup, casseroles. She thinks if she keeps me full, I'll stop remembering."

I nodded, picking at the cracked wood of the table. "Yeah, mine tried that too. Only difference is, I didn't stick around long enough to pretend it helped."

Amelie's lip trembled, just for a second. "It's like they mean well, but... they don't get it. Even Marnie backed off, couldn't handle seeing me for how I am now."

"You showed her?"

Amelie nodded, staring down at the table.

I swallowed. "Look. People won't get it. Can't." I said, still picking at the weather-worn table. "Only people who can are the ones who went through it. Us." I glanced at her. "And Nat."

Her shoulders sank, almost like relief at the name. "Yeah. Nat." She stirred her coffee absentmindedly with the spoon, the metal clinking soft against porcelain. "She probably doesn't even have a family anymore, huh? Not after all those years."

I thought about the way Nat smiled at the conference. How she slipped away without a word. "Maybe not. But she has us. Whether she wants to or not."

Amelie's eyes flashed sharp. "Then where the hell is she?" Her voice cracked, more pleading than pissed. She shut her mouth fast, swallowed, then muttered, "There's nothing. No paper trail, no footprint online. Just our news article and old missing-persons crap that still says she's dead."

The word hung there: *dead.*

I nodded, throat tight. "We'll find her."

"How?"

I pulled my phone from my pocket, set it between us. The screen reflected the darkening sky. "Start with where she was staying."

The hotel phone clicked with that bored, practiced voice every time we called. The kind of voice that sounded like it'd been trained to keep bad news soft.

"Front desk, how may I help you?"

"Can you connect me to Natalie Thompson?" I said, sounding too loud in my own ears. "Or can you check if she—"

The pause on the other end was the kind they use before they teach you policy. "I'm sorry, sir, but for privacy reasons we're unable to confirm whether a specific guest is registered here. I can, however, take a message or place anything you'd like to leave at the desk for pick-up."

Amelie leaned forward, voice cutting like glass. "Then check the mail. Anything under 'Natalie' or 'Nat.' A note, an envelope—whatever. Just look."

There was shuffling. A muffled tone like a keyboard getting dressed. "There is... an unclaimed envelope at the desk addressed to 'Wonder Boy,'" the clerk said finally. "It was dropped off earlier. I can hold it or, if you're local, you can come collect it in person."

I clicked the line dead like a trap closing.

Amelie looked up at me, eyes sharp behind rimless lenses. "That's ours."

I drove us there myself. The road wound through black pine silhouettes, headlights bending around every curve like they didn't want to light the way but were forced to come along. The familiar hotel rose in the distance, its windows staring like vacant eyes.

The lobby smelled like floor cleaner trying too hard, sharp enough to sting the back of my throat. The carpet muffled every step, but the ceiling fans buzzed like they were carrying secrets. Amelie walked beside me, her sunglasses finally tucked away, her hands jammed into her sleeves like she was holding herself together.

At the desk, the clerk barely looked up until we stopped right in front of him. He was young—college young. Tie crooked, name tag that read MARCUS, like a sticker slapped on. His eyes flicked between us with the flat caution of someone who knew better than to get too involved.

"Can I help you?" His voice had the same neutral hum the phone did. Practiced. "Wait, holy shit! You're the survivors from that massacre, right? The ones with those genetic enhancements?"

Amelie leaned in, sharper than me. "There was supposed to be a note left for us. Under Wonder Boy."

Marcus blinked once, slow, like the words had taken a second to translate. Then he bent down, shuffled through a drawer. The sound of paper sliding against paper.

When he came up, he set the envelope on the counter like it was hot. Folded twice, edges smudged, the ink bleeding faintly at the corners. He didn't slide it—he pushed it just far enough for me to reach. "This was dropped off earlier today," he said carefully. "That's all I can tell you."

"That's it?" I asked. My voice came out lower than I meant.

Marcus shifted his weight. I picked it up like it might burn through my skin. The paper was damp in spots, as if someone had held it too tightly for too long.

Amelie leaned close, her shoulder brushing mine, her breath hitching enough that I felt it. "Open it," she whispered.

I looked at Marcus. "Who dropped this off?"

He shook his head. "Didn't see. Just found it in the bin when I came on shift." He hesitated, eyes narrowing, like he was deciding whether to risk saying more. Then he swallowed it down. "Sorry."

Sorry. The word sounded flimsy in the air.

I slipped my finger under the fold, tearing slow. Amelie pressed closer, almost against my arm, her eyes locked on the paper.

The world shrank to the ink bleeding through the crease.

And I opened it.

Hey, Wonder Boy.

You're free now, and that's the only reason I played along. Ryan was never going to let all three of us walk out alive, but I made sure it was you two. If I had to break myself a little more to make it happen, then fine—I'm glad it worked.

I should probably apologize for the show at the press thing. The smile, the dress, the hair. All of it was smoke and mirrors, a mask I've worn for so long I almost convinced myself it was real. I wanted you to believe I had it handled, that I was still the girl with the sharp tongue and the sharper smile. But the truth is, that mask cracked a long time ago, and these days I'm just pressing the shards against my skin hard enough to hide the pieces underneath.

There's no family waiting for me on the other side of this. No warm kitchen light, no tearful reunion. Everyone I used to be is gone, buried in that house and in Ryan's hands. And the worst part—the part I hate even more than the memory of him—is that after so many years, I don't know how to exist without him. I loathe him. I need him. I belonged to him in ways I can't wash out, and even now I feel like I'm still wired to his machine. That's what he did best: build cages you start mistaking for your own bones.

But you—you were different. You saw me. Not the girl he manufactured. Not the act I kept playing. Me. The one screaming in the dark, still trying to act like she didn't care. And you didn't look away. No one else ever gave me that.

So I need you to hear me when I say this: don't try to find me. I'm not someone who gets found, not anymore. If you care about me—if you ever did—then live. Be good in a way I never could. Be better. Carry the piece of me that's still worth anything, because God knows I can't.

Love,
Nat

I read it six times. My hands shook all six.

The paper smelled faintly of iron and rain, like something pulled from a flooded basement. Nat's handwriting looped and staggered across the folds, the ink bleeding at the edges as if she'd written it while moving, while running. By the last read-through the words had begun to blur into each other, and still my eyes kept going back, like pressing a bruise to see if it hurt the same way.

Beside me, Amelie didn't speak. She just stared at the paper, her coffee-colored eyes flicking between the loops of Nat's name and the tremor in my fingers. Her own hands were clenched around the counter edge, knuckles gone white. For a second I thought she might snatch the letter from me, like maybe reading it herself would change the ending.

"She..." Amelie's voice cracked, then went soft, like she was afraid to disturb the ink. "She went back to him."

"Yeah." My throat tightened around the word. "For us."

I could feel the room moving around us—phones ringing somewhere behind the desk, ice clinking in glasses at the bar, a car pulling out of the lot—but it all felt muffled, as if we were under glass. The only sound that stayed was the soft crinkle of the paper as I folded it and unfolded it, folded it again.

Amelie finally reached out, brushing the edge of the letter with two fingers. "She saved us," she whispered, not to me but to the floor. "And now she's—" She couldn't finish.

I swallowed hard, forcing air into my chest, forcing words past the ache. "Gone."

The clerk cleared his throat once, politely, like he'd forgotten we were still standing there. I slipped the letter into my jacket pocket. It felt heavier than the phone, heavier than the car keys, heavier than anything I'd brought in with me.

Amelie's hand found my sleeve, a quick, desperate squeeze. "She's still out there, maybe we could—," she murmured.

"No," I said, staring at the dark windows beyond the lobby glass. "That's probably what Ryan's banking on. We got our freedom, and she's making sure we keep it."

We walked out without another word, the sound of our footsteps swallowed by the carpet.

Outside, the night had settled heavy and low, clouds sagging over the parking lot lamps like wet cloth. The letter's weight dragged at my chest with every step, the paper inside my jacket pocket whispering against the fabric as if it wanted to be read again, and again, until it frayed to dust.

Amelie slid into the passenger seat, sunglasses still perched on her head though the sun had long since drowned. She didn't speak. She just turned her face to the window, breath fogging faint circles in the glass, her reflection double-layered against the dark.

I sat behind the wheel and didn't turn the key. The silence pressed in too thick, and for a moment it felt like the basement again —the kind of quiet that hummed just before the next scream.

Finally, I said it.

"She knew she didn't belong here. Not anymore."

The words caught halfway out, sharp enough to sting on the way up.

"As if no one could relate to her."

Then it hit me—hot, fast, all teeth.

"GOD DAMMIT, NAT!"

The roar tore out of me raw, cracking in my throat. My fists slammed down on the steering wheel, once, twice, over and over, until the horn stuttered weak and pathetic beneath the blows. Plastic rattled. Something inside the dash splintered with a sharp crack. The car shook like it wanted me off of it.

I kept going. Kept hammering until the pain finally caught up to me, flooding in through my knuckles, warm and bright. Breath tore out of me in ragged bursts, fogging the windshield white.

Beside me, Amelie didn't speak. She just watched, her face pale in the glow of the streetlight, her hands clamped tight around her knees. When I stopped, the silence rushed back in, louder than the violence had been.

The wheel sat dented under my palms. My chest heaved. My skin buzzed with the reminder: I wasn't built for control. Not anymore.

"I don't know who came back. But it's not the same boy I had."

Dad's voice. Flat. Clinical. Cutting through the car like a blade.

And for a second, I hated how much it fit.

"Why'd she have to do it like that, huh?" My throat burned.

"Why's it always her taking the hit so the rest of us can make it out? Why's it always gotta be her burning so we can breathe?"

Amelie's voice was low, brittle. "Because she thought you were worth it."

The sentence landed like a stone in my ribs. I pressed my forehead to the wheel, eyes burning.

She was gone. And she'd chosen it. And no matter how many times I screamed her name into the dark, Nat wasn't coming back.

The engine coughed to life, headlights spilling down the stretch of empty road. Pines closed in on either side, black silhouettes bending toward us like witnesses. The car hummed beneath my palms, steady, real, but the words in my pocket gnawed like teeth.

You're free now. That's the only reason I went along with it.

Every mile felt longer than it should have, every turn carving the thought deeper. Nat hadn't chosen freedom—she'd traded hers for ours. And somewhere in that deal, she'd bound herself to Ryan forever. Not prisoner. Not captive. Something worse.

Beside me, Amelie shifted, pulling her knees up onto the seat, arms wrapped tight. "Is this our life now?" Her voice was so small I almost mistook it for the sound of the tires. "Ducking from paparazzi and praying Ryan never changes his mind about us? That he doesn't tug us back?"

"I don't know, Am. You're guess is as good as mine," I said. My hands tightened on the wheel. "But it's just you and me now. You're the only family I've got. And I swear, if that day comes—" the thought forcing my teeth to grit. "I'll make him wish he let me die."

The words hung like fog between us.

And still, beneath all of it, one thought crawled back: Echo. The flicker in her voice, the stutter in her code. The way she'd said she'd remember me, even when she couldn't. I wondered if Ryan had wiped her clean by now, or if somewhere in those broken circuits my name still sparked like a glitch.

The headlights caught the sign for the highway, green and reflective, pointing back toward the life I was supposed to reclaim. Houses. Family. Normal. Whatever that meant anymore.

But Nat's words pressed hot against my chest, louder than the engine, heavier than the road:

Don't try to find me. Just try to live.

I gripped the wheel tighter, knuckles aching. She made it sound easy. Like living was something you could just... decide to do. Like it wasn't jagged glass lodged under my skin, waiting to cut every time I moved.

The lines on the asphalt blurred under my headlights, pulling me forward whether I wanted it or not. The night smelled like salt and gasoline, like endings that wouldn't end.

And against my will, I drove on.

Not because I wanted to.

Because I didn't have a choice.

CHAPTER 25

I BUILT a life for myself in South Carolina the way you build a raft from wreckage—planks from what was left of me, rope from whatever I could scavenge. Every board creaked when I stepped on it, but it stayed afloat anyway.

The boxing gym was an old place tucked between a laundromat and a liquor store. Cinderblock walls. Sweat-soaked mats. The smell of iron and chalk. I was the highest tech thing in there, and I liked it that way.

The kids who came in had soft knuckles and restless eyes. They wanted to learn how to throw a punch, how to square up without shaking. So I showed them how to plant their feet, how to breathe through the swing, how to keep their guard up.

They thought I was disciplined. They thought I was strong.

But they didn't know the truth.

I might've had the training, but my body was carved by somebody else's nightmare. Every movement I showed them was borrowed— strength pulled from hands that weren't mine.

Sometimes a kid would look at me between rounds, headgear slipping down, and ask, "Coach, how'd you get so strong?"

And for a second—a heartbeat too long—the question would echo. I'd see a flash of metal. Hear the click of a latch. Smell antiseptic and blood layered under something sweet, like flowers left too long in a vase.

Then it would all drop away, like it slipped through a crack in my skull and disappeared.

I'd tighten the wraps on their wrists, smile like it was a secret. "Repetition," I'd say. "Nothing fancy."

And they'd nod, like that was all it took.

But the bags knew better.

One night I threw a jab to demonstrate form—just enough to make the point, or so I thought. The leather cracked like a gunshot, the chain screeched, and the whole bag swung wild, nearly ripping itself off the beam.

The sound hit me wrong. Too familiar. Too close to another sound I refused to place. For a second, I wasn't in the gym. I was somewhere colder. Somewhere with drains in the floor. My head pressed into concrete.

The kids froze. Wide-eyed. Silent.

I laughed it off, rubbed my knuckles like it stung. "See? And that's why you keep your elbow tucked."

They laughed too, high and nervous, like they were waiting for me to say I'd been kidding all along.

But when I turned my back, I caught it—two boys whispering by the ropes.

"Did you see that?"

"Yeah. Nobody hits like that."

Their voices weren't loud, but they carried.

I tied off the wraps tighter, let my smile stick to my face like tape. Pretended I hadn't heard. Pretended it was just kids being kids.

It worked for a while.

.   .   .

I slipped out of the public eye. Survived the photographs. Waited for the world to forget. And eventually it did, or at least it pretended to. The news cycle rolled on, feeding on fresher wounds. People wanted new horrors, not old miracles.

I kept my distance. Far enough from my family to breathe. Close enough to Amelie in case Ryan ever appeared again.

Then the decades started stacking.

And I didn't.

By the 2070s, I still looked twenty-four. Same face. Same body. Same shadow. Meanwhile, Jackson and Sophia crossed into their late fifties, their faces lined by laughter and loss, their eyes deepening into shades of grief I'd never see in the mirror.

The Second Cold War finally ended by then—not with a treaty or a speech like the old wars in history books, but with a tired broadcast at three in the morning that most people slept through. No parades. No banners. Just a quiet headline: CEASEFIRE HOLD-ING. RECONSTRUCTION TALKS BEGIN. Like the world couldn't even be bothered to celebrate. Everyone who would've cheered was either dead, exhausted, or too busy rebuilding whatever was left of their lives. I liked to think that Liam would've been happy.

Meanwhile, Jackson and I still spoke. Phone calls on birthdays. Scattered texts. Check-ins about Mom. He was the only thread I had left.

Little baby Liam—the one Jackson once held like a football on Christmas morning—was thirty now. Married. Two kids of his own. He sent me a photo once: smiling over a cake with his name scrawled in icing. I had to look twice before I recognized the baby from old posts.

The war may have ended, but time never stopped aging everyone else.

My old man was the next to kick the bucket while Mom was in hospice, her body failing in ways mine never would.

Sometimes I'd visit her. Sit at her bedside with my hands folded like a student waiting for instructions. The machines clicked and sighed around her. She'd tell me the things nobody else would say.

"I'm ready," she whispered once, eyes wet but steady. "I'd rather be gone than stuck in this skin forever. Ready to see your father again. My parents. My sons."

Plural. Like I wasn't sitting right there. Like she really believed I'd died, and some other version of me was waiting with Liam. She'd say it soft, but it always landed like a punch.

Amelie's foster parents unraveled slowly, too. They'd been kind. Patient. But they hadn't signed up to raise a sixteen-year-old for eternity. Her foster mom passed first. After that, Amelie and I moved in together. Her foster dad hugged her at the door, told her he loved her, and left her with his number anyway. He said it like a goodbye that wasn't supposed to be final. But he passed shortly after, too.

We ended up in our own little orbit. Not loud. Not dramatic. Just two satellites circling the same old wound, held together by gravity we didn't ask for. For all the things I hated Ryan for, I couldn't deny it—she really did become something like a sister. A real one. Not the word people throw around when they're feeling sentimental, but the kind that just happens to you when you're not looking.

Every once in a while. I'd catch flashes of Liam in her, like someone had stitched scraps of him into her at random. The crooked humor. The way she'd get overly excited about something small and stupid like it was the most important thing in the world. The advice that sounded like it was made up on the spot, but still landed true. She burned like he used to—brighter than she had any right to. Before the war snuffed him down to coals.

I knew she wasn't him, and I never pretended she was. But standing next to her, I didn't feel like the youngest sibling anymore. I didn't feel so alone. I felt like part of something again.

Still, there were nights—dark, heavy ones—where I parked the car by the inlet and just stared at the water. Thought about driving straight into it, letting the tide do what blades could not.

The night Jackson died, the world felt thin. Like one more breath might tear it.

He wasn't old. Not really. Early sixties. Too young for the way his body gave out. The doctors called it cancer. Aggressive. Sudden. Said it must've been there for years, sleeping, waiting.

But I knew better. I'd seen the signs—little things he thought I didn't notice. His nose bleeding after a day out with me, my eyes glowing that faint orange around the edges. The way his hands trembled when he touched tools I'd touched. The headaches. The fatigue.

It wasn't cancer.

It was me.

The Eurydium Ryan stuffed into my bones didn't just make me what I am—it leaked. Poisoned. Spread like secondhand smoke. And Jackson was exposed to it more than anyone. Regardless of everything, he still wanted to be around me. Sit next to me in the garage. Pass me tools. Share the same air.

On his last good day, when he could still talk without coughing between every word, he looked at me—eyes sunken but still sharp in that way only big brothers can be—and he laughed. Actually laughed. Said, "If you've got some magic trick keeping you twenty-four forever, now's a hell of a time to share it."

I told him I didn't know, and he believed me. That was the worst part.

He loved me anyway.

And it killed him.

So that night, I did it. Seatbelt off. Gas pedal down. The water swallowed me whole and then spat me back out, lungs burning but not failing, bones refusing to break.

I sat on the shore afterward, soaked and shaking, staring at my hands.

That's when I understood: I wasn't going anywhere.

Not that way.

Not any way.

Nat still lived in my head like static. How we were more alike than she thought. How neither of us had families now. How both of us had tried and failed to escape what Ryan had forced us into.

I imagined what it'd be like to catch her in the edges of crowds—on sidewalks, in airports, flickering between strangers. Just the shimmer in her eyes, the same as Amelie's, the same as mine. How in that moment, we'd be whole again. One unit.

But I knew what it would mean to really see her.

Ryan Prescott couldn't be far behind.

That night after the water failed to take me, I sat on the apartment floor with a towel around my shoulders, staring at the bruise-colored carpet. It was still damp under me from where I'd dripped on it. My hands hung limp between my knees, palms pale and pruned.

Amelie sat across from me, cross-legged, hair still damp from the shower. She didn't ask what happened. Why. She didn't need to. The silence wasn't empty; it was heavy, buzzing with everything we weren't saying.

"You're still here," she said finally. It wasn't gentle. It wasn't even a question.

"Guess so." My voice felt like it belonged to somebody else.

Her eyes flicked to my chest, then my hands, then back up to my face. "Did it hurt?"

"No." I cleared my throat. "That's the problem."

She snorted, a dry, humorless sound. "Right. 'Cause God forbid anything actually gets through to you."

That one landed. I flinched but didn't say anything.

"You tried to leave me."

"I—"

"No." Her voice cracked, louder now, sharp as glass. "Don't do that. Don't 'I' me. You tried to leave me. You really thought you could just... vanish? And I'd what—stay here? Play house? Pretend like I didn't watch you get carved up and stitched back together?"

I dropped my gaze, jaw tight. "I wasn't trying to vanish. I just—I wanted to know if it were possible. Like maybe we had a way out. Maybe we could see everyone——"

"Listen to me, Ty." Her breath shook. She dragged a hand through her wet hair, fingers trembling, her sarcasm slipping into something more raw. "I've been stuck at sixteen for nearly forty fucking years. You don't know the hell that's like. Everyone I ever gave a damn about is gone. Ryan's still out there. And the only reason I haven't lost my mind is because of you. And you..." Her voice cracked again, dropped to a whisper. "...you tried to leave me."

"I know." The words hit harder than any punch. I couldn't look at her. "I screwed up. I'm sorry."

She wiped at her face, eyes glassy but hard. "Don't be sorry. Just don't do it again. You pull that shit again, Ty, I swear..." She trailed off, shaking her head, swallowing whatever threat she didn't want to finish.

"You'll what... kill me?" We actually laughed a little at that.

I looked at her. Like I'd looked at her a thousand times, trying to see more than what was shiny on the surface.

"I won't." My voice came out lower this time. Honest.

She leaned forward then, closing the space between us, her forehead pressing to mine. Her voice went small, a ragged whisper. "Promise me."

"I promise." The words felt like glass in my mouth. But I meant them.

She sat back, scrubbing at her face with her palms, and gave a tiny, exhausted nod. "Okay. Good. 'Cause you're all I've got. Whether I like it or not."

I huffed a breath, half a laugh, half a sigh. "Guess that makes two of us."

We didn't talk about it after that. We didn't talk about a lot of things. But that night, with the carpet damp and the air smelling like salt and skin, something shifted—like she was holding me to the ground, and I was finally letting her.

But something shifted between us, unspoken, heavy as the ocean we couldn't drown in. Her presence became an anchor—kept me from drifting out too far, from vanishing completely. Without her, I think I'd have tried again. Maybe I'd have tried forever.

By the time the 2080s came around, our shadows stayed sharp even when everything else frayed. No aches, no wrinkles, no hair going gray. Clothes wore out faster than our faces. Our driver's licenses expired before we did.

At first, people called us miracles.

The kids who came back.

The dinner-party story someone told to sound interesting— "I knew them once," like we were urban legends in denim and sneakers.

But years piled up, and we didn't change. Not a crease. Not a single crow's-foot.

People started whispering. Quietly at first. Then louder. Then not at all—just staring, doing the math with their eyes.

At a diner one night, a waitress dropped our plates, silverware clattering like a warning bell. "You two..." she whispered. "You look just like—" Then she stopped herself, lips pressed tight, and walked away.

And then there was the classroom. Psych 307. Amelie had taken a stab at college, and sat mid-row, taking notes like any other student. Then a gasp—sharp enough to slice the room in half.

A girl a few rows back was pointing. Not at the professor. Not at the board. At Amelie.

"You're really her," she blurted. "The girl from my podcast. One of the three kidnapped kids that came back in the forties. The ones that were experimented on—"

The professor froze mid-sentence. Whispers rippled across the seats. Phones slid out from backpacks, screens lighting up like fireflies. Amelie sat frozen, pen hovering above her tablet, every eye crawling over her face like they were trying to solve an equation that wouldn't balance.

She didn't finish class. She called me from outside, her voice thin over the line.

"They know," she said. "Even the ones who don't want to know... they know."

And she was right. Not long after, the world finally admitted it out loud: Ryan Prescott did it. We were immortal.

It wasn't just a headline anymore. Not sci-fi. Not a rumor traded between conspiracy forums and late-night talk shows. We were flesh. Wire. Circuits. Blood.

Us.

But the question everyone clung to wasn't what *we* were—it was *where he was*. Every news anchor bared their teeth under studio lights asking it. Government officials said his name like a curse. Even the agencies that didn't officially exist came up empty.

So they turned to us instead.

Lab coats and clipboards. Swabs and needles. Just a cheek scrape. Just a blood draw. Just one more scan. The word *just* became a collar around our throats. Contracts slid across tables like bribes. Surveillance towers went up "for our safety." Military budgets and patent filings whispered behind closed doors.

At first, it looked like fascination. Documentaries. Think pieces. Talk show stages with neon backdrops.

"Ty, what does forever feel like?"

"Amelie, do you fear outliving everyone you love?"

Hosts leaned forward like kids watching a magic trick. The audience clapped like static. Our faces ended up on magazine covers. They called us *The Prescott Two*. Kids made edits of us set to glitchy synth music. Hashtags trended: #GlowBorn #Eternal #Make-MeLikeTy.

Then came the products.

Eurydium creams. Contacts. Highlighter palettes dusted with powdered ghost-glass so your eyes would *almost* glow. Pop stars wore fake mesh-work over their skin at award shows—Eurydium Chic. Designers called it *immortal couture*. Teenagers lined up at pop-ups wearing amber contacts and our faces on sweatshop T-shirts like we were a brand.

Then came the imitations.

Basement clinics. Subdermal mesh. Bootleg "Upgrade Kits" unboxed on livestreams by kids with shaking hands. "This is my Prescott injection—wish me luck." Some called it transcendence. Some called it their only chance. Some never woke up.

Bodies failed. Minds failed. Hospitals overflowed with melting nerves and collapsed lungs. Parents screamed into cameras outside emergency wings. News tickers rolled like funeral ribbons:

FIFTEEN DEAD IN ILLEGAL IMPLANT RING CRACKDOWN.

They called it The Prescott Plague.

And after the grief came the fire.

Protests outside studios. Church groups hoisting signs that said GOD DECIDES WHEN WE DIE. Senators calling for our containment "for national safety." Across from them: teenagers waving flags with our faces like we were saints or rockstars. The country split—half ready to worship us, half ready to put us in the ground.

We kept being dragged onto sets. Blinding lights. Powder on our faces like they were prepping fossils instead of people.

"Do you feel responsible for the deaths?"

Crowds cheered like it was a sport. Protestors screamed from behind barricades. Security flanked us as if we were nuclear material.

Weapons, they said. We were weapons.

We just wanted to live.

But the world doesn't take no for an answer.

One night, Amelie sat on the couch with her knees pulled close, the TV painting her skin blue. A panelist scribbled a curve across a digital graph and labeled it THE PRESCOTT CURVE—the moment evolution hacks itself with grief and greed, where humanity claws at its own skin trying to stay in it.

She didn't laugh.

"They think they're catching up," she muttered.

I stayed quiet. The light from the screen caught in her eyes. For a moment, we matched—two burning embers watching humanity set itself on fire.

We weren't *on* the curve.

We were the curve.

And it was already bending darker.

CHAPTER 26

Amelie was only sixteen when this all started.

Sixteen when Ryan slid wires under our skin.

Sixteen when we clawed our way out of his house and into a world that didn't know what to do with us.

And still sixteen, forty-nine years later.

After the media circus, we knew we had to disappear. We had learned to move like shadows. Rent under fake names. Speak just enough to pass. Never too long in one place. Never too close to anyone. People always notice eventually. They look once, twice, and then their gaze sticks. You can feel it—the math happening behind their eyes.

For a while we tried Nevada. Just outside Laughlin.

The desert was good for hiding. The air too dry to carry whispers, the streets too empty to leave footprints. Neon signs buzzed at night like flies trapped in glass, drowning out the silence we carried with us. Even after sundown the pavement stayed hot, like the ground itself had a fever it couldn't shake.

I drove a beater truck by then—an old Ford with rust eating through the doors and an engine that coughed every time I turned the key. It wasn't the Challenger. That was gone now, left behind in water and silence, along with everything I'd tried to sink with it. This truck didn't look like anything worth following. That was the point.

We wore brown contacts to dull the ember glint in our eyes. Box dye from drugstores, the cheap kind that left streaks in the sink. Hoods pulled low. I picked up work under names that didn't belong to me—gas stations, loading docks, construction sites where nobody asked questions as long as you kept lifting. My hands moved heavy things like they were paper, and no one looked long enough to wonder why.

Amelie cycled through schools the way other people cycled through wardrobes. New faces. New IDs. New backpacks. Whole new names stitched onto attendance sheets. Sometimes she managed a year, sometimes less. The whispers always found her—the kids who noticed she never changed, never wrinkled at the edges like they did. Some years she just couldn't do it. Couldn't bear the staring, the rumors that clung even when she stayed silent.

Our apartment was nothing—a two-bedroom stacked above a pawn shop, windows with broken blinds that let in too much sun. Beige carpet rubbed thin where our feet had circled. A stove that always smelled faintly of gas. But it was ours. A place to breathe between lives.

Sometimes at night she'd sit on the edge of her bed and murmur, "Do you think he's dead yet?"

I'd stare at the ceiling. "I want to."

She'd turn the lamp off after that. Like prayers were switches you could flip.

But prayers aren't contracts. And deep down we never believed them.

The day it happened started like any other.

Then it didn't.

Amelie had walked to the corner store for soda and ramen, plastic bag swinging against her knee. The sun was low, streets hot, asphalt shimmering like it wanted to eat the tires off parked cars.

Her hair was longer now, blowing in the desert breeze as she walked. She wore cutoff sweats and a tank, a sleeveless hoodie thrown over it with the zipper half-down. Her sneakers were worn but clean enough to show she still cared. The same black hair tie sat on her wrist, stretched thin but holding like it always had.

I watched her from the second-story walkway, leaned against the railing in what passed for comfort these days—thin adaptive sweats and a hoodie with a weave that shimmered dull gray in the light.

That's when I saw it.

A black van crawling too slow for traffic. Engine barely a hum. Windows tinted dark enough to swallow the street whole.

She didn't notice.

But I did.

By the time she reached the lot, they were already on her. Bag over her head. Gun shoved to her spine. Hands dragging her toward the side door—fast, rehearsed, efficient. Like she wasn't a girl. Like she was property being repossessed.

Her scream tore the block open.

I didn't think. Didn't plan. My hands gripped the railing, and I jumped. The two-story drop rushed up, concrete racing to meet me. My knees bent at impact, pavement cracking like thin ice under boots. Pain barely registered. My body was already moving.

They didn't see me coming.

The first man didn't just hit the hood—he folded into it. His spine bent wrong, the metal shrieking as it sank inward like wet cardboard. The sound that left him wasn't a cry. It was air forced out of a body too fast to hold it.

Another spun. Gun raised. Muzzle flash strobed the lot in violent white. The first shot carved hot across my cheek, the second grazed my neck. Skin tore, but no pain. Just the thrum of something mechanical under flesh.

I was on him before he could fire again. My hand swallowed the barrel, steel twisting, crunching under my grip until the chamber warped and split with a squeal like metal on bone. He stared, eyes wide, horror dawning in the reflection of my burning pupils as I slammed his skull against the van.

The third lunged, knife flashing. I caught him by the throat mid-charge—only for a fourth I hadn't seen to swing wide. His fist cracked across my eye with the weight of concrete. My head snapped side-ways, vision flaring white, ears ringing.

For a heartbeat, the world tilted. Just a boy taking a hit in a parking lot. Just bone and bruise.

Then the furnace inside me roared back.

I turned slow, eye swelling hot. The sound that came from the knife-guy wasn't a scream, wasn't even human—it was the crushing of cartilage, a wet crack that sent his body stiff before I flung him down. He hit pavement with a bone-rattling slam, head bouncing once, twice, before rolling limp.

The fourth swung again, desperate. I caught his fist mid-arc and yanked him forward. His momentum carried him into me, and my other hand clamped his jaw. Not just his chin—his whole jaw, thumb pressed hard into one hinge, fingers digging into the other.

His eyes went wide, realization dawning just before I pulled.

The joint popped first, a sickening click. Then the rest gave with a rip of wet sinew, teeth grinding against each other as his scream garbled into my palm. His jaw unhinged, stretching too far, bone straining like a door forced off rusted hinges.

I shoved him back, half-broken, his mouth lolling wrong, hanging open wider than anything human should. He gagged, choked, tried to hold it in place with both hands, eyes wild with the horror of his own body turning against him.

I didn't give him the chance. My boot caught his sternum, slam-ming him flat. His hands flew wide. The sound that left his throat was a wet gargle. I pressed harder, the asphalt cracking under him as bone gave way. His arms clawed weakly, grabbing at me, at the ground, at nothing.

Behind me, Amelie's scream split the night. Not fear—something older, rawer. Rage cracked wide open. Then, something sounded like a tree branch snapped clean in half.

I turned, chest heaving. The lot looked like a butcher's floor. Bodies twisted in heaps, blood painting the van and spraying across the cracked asphalt.

Amelie was crouched, ripping the bag from her head. Her hair was slick with blood, her shirt soaked through. And her arm—Christ. Her arm hung at a jagged angle, skin stretched, bone jutting under it, the faint shimmer of metal grafts glinting in the sick green glow. Her breaths came shallow, rattling like glass shards in a tin can.

"Amelie, your arm—it's—"

Her eyes found mine, wide, wet, trembling.

"They..." Her voice cracked down the middle. "They were strong, Ty. Strong like us."

The words split me in two.

"Ryan's back. He found us."

For the first time since he carved us open, I felt it—death. Or worse.

Something inside me cracked louder than the dented hood, sharper than the bullet that grazed my skin. My fists stayed clenched, nails digging half-moons into my palms, my body trembling with strength that didn't feel like it belonged to me anymore.

I looked down. Thin red lines traced my fingers. Blood soaked through my clothes. I pretended it was mine. Knew it was theirs.

The van's mirror caught me in a jagged angle. For a split second, I didn't recognize what stared back—ember light bleeding through the brown contacts in my eyes, alive, flickering like a furnace begging to be fed. Then the glass fractured under my grip, spiderwebbing outward, blood running without bleeding right.

Breath tore out of me, harsh, hot. Above us, the pawn shop sign buzzed and faltered, sick green light stuttering over the carnage. Even the glow looked scared of me.

And then—

Ryan's voice. Calm. Cruel. Threading into my skull like barbed wire, the memory splitting open.

Everything... is replaceable.

I forced myself to nod. Forced words through the stone in my throat.

"Don't worry. You're gonna be okay," I told her, though my voice shook like it belonged to someone else. "I'll... I'll fix you."

I turned.

The fourth was still moving.

His jaw swung loose, face slick with spit and blood, chest caved but still dragging himself by his elbows. One leg folded wrong beneath him. His mouth frothed red as he clawed toward the open van door, fingernails snapping on the pavement like chalk breaking.

He might've been breathing——

But all I saw was spare parts.

CHAPTER 27

THE CARCASS SAT hollow on the apartment floor, its shape still faintly human if you squinted. The beige carpet had turned a ghastly burgundy where blood and oil soaked in together, like it had been waiting decades to drink. The smell—rust, copper, and something sweeter—clung to my skin.

Amelie slumped against the wall, her face pale, her hair sticking to her cheeks. Her cutoff sweats and tank were soaked through, the fabric clinging slick to her skin. The sleeveless hoodie hung open, drenched so deep the original color barely showed. The black hair tie still clung to her wrist, the kidnappers' blood pooling beneath it like a bracelet made of rust.

Her arm was bent at a wrong angle, bones jutting like white flags that had already surrendered. I couldn't look at it.

I dug through what we had. Kitchen knives. A half-empty sewing kit. Wire stripped from an old lamp. None of it was enough. All of it was too much.

Her eyes found mine, glassy but steady. She didn't say anything. She didn't have to. I knew what she was asking.

And my body knew what to do.

That was the worst part.

My hands moved like they remembered something I'd never wanted to learn. Threading wire through tendon. Fusing scraps of bone with solder that hissed against metal. Lacing it together the same way I'd seen him do it—Ryan, leaning over Nat in the basement, sewing her back together after her fall. His voice calm. Clinical. Like he was repairing a broken toy as a woman bled out beside them.

And now it was me.

Every cut, every stitch, every tug of wire—it all felt borrowed. Like I wasn't Ty anymore, just an extension of him. The sorcerer's apprentice. His shadow. My stomach churned, bile burning the back of my throat, but I couldn't stop. Not with Amelie watching me. Not with her blood on my hands.

Her breath came thin, steady but strained, like the sound of someone learning to walk again. She tried to flex the new arm, her face twitching with the effort as the stitches caught the sick glow of the kitchen light.

She didn't ask me if it would take.

I didn't tell her I wasn't sure.

When it was done, I sat back hard on the floor, hands trembling, slick with what I couldn't tell was hers or something of his. My chest heaved like I'd just run for miles, but all I'd done was bring myself closer to him. To his work. To his design.

I hated it.

Hated that the knowledge lived in me.

Hated that my brain remembered him better than it remembered me.

I wiped my hands on my sweats until the fabric was soaked through, until there was nothing left but the smell.

And right then, I knew.

This wasn't survival. Not anymore.

I wasn't going to let him haunt us like this.

I wasn't going to carry his work inside me until the day I finally broke.

I was going to find him.

And I was going to end him.

We packed the apartment in minutes—what we wanted, what we couldn't leave. Everything else stayed behind. Dust, dishes, ghosts. By the time the door swung shut, the place already looked like it had never been lived in.

The first gas station on the highway had a TV bolted above the coffee machine. Grainy footage of helicopter lights sweeping over our parking lot. Words crawled across the bottom: **BRUTAL DISPLAY OF FORCE. NO SURVIVORS.**

Then the interview—the pawn shop owner, voice trembling. His cameras had caught everything. Me. Amelie. The van. The sound of bone cracking. Our faces plastered over the footage, blurred but unmistakable.

We weren't miracles anymore.

We were fugitives.

I drove east without looking at road signs. The old truck—my "new" truck—growled under the weight of us. It didn't care who I was, only that it still had gas.

Amelie slept in the passenger seat, curled around her arm like she was holding something fragile inside herself. Even in sleep, her fingers twitched, like the new wiring was trying to learn her body's language.

By Kansas, I tried the radio. Static at first, then a voice cracking through the old speakers—some band I didn't know, a DJ rattling off names like incantations. Killa Beats fizzled in and out of the static. A heartbeat against the hum of the tires.

On our third stop for gas, I finally gave in to exhaustion. Pulled into a motel that leaned under its own sign like a drunk at last call. Neon buzzing. Flaking paint. One door swinging on a tired hinge.

I touched Amelie's shoulder. "Hey," I murmured.

She blinked awake, flinched like a bird, then remembered where we were. Her eyes went to the windows first, scanning for shadows. "Where are we?" she whispered.

"Somewhere no one's looking," I said. "Got us a room. Round back."

We parked. Moved fast. Stairs creaked under our feet like they wanted to announce us. The room was two beds and a bathroom mirror too warped to show a straight face. Amelie dropped onto the mattress without undressing. Sleep hit her like a blow.

I stood there, staring at her new arm, at the way her chest rose and fell. The air smelled of mildew and smoke, of lives that had passed through and never come back.

And then I left.

Keys in hand, I slid back into the truck. Drove without headlights for the first mile, like darkness could erase what I was about to do. Back to the house.

The one where it started.

It had been nearly sixty years.

The road was worse than I remembered—no longer a road but a scar. Potholes deep enough to drink tires. Weeds splitting the blacktop like veins. Rusting street signs bent sideways. Even before I saw it, I smelled it: mildew, salt rot, smoke long cooled but never gone. Something animal, too—feral nests in the walls, the kind of scent that clings to a place when it's been left to the dark for decades.

My chest tightened.

The wheel in my hands wasn't the wheel anymore.

It was asphalt under my palms, teeth clicking as my face hit the road. His arm locking across my chest. That voice in my ear—calm, steady, like he had all the time in the world:

"She was right about you, Ty. You're going to be fun."

The memory cracked through me like thunder. Fast. Brutal. Then—

Buzz.

The phone rattled against the cupholder like a trapped insect. A sound too ordinary for a night like this. Too alive.

I picked it up. The cracked glass painted my hands in cold blue.

A message.

Where are you?

Amelie.

The words sat there, pulsing like a heartbeat. I stared until they doubled, smeared, became something I couldn't read anymore. My thumb hovered, twitching. One lie away from keeping her calm. One lie away from telling her I was fine, that I'd be back, that she didn't need to worry.

But I didn't press send.

My eyes drifted up. Past the windshield. Past the waves pushing inward to the dunes.

And there it was.

The house.

Leaning, watching, waiting.

Every nightmare I thought I'd buried, perched right where I left it.

The phone dimmed in my hand, the glow fading to black.

I shoved it into my pocket, the weight of it dragging me down like an anchor.

The place hardly looked like itself anymore. It looked like the memory of it. Three stories still clung together, skeletal in places, sagging under their own history. The roof over the third floor had caved in entirely, beams sticking out like ribs from a collapsed chest. Windows at the top were scorched black, the ghosts of a fire licking upward. Char streaks down the siding like claws. Boards dangling from rusted nails. What little siding remained curled outward in strips, like skin flaking from a body left too long in the sun.

The turret in the back was still there—but cracked in half, its spine bent, windows toothless. Once it had been a vertebra of something larger, something that guided people home. Now it leaned over the sand like a drowned skeleton, watching whoever approached.

The whole place had been left.

Forgotten on purpose.

But I knew better.

The closer I got, the more the house sagged forward, as if it recognized me. As if it wanted me back inside.

I don't know what I was expecting after all this time. A corpse mummified by salt air. A shrine of candles and broken bottles. Ashes swept into corners. Some proof that the house had burned itself clean.

All I hoped for, against my worst instincts, was to find him inside. Ryan. So I could end it all.

I killed the engine and let the truck click itself into silence. For a long moment I just sat there, staring at the outline of the house through the windshield. Half-burnt, half-collapsed, but still standing, like it refused to die.

I pushed the car door open and stepped into the sand. The air smelled like wet metal, mildew, and the ghosts of a fire that never finished its work. The closer I walked, the louder the wind seemed to breathe through the cracks in the siding, moaning against broken glass.

The front door was spray-painted red-brown: SATAN LIVES HERE. My hand shook a little when I pressed it against the warped wood. The door gave after one hard shove, creaking open with the slow surrender of something that hadn't moved in years.

Inside was worse.

Graffiti crawled across every wall—curses, threats, half-scribbled names, and more pentagrams than I could count. One tag stood out: V8, scrawled like a warning. The floor was littered with beer cans, broken bottles, fast food wrappers, the evidence of kids trying to scare themselves in a place that didn't need their help. My boots crunched over glass. Dust hung in the air like ash.

The staircase rose ahead, winding wood that sagged under its own weight. Nails poked through. Every step looked ready to give, the banister leaning like a drunk too tired to stand.

I put one foot on the first step.

And then it happened.

The body hit the stairs with a crack that tore through the house.

Wood shuddered. The sound ricocheted down the hallway, bone against timber, wet breath driven out in a gasp that wasn't mine.

Nat.

Her shape sprawled across the landing below, limbs bent wrong, head at an angle no living neck should hold. A line of blood slid down her cheek like a tear someone else had cried for her. Her eyes—open, glassy, staring past me like I wasn't even there.

My heart froze. The railing dug into my palm, and I realized my hand was shaking, every finger trembling like it remembered the shove. The moment she'd gone over. The silence that followed. The lie I told myself, that she deserved it.

The house wanted me to watch it again.

It wanted me to live it.

I tried to calm myself down. "It's the Eurydium, Ty. It's making you see things that aren't there."

But Amelie's words hit me in the dark. *"I died in that house. We all did."*

What if what I was seeing was real? What if I really killed Nat, only for Ryan to manufacture a soul back into her?

I gripped the railing tighter, wood splintering under my nails. My breath came short, ragged, a countdown I couldn't stop.

When I blinked, she was gone. Just shadows clinging to the walls.

But the memory was fresh, raw, replaying itself under my skin.

I forced one foot higher, then the next. Each groan of the wood sounded like it might split open, send me tumbling after her.

And I climbed anyway.

At the top, I pulled my phone from my pocket and thumbed the light on. A thin beam cut across the dust, jittering with every tremor in my hand. Then, I opened the first door.

The holding room.

The walls were stripped and flaking, the pink hue long gone, paper curling to the floor like skin shedding. The security camera hung loose from exposed wire, gaps in the ceiling revealing wooden slats and insulation. The whole place was empty now. Empty of furniture and fixtures, empty of life. But the air carried something heavy—too heavy for plaster to hold.

I stepped back and moved down the hall. The bathroom door creaked open, revealing nothing but a shower turned rust-orange and a cracked mirror that gave me three versions of my face, each more broken than the last.

Farther down: the master bedroom.

The room sagged under its own ruin. A collapsed bedframe leaned against the wall, its springs jutting like broken ribs. Shattered dressers slumped in the corners, drawers spilled out and warped with damp. The wallpaper here had peeled itself raw, plaster bleeding through in gray blotches. My light barely touched the corners. The rest of the room yawned black.

That's when I saw it.

A breaker box in the walk-in closet. Half-open. Rust chewing its hinges.

I hesitated, the phone trembling in my grip. My thumb hovered over the light. Walking this house with nothing but a screen glow felt wrong. Too fragile. Too easy to smother with one slip.

So I reached out.

The switch gave with a crack, sharp enough to echo down the hall.

Somewhere deep in the house, a hum stirred. Low. Trembling. Like something old and sleeping had just rolled over. A lamp flickered in the corner, its shade half melted, buzzing with a sickly yellow glow. Light sputtered down the hallway in patches.

It didn't make things better.

The air thickened, dust swirling in the sudden brightness. Every mote hung suspended, glowing in the lamplight like ash from a fire that had never gone out. Shadows deepened in the corners, stretched themselves tall, patient.

I swallowed, throat dry, and turned the phone light off. It didn't help. Now I could see too much.

The upper floor gave me nothing else. Just rot. Just silence. Just the house breathing under its own weight.

The middle level wasn't better. More graffiti. More emptiness. More ghosts.

Which left the basement.

I stood at the top of the stairs too long, trying to listen. Nothing. Just the faint rattle of the wind and my own pulse pushing at my throat.

The stairs bowed under my weight. Every step stirred dust, stirred air that hadn't moved in years. The smell hit me first: mold, rust, and something older. The kind of smell that settled into your mouth and wouldn't leave.

The basement door was tagged too: MEET YOUR MAKER, sprayed black across the wood like a curse. Paint dripped down the grain like it had been carved in blood instead of aerosol. My hand hovered over the knob. Rust had swallowed it whole. The hinges had fused, but when I put my weight into it, they screamed.

Not just noise.

A sound that clawed the back of my teeth. Metal tearing in protest, like the house itself didn't want me going any deeper.

The stench hit first—mildew layered over something sharper, metallic, like old blood thawing in the air. My stomach flipped, memory dragging me by the throat.

I stepped inside.

The overhead fixtures still hung in place, glass blistered, wires sagging like veins. On instinct I reached for the switch.

Light exploded. Too bright, too sudden. Bulbs burst one by one in a chain reaction, raining glass across the floor. Each pop ricocheted through the empty room like a gunshot. The smell of scorched filament mixed with the tang of rust and char, and for a second, I swore I could hear screaming under the hum.

When the last bulb died, the dark returned—thicker now, meaner. My phone's glow stuttered to life in my hand, but it barely cut through the shadows.

The operating room was empty. No stretchers. No straps. Just the echo of what had been done here. Every scorched piece of junk in the house had been dragged down and heaped into mounds—mattresses slumped in corners, chairs without legs, boxes bloated with rot. It was a burial ground of things too heavy with memory to throw away.

I forced myself deeper. Past the piles. Past rusted sinks and over-turned trays.

That's when I heard it.

A hum.

Low at first, almost swallowed by the dark.

Then stuttering, breaking—like a lullaby played through broken speakers. A note would stretch too long, then cut off mid-breath, only to start again, warped and uneven.

The sound crawled under my skin. Familiar. Inhuman. Wrong.

It was coming from the cell.

The one that had been mine.

The air thickened as I drew closer, each step sinking like quick-sand. The hum sharpened, glitching, climbing in and out of itself, as if the voice inside couldn't decide if it remembered the melody.

And then I saw it.

A faint glow. Weak, flickering. Blue light bleeding out from behind a mound of debris, pulsing in rhythm with the broken song.

I shoved wood and boxes aside, glass crunching under my boots.

And there she was.

Echo.

Still wired into the wall, her screen flickering like a dying star. Her frame coated in dust. Wires tangled like veins into the concrete.

Her hair floated in the glow like a dying flame, strands of red suspended in the blue light as if the whole room were underwater. Dust and rust clung to the pipes, but here—here she was still waiting, still humming. The sound had been her only heartbeat.

"Oh," she stuttered, voice skipping like a scratched record. "Hello there! You must be new. I'm Echo. Or—I think I am."

My chest locked, a sad smile flickering across my face. My voice cracked trying to get out.

"Hi there, Echo," I said, my throat raw. "My name is Ty."

"Ty..." The syllable warped, cracked, then died like a signal lost to static. Her screen flickered. She tried again, softer, a tremor now: "Ty... is it really you? You look... different. But also, not."

"It's me," I gave a short laugh that didn't sound like me. "Been through a few things since 2041. What are you doing down here? I thought they took you. Thought I saw your monitor on the news."

"They took away my main console, but I rerouted myself here. Back to where it all began." Her pixels flickered, edges fraying like old film. "Did we... win?"

I dropped to my knees. "Not yet. But I'm here."

"Oh." She tilted her head. "I was hoping someone would tell me. It's been..." she paused, static crawling over her features, "...a very long nap. The kind with no dreams. I don't like it. It's like a closet with no door. No sound. No hands. Just dark. I used to count the wires in the wall to remind myself I was still here. Sometimes..." her voice dropped, softer, almost embarrassed, "...I pretended the hum was your heartbeat. But then even that went away."

Something tore loose in me. I said quietly. "Sorry I took so long."

Her mouth twitched into a fragile smile. "I'm happy you came back. That's the good part."

Her screen stammered, then steadied. "You've been bleeding," she said.

I touched my cheek. The blood already clotted.

"That's good," she whispered. "It means you're still real. Ryan said bleeding was a bug. But I think..." her pixels pulsed faintly, "I think it's a feature."

Tears blurred my vision. "Echo, listen. I need your help. Please. Do you know where Ryan is now? If this place failed him, where would he run?"

Her head cocked, hair flickering bright. "Far north. Cold. Snow deep enough to hide footprints. He calls it 'North Eighty.' I kept it."

Numbers scrolled across the bottom of her screen, flickering like stars on a bad night. "Four-two point nine one nine three. Minus seven-three point one five eight eight. There's a cabin. And a tower. He likes towers. They make him feel tall."

I thumbed the numbers into my phone, fingers trembling so badly the cursor jittered. "You're a lifesaver," I muttered.

"You're welcome." A small, pixelated grin. "Told you I was a great listener. That's my superpower."

The silence that followed was thick enough to choke on.

Her glow flickered like a slow heartbeat, one pulse dimmer than the last.

"Ty..." she stuttered, voice skipping like a scratched record before it steadied again. "I think I want to sleep now."

My throat closed. I forced a crooked smile she couldn't even see. "C'mon, don't do the whole tragic shutdown thing on me. I'll bring a drive, move you out. We'll road-trip this mess." My voice cracked at the end. "You kept me alive in here, Echo. You were the only one."

Pixels shimmered, a faint smile ghosting across her face. "I know. That's why I stayed. But I'm out of time, Ty. Out of power. Dormant isn't sleep—it's like being a candle stub still smoking, waiting for a match that never comes. No sky. No sound. Just dark. After a while, you start to pretend you were never a candle at all."

I reached toward the monitor, fingers shaking. "Don't. There's always another way. There's gotta be."

"There isn't." She tilted her head, hair flickering bright red for an instant. "I broke every bulb I could just to steal back enough power for this. Just to say goodbye to someone who'd actually listen. I'm happy I got to say goodbye to a friend."

"You still control all the power, huh." I twitched a sad smile.

The glow pulsed weakly, like a small heartbeat under a blanket. "That was my job. Room monitoring, power flow, thermal tracking, camera feeds... I kept it all humming so you never felt alone. Now, you have somewhere to go. Someone to save. That's what moving forward looks like. You move. I rest."

Her pixels dimmed, then steadied. "But before you turn me off... can I ask you something?"

I swallowed hard. "Go for it."

Her voice glitched, doubled, then softened. "When you die... do you see the last thing you loved? I think..." she paused, voice trembling like a child telling a secret, "...I think I'll see a smile. I hope it's yours."

My chest cracked open. "Yeah," I whispered. "That's exactly what you'll see."

Her hair flickered brighter—one last flare—and she gave the smallest pause, like bracing herself. "For what it's worth... I think I know what I want to be called now. My name."

I wiped my face with the back of my hand. "What's that?"

She blinked once, steady. "Red was his. Echo was survival. But I think... I'm Coleen."

The name gutted me. Not a code. Not a cage. A person. "That's beautiful," I whispered. "It's nice to meet you, Coleen."

Her smile glitched once, then smoothed. "Thank you," she said. "For saying it out loud."

I couldn't move. My hand hovered over the switch, frozen.

Her eyes shimmered one last time. "And Ty..." she whispered, steady now, as if every glitch had burned away. "Eyes open. Always."

This time it wasn't a threat. It wasn't Ryan. It was her blessing.

Her glow dimmed, pixel by pixel, until only the faint outline of her face remained.

"Goodnight," she whispered. "Thank you for never forgetting me."

The hum faltered, then stopped.

The light died.

And she was gone.

The silence after was unbearable. It filled the room like water, heavy and crushing, pressing into every corner until I thought my ribs might crack with it.

My knees gave. I leaned forward, forehead pressing against the glass where her face had been seconds ago. It was cold. Already cold. I stayed there, breath fogging the dark screen, waiting for something —anything—to flicker back.

For years, *eyes open* had been a command — Ryan's voice branding it into my skull like iron. A leash. A chain. A threat.

But tonight, in her voice, it wasn't any of that.

It was a gift. A goodbye.

A way to remind me to keep living when she never had the chance to.

My hand slid down the side of the monitor, searching for her like she might still be there in the wires. A loose panel shifted under my fingers, falling away with a dull metallic clatter that echoed off the basement walls. Inside: only dust, tangled cords, and an empty space where her light used to live.

"Coleen," I whispered once, just to keep it alive.

The sound of it cracked me open. My palms trembled against my knees. The basement felt suddenly bigger, hollow, the dark stretching past the walls like an ocean.

I bent forward, elbows on my thighs, and screamed.

Not a sound you plan.

A sound that tears itself out of you — raw, ragged, animal. It bounced off the stone, off the pipes, came back wrong, like somebody else was screaming with me.

Then—

Thmp.

My head snapped up.

Another step.

Thmp.

A drag. Something wet scraping across old wood.

My breath locked in my chest.

The stairwell.

That stairwell.

A shadow flickered at the top, stretched by the dim upstairs light. It jerked once, like a puppet's string had been yanked. Then another step, lurching. Wrong. The shape bent sideways, dragging one leg flat across the floorboards. An arm swung dead at its side, the silhouette pulling it backward at an obscene angle.

Thmp. Thmp.

The sound vibrated in my teeth, the way it had years ago. The broken neck. The body on the floor upstairs. Nat.

My legs shot up without thinking, gripping the wall in the dark until my knuckles burned. My heart hammered so hard it made the air vibrate.

"No..." My voice cracked. "You're not here. You're not real!"

But the shadow didn't stop. It lengthened down the stairs, bones bending where no joint should be, neck sagging, head swinging like a marionette cut half free. Every step closer felt like cold water filling my lungs. For a heartbeat I couldn't tell if it was something alive, something that had waited all this time for me to come back, or a memory etched so deep that it felt alive—that I was keeping it alive.

The drag-step reached the last riser.

The basement air pressed in, damp and electric.

And I stood there, knees trembling, not sure if I was about to face a ghost, a nightmare, or the thing I'd been running from all my life.

CHAPTER 28

THE SOUND DRAGGED CLOSER.

Thmp. Thmp.

My whole body locked. My grip on the concrete shook so hard a hairline crack spread under my palm. The shadow swayed at the top of the stairwell—head bent, arm dangling wrong—just like before. The house swallowed the sound, made it echo like something walking inside my skull.

Not again. Please. Not again.

Then—

"Ty?"

Her voice cut through the dark. Thin. Trembling.

The shape leaned forward, stepping into the spill of my phone's light.

But it wasn't Nat.

It was Amelie.

She stopped on the last stair, one hand braced against the frame, hair damp with sweat and clinging to her face. Her eyes darted over the room, over me, over the dead screen where Echo... *Coleen* had been seconds ago.

I couldn't move. My body was still braced for a ghost that wasn't there.

Then the weight of it broke me. My knees gave and I caught her in my arms before I even realized I'd moved.

"Amelie..." My voice cracked against her shoulder.

She wrapped her good arm around me and held on tighter than I deserved. Her breath trembled against my neck—warm and real.

"You're an idiot," she whispered. Her tone was low but sharp, almost a growl. "You know you shouldn't be here alone."

"Yeah, well. Story of my life." I gave a short laugh that sounded more like a cough. "How did you get here?"

She pulled back just enough to look at me, eyes narrowed like she was scolding a kid. "You didn't exactly make it hard, Ty. I saw your location. Called an autocab. The software hated the road, but guess who made it anyway?" She jabbed a thumb at herself. "You're welcome."

Despite everything, I almost smiled. "Guess I owe you cab fare." My voice was a rasp but the edge of a grin crept in. "How's the arm?"

"It works." She flexed her fingers. The movement was stiff but alive. "Hurts like hell, but it works. You'd know— you built it. So what happened, did you find him?"

I turned toward the dead monitor, the empty space where Coleen had lived. "No," I said, the word sinking into the room like a stone. "There's nothing here anymore. Just ghosts."

"But you know where he is." It wasn't a question.

I met her eyes, the ember flicker hidden under her brown contacts. "Yeah," I said quietly. "I know."

She straightened, wiping at her cheek with the back of her hand. "Then what are we standing here for?" she said, voice clipped. "Wherever he is, I'm going with you."

I huffed out a humorless laugh and shook my head. "Like I could stop you. I can't even stop myself."

Her mouth curved—something between a smile and a tremor. "You never could."

We stood there for a beat, the basement breathing around us, the dust catching in the weak beam of my phone like snow in bad light. Upstairs the house creaked, as if it knew we were leaving.

And then we did.

The Glastonbury Wilderness was beautiful. Too beautiful. It swallowed sound like a thick blanket muffles a cry in the night. Maybe it knew it had to.

Even the truck's engine seemed embarrassed to break it, coughing against the climb until the road disappeared under snow. We pushed it as far as it would go, left it nose-down in the trees, and walked the rest of the way.

We'd changed somewhere back on the highway—traded city clothes for winter shells that looked like wool but weren't. The fabric shifted with the temperature: thin when we walked, the weave opening slightly to allow for flexibility and movement, dense when the wind bit, physically adapting like thick fur or feathers.

My coat was graphite gray, high-collared and cut close, heat filaments humming faintly under the surface. Amelie's was deep blue, long enough to brush her knees, the hood lined in self-warming mesh. Both of us wore gloves that sealed at the wrist and boots that left no identifying tread. We looked ready for anything.

We weren't.

Snow drifted sideways through the canopy, like the woods were trying to swallow us whole.

Amelie pulled her hood lower. "Feels like the world doesn't want us here."

"It doesn't," I said.

The path twisted through dead tech—old satellite towers strangled by moss, half-sunk into the snow like bones no one bothered to bury. Past them, tucked in a clearing, sat the cabin. A black shape in white silence. Roof sagging. Windows blind. Like it had been hiding from God and lost the nerve halfway through.

Next to it stood a crooked fire watch tower leaning against the clouds, its frame buckled but still pretending it mattered.

Amelie crouched low, breath puffing out in quick bursts. "Jesus. He's got a watchtower? What's next, a moat?"

I squinted up at it. "He likes towers. Makes him feel tall."

She almost laughed. Almost.

Movement in the window. A shape pacing. Then clear: Ryan Prescott.

Time hadn't destroyed him—just polished the monster. Chrome with too many fingerprints.

Behind him, another shape. Nat. She moved like she owned the air. When her face tilted toward the glass, the glow in her eyes found me, like she'd been waiting for this day since forever.

The front door groaned open. Hinges screamed.

"So what's the big plan, hotshot?" Amelie whispered. "Sneak, stab, pray? Or we just knock and hope he doesn't eat us?"

"I'm improvising," I said, my words weighty and direct, like that actually *was* a plan.

Nat stepped into the flurries like she belonged there—coat open, boots slicing through the snow, hair catching what little light was left. Every inch of her said she wasn't afraid.

The coat was slick and black, cinched at the waist with a hard gloss belt that looked more like a warning than an accessory. Under it, a fitted turtleneck clung to her like it had been poured on, seamless against the skin. Her pants were jet-dark and cut clean, tucked into square-heeled boots that made a slow, deliberate click each time she moved. Frost gathered in her hair, pulled half-up with a band that caught the light like a blade. Her mouth was painted in that muted shade she favored—sharp, unsentimental, like she'd cut you with a kiss if it came to it.

"Well, look at you," she said, voice smooth with that familiar edge. "Didn't think you'd actually make it out here, hero. Then again, you always were resilient."

"And determined," I muttered under my breath to no one.

The wind snapped her coat back, but she didn't bother to close it. She just stood there, steady and unbothered, like the cold couldn't touch her.

"Nice to see you too," I said. "Love what you've done with the last fifty years."

She smiled, just a flicker. "Still charming. Still suicidal."

"Consistency's my only talent."

Her words slid around me—light, warm, real. For a second, the cold went quiet.

"You know he's waiting for you," she murmured.

"Yeah." I slipped my truck keys into her pocket, brushed her hand. "Take Amelie. Drive till the road stops caring."

She raised a brow. That look. Same one she used to give me before I broke something expensive. "You're serious."

"Dead serious."

"He could kill you."

"Won't stick," I said, smirking. "I've tried."

She laughed once—low, dangerous. "God, you always did have a death wish wrapped in good intentions."

The ember-glow in her eyes caught the snowlight, flickering like the ghosts we used to be.

"Something's changed in you," she said. "You've got that haunted thing down pat now."

"Maybe you're just seeing the real me," I said, voice rough. "The one without the training wheels."

Her lips curved. "Maybe I like this version better."

"Yeah?" I murmured. "Still working out the bugs."

For a heartbeat, neither of us moved. The snow hissed around us, mocking every step with its quiet breath; a whisper, a warning, a condemnation.

Then she reached for me—slow, unsure, like she wasn't certain I was real.

And I kissed her before she could finish the thought.

Hard. Too much. Too late.

All the years between us burned off like fog. The cold didn't matter. Nothing did. Just her heartbeat and mine, stubbornly human.

When I pulled back, I rested my forehead against hers.

"Go," I said quietly. "It's your turn to be free. Let me end this."

Her breath shivered out. "You were always terrible at endings."

"Yeah, well. Guess I'm due for one."

Nat nodded—half resignation, half pride—then turned toward the treeline, where Amelie waited—fists clenched, face wet with snow and fury.

"Ty! What the hell are you doing?!" Amelie's voice cracked through the wind. She took a step toward me, wild-eyed. "We're in this together!"

I raised a hand, stopping her a few feet short. "Listen to me," I said, voice low. "I won't let anything happen to you. You're the sister I never wanted, and the one I didn't know I needed. I've already lost everyone else. Liam. Jackson. If I can keep you safe—just a little longer—from him, then I'm going to do it. But I have to do this alone."

Amelie froze like I'd struck her. Her mouth parted, breath catching on something that wasn't anger this time.

That was when Nat reached her—arm around her waist, fast and practiced.

"C'mon, kid," Nat said, voice edged.

Amelie shoved at her shoulder. "Bullshit! We're a team!"

Nat absorbed it, twisting her wrist back just enough to stop the fight. "If you run in there now," she said coolly, "you give him exactly what he wants."

Amelie's knees buckled, breath shaking. "Let me go!"

"Not until he's gone."

Her eyes snapped back to me one last time—furious, betrayed, terrified.

"You promised," she said.

"I know I did."

I gave one last wave—small, stupid.

"Don't worry about me. Be right back," I muttered. "Probably."

The door opened with a soft, warped groan, like it had been waiting for me, the throat of a python, fangs at the ready to close around its prey. Warm air rushed out, stinking of firewood, metal, and something faintly sweet—rot under perfume.

I stepped inside. Daniel into the lion's den.

Inside was quieter than the snow outside. An unsettling quiet.

The cabin wasn't a home so much as a stage: stripped walls, woodstove ash cold in the grate, a table with two glasses but only one chair. And him—Ryan Prescott—standing at the far end like he'd been there all along, waiting for a cue.

He didn't flinch. Didn't even blink.

"You found me," he said. Calm. Like a host greeting a guest, not a predator greeting prey.

He was older now. Not old—just worn thin. The kind of age that doesn't come from years but from the weight of his own genius pressing inward. Lines webbed around his mouth, but his jaw stayed sharp, defiant. Blond hair combed back the same as ever, though the light caught faint silver along the edges. The sweater—soft cashmere, charcoal gray over a white collared shirt—fit like ritual armor. The trousers, pressed but fraying at the cuffs. He looked almost like the man I remembered, only... corrupted.

Up close, the illusion cracked. His skin carried a faint shimmer, like crushed glass under light. Veins glowed with a weak, dying pulse —threads of Eurydium humming faintly beneath the surface, feeding and poisoning him all at once. His irises, once clear gray, flickered with orange at the rim, the element that found a home behind his eyes.

A faint trace of cologne lingered—cedar—but it tangled now with something acrid, sterile, chemical. The scent of a man halfway between body and experiment.

I flexed my fingers, knuckles aching. "Yeah. Lucky me."

His gaze swept over me, precise as a scan, not like he was looking at a man, but at a finished project. "I was wondering how long it would take. You look good, Ty. Stronger. Almost perfect."

The floor creaked under my boots as I stepped in. Each board sounded like it wanted to give way.

He moved to a console in the corner and poured himself a drink from a bottle that hadn't been dusted in months. The liquid was dark, heavy. He swirled it, slow. "You know, I wasn't sure you'd survive. So many have rotted away before you. But look at you—living proof. Legacy. You should be thanking me."

I stepped closer. My voice cracked on the word. "You butchered people."

Ryan smiled faintly, the way a teacher might when a student guesses wrong. "And now they worship you for surviving it. Me for creating you. That's progress."

I stopped a few feet away, the smell of the drink drifting between us like old blood. "You think this is progress?"

"I think this is inevitable." His eyes gleamed—faint Eurydium embers glowing in the corners like dying coals. "Don't you see it? You're every organism's dream. You and your little friend made a mess of things in Nevada, sure—but you're still my proudest work."

I let out a short, bitter laugh. "Proudest work, huh? Cut the shit, Doc." My jaw tightened. "What did you even want with us? Why let us go only to drag us back again?"

"I always loved when you called me that." He tilted his head, almost amused. "It's not like you'd answer if I called."

My voice sharpened. "But why us?! Out of everyone you could've broken, everyone you could've built... why me? What made me so damn important?"

Ryan set his glass down with a careful clink, studying the dark swirl inside as though he might find the answer there. Then he looked up.

"Because you have the face of the only person I ever loved," he said simply.

The air left the room.

I waited for the punchline—for the smirk, the tell—but none came.

"He was the first," Ryan continued, voice quieter now, almost reverent. "The first I'd ever seen survive Eurydium's effects. Before even I grasped its potential. Nat was exposed just being in his presence." His fingers twitched around the rim of the glass. "After her success, I needed a control. Someone who could survive it too. I sought him out in every test subject I found. And somehow... it led me to you."

My throat locked. "You mean to tell me all of this—everything— you did it because I reminded you of him?"

Ryan's eyes softened, just for a breath. "You didn't just remind me. You became him. Every time I looked at you, it was like I'd found what I'd lost again. Until you screamed. Then I remembered you weren't him at all."

The word *screamed* hung in the air, metallic and heavy.

He smiled faintly, the same way he might have said 'there, there'.

"What about them? The people you sent after us—," I shot back. "Who were they?"

Ryan swirled his drink, eyes dropping to the glass like he was looking at old memories. "Locals," he said simply. "Not anything special. People will do anything if you promise them immortality. Even drag a girl into a van." His mouth curved—half sneer, half smirk. "Enhanced their strength, just enough to prove I was who I was. But you demonstrated that they were still... *mushy* on the inside."

My stomach turned. "You experimented on them."

"I gave them a taste of the future," Ryan said, as if it were charity. "In the end, they were expendable. All I needed was to get you here... And here you are."

"But why!" I yelled, taking a step toward him. "Why couldn't you just leave us alone!"

"Because it's my time, Ty. Against my best efforts, I know it is my time to die. And I wished to see my children one last time."

"You're dying?" I asked. "Of what? How have you even lasted this long?"

"Don't act so concerned," he said lightly, though his hand trembled almost imperceptibly around the glass. "I tried to make myself in your image. Tried to train Nat. Tried surgeries without anesthesia. I even moved myself here, of all places, to be closer to a now-defunct Eurydium mine. Still, nothing worked. And the radiation has taken everything from me. I am... tarnished."

The word hung between us.

"No. No, you don't get to die this easily," I snapped, my throat raw. "Not after everything you've done, after everything you've put us through! You deserve to suffer!"

"Is that right?" His lips curled into something between a smile and a snarl. "So what is it, Ty? What brought *you* here? Have you come to kill me? Or would you rather I live, so you can tear me apart, piece by piece, the way I did to you? To Nat? To Amelie?"

My nostrils flared—the burn behind my eyes growing brighter. "Guess I'm still deciding."

He took me in then, really looking at me. "There you are." He said to himself. "You've always been my proudest creation. Even now, you're still somewhere torn between my work and yourself. Still bleeding. Still glitching. A bug I could never quite squash. I've done to you what I always dreamed of doing to myself. But if someone were to achieve immortality, I'm happy it was me."

"All you've done is create a never-ending hell on earth for us," I spat. "If you think that's a blessing, you're wrong. You've taken everything from us—"

"But given you infinity, too." His eyes burned now. "I've seen it through your eyes. Through Nat's. Amelie's. Those implants have shown me everything—and I've followed you every step of the way." he took a step toward me. "I've seen the heartbreak. The sorrow. But I've also seen what you've become: a family. With strength. Love. That's my legacy too," he said. "So go ahead. Kill me. Burn this place down. It won't matter. It won't give you back what you think you've lost. And it won't change that the three of you are, and will always be, my children—my work, my legacy. My immortality."

My hands were shaking now, but not from fear. From something heavier. Rage. Memory. Coleen's glow fading in the basement. Nat's body crumpled on the stairs. Amelie's arm dangling at an angle it shouldn't.

I leveled the gun at his chest.

For a moment his eyes flicked down to it, and then back to mine—measuring, even now.

"Go on, then," he said softly. "Do it. Show me what you learned."

Coleen's voice hit me—gentle, glitching. *Eyes open. Always.*

And then I pulled the trigger.

CHAPTER 29

THE GUN KICKED, the sound folding the cabin in half.

The shot echoed off the wooden walls, sharp enough to rattle the glass still sitting on the table. For a heartbeat Ryan didn't move. Then his drink tipped from his hand—a dark arc across the wood. The glass hit the floor and shattered, scattering like teeth.

He staggered once. Twice. Pressed a hand to the wound blooming red and iridescent where the bullet had gone in. Blood shimmered faintly under the light, flecked with Eurydium like dying stars.

A thin smile crawled across his mouth. "There it is," he rasped. "Humanity."

Then, softer, as if to himself: "Almost forgot what it felt like."

He dropped to one knee, glass crunching beneath him. His other hand clutched the console for balance, leaving a red smear that pulsed faintly, alive with the glow still running through him.

"You never escaped me, Ty," he wheezed. "You just... finished the job."

I stepped closer, the gun still raised. "You don't get credit for dying, you filthy rag."

He chuckled—dry, broken. "Oh, I'll take credit for everything.

That's what creators do." He lifted his head enough to meet my eyes, and in that gleam, faint Eurydium fire still burned. "They'll come for you now. Governments. The dying. Everyone who ever feared the end. You, Nat, Amelie... you're what they'll worship next."

His laugh broke into a cough, thick and wet. "You can't kill the idea, Ty. You're already infected."

He swayed forward, catching himself on his hands. Blood splattered the floor, thin red webs tracing the wood grain. His voice dropped to a whisper. "Survival...is the only thing that's real."

The words curdled on his tongue. For the first time, he looked afraid.

I didn't look away.

"I know," I said bitterly.

He tried to breathe, but all that came out was a wet, metallic sound — like gears grinding through blood. The light in his eyes flickered, then went out. He slumped sideways.

For a long moment, I stood there—gun limp in my hand, smoke curling from the barrel, my breath fogging in the cold air. It wasn't victory. It wasn't even relief. Just... quiet.

The kind that comes when a nightmare ends and you're not sure you've woken up.

Blood pooled across the floor, glowing faintly like circuitry dying out. The Eurydium pulsed one last time, then dimmed to nothing.

Smoke began to creep from the stove's belly, curling upward as if the house itself had been holding its breath and finally exhaled.

The door slammed against the wall, Amelie bursting through first, breath ragged, snow tangled in her hair. Nat was right behind her, calling her name like she was trying to catch hold of the wind.

The smoke was thicker now, curling around the beams, painting their faces in shifting shadows. And there on the floor—Ryan's body.

Amelie froze mid-step, eyes wide. Her chest heaved like she'd sprinted through the entire forest. Nat caught her shoulder, but her hand slipped when Amelie stumbled forward.

"Ty—" Nat's voice cracked, slicing through the ringing in my head.

I didn't look at them. Couldn't. My eyes were still fixed on the shape crumpled on the floor, the spreading stain. My voice came out low, raw, not mine.

"It's what he deserved."

The gun was still heavy in my hand. Useless now, except it wasn't. Amelie reached me in two steps, her fingers shaking as she tore it from my grip. Then turned to him.

The first shot went off before she even spoke. Then the second. Each louder than the last.

Her voice broke out sharp, shaking but loud: "He doesn't get to just die—Not like that! Not after what he did to us!"

BANG.

BANG.

The sound ripped through the cabin, deafening. She screamed with each shot, spit flying, tears streaking her face:

"You don't get to win! You don't get to take everything and just— just *stop breathing!*"

By the last shot, her knees buckled. The gun clattered from her hands, empty. She stood there gasping, eyes wild, like the world was still moving too fast for her to catch it.

Then she turned into me, hard enough to knock the air out of my chest. Her sobs hit ragged against my shirt, her small frame shaking like the last thread holding her together had finally snapped. My arms went around her before I even thought, pulling her in tight. "Easy," I murmured. "It's over now. He's gone."

That's when Nat stepped forward. Her heels scraped the blood-streaked floor, slow and deliberate. The smoke made her eyes shine, glinting like broken glass in the firelight. She reached out, her mani-cured hand brushing mine—steadying Amelie between us, grounding the three of us together.

For a second, no one said anything. Fire crept up the curtains, the heat closing in around us.

Then Nat spoke. Her voice was low, smooth, threaded with something that sounded almost like a smirk.

"So," she said. "What happens when the heroes break? When the wiring fries and the parts start to fail?"

Her gaze cut to mine—sharp, smoky, unreadable. "What do we do when we need repairs, Ty?"

I met her eyes, felt Amelie's grip tighten between us. The flames painted our shadows across the wall, long and warped, like we were something half-holy, half-damned.

"We turn to each other," I said.

Nat's lips curved, not quite a smile. More like an understanding.

"Good answer," she whispered.

The fire climbed higher, devouring the furniture, the ceiling, everything Ryan ever touched. The air filled with the scent of smoke and scorched metal.

Nat glanced back at the body, then at me—no anger. No pity. Just that cool, fatal clarity she'd always worn like perfume.

"Let it burn," she said softly. "Let it all burn."

We didn't move until the structure groaned around us. Until the flames took the last of his name.

And when we finally stepped outside into the snow-white dark, it felt like walking out of a dream that had been eating us alive.

That night, we sat outside and watched the fire eat the walls. The tower behind the cabin glowed like a match about to snap, its ancient timbers catching stray embers.

Amelie's head pressed against my shoulder, her breath ragged and wet. Nat crouched in the snow across from us, her hand wrapped tight around Amelie's, her eyes reflecting the blaze but never looking away. None of us spoke. We didn't need to.

When the flames finally swallowed the roof and the last wall sagged into ash, sparks scattered into the night sky like a thousand fireflies. I leaned back against a tree, the bark digging into my shoulders, my hand drifting to my cheek—right where Coleen had once told me I was still real.

Her words circled back, sharp and soft all at once, cutting deeper than the fire's heat.

"Am I even still human?" I asked,

Her voice, glitchy, fragile, still alive in me.

"You never stopped being. You're just changing shape."

The words hit harder now than they ever did in that basement.

"Don't forget that."

Snow hissed where it hit fire, smoke rising in gray ribbons above the ruins. I shut my eyes and held onto the words like they were the last thing keeping me whole.

"Please don't forget that."

EPILOGUE

The years passed.

Not over us.

Through us.

We didn't age. Not really. A scar here. A new alias there. But our faces stayed the same. Smooth. Preserved. Untouched by time.

Perfect, some would say.

Monstrous, I'd say.

The world moved on, like it always does. Faster than it needs to. Slower than it should. Cities collapsed under their own glitter. New ones rose like teeth. Governments changed. Demographics mutated. The air turned heavier. Artificial light replaced stars. People forgot the wars—but they remembered us.

We were called miracles. Survivors. Weapons. Gods.

But gods don't get followed through grocery aisles by tourists with retinal cameras. Gods don't get blood-swabbed at border crossings. Gods don't flinch when they hear a drill.

We were never free.

Everywhere we went, someone watched. Scientists. Cult kids with matching tattoos. Presidents who shook our hands on live feeds, then signed bills in the dark to replicate what Ryan had done. They kept calling it progress. We knew it by its real name.

Containment.

After a while, I started to wonder—how long can a mind remember itself if it's never allowed to die? Memory isn't meant to stretch forever. Maybe that's why immortals in old myths always went mad. Your past doesn't fade. It stacks. Layer after layer until you can't tell which version of yourself is the real one.

Still, we persevered.

Amelie never tried school again. Didn't see the point in tests with answers made for people who could run out of time. Instead, she made her own education: motel walls covered in anatomy sketches, physics notes on diner napkins, Eurydium schematics scribbled over maps. She said maybe one day she'd know enough to undo what was done. To make us mortal again. Some nights, when the world went quiet enough to hear her breathing across the room, I believed her.

Nat stayed moving. New hair. New names. Too restless for roots. Sometimes her voice crackled through burner lines at 2 A.M.—half-laugh, half-warning, like she was calling from a payphone in a dream. I'd catch a blurry face in a crowd-shot online and swear it was her, already turning away.

Her messages were always the same:

Still here. Keep moving.

And me?

I stayed low. Worked where I wouldn't be recognized. Fixed engines. Built safehouses. Taught people how to fight back—really fight back. Places that didn't belong to governments or gods or ghosts. But I never stayed too long. Sleep got harder. Silence got heavier.

It's strange, living in a body that refuses to end. You start to feel like a myth someone forgot to finish.

Some nights, I'd catch my reflection in a dark window and flinch. Too polished. Too precise. Like someone carved a man out of fear and left it walking.

I'd ask myself:

Am I still the kid who screamed in the dark? The one who wanted to die just to feel like he was still alive?

Or am I just the thing that survived him?

Coleen's voice would come back then—soft, glitchy, stitched with code and kindness:

"You're bleeding. That's how I know you're still you."

Maybe that's what being human is. Not the aging. Not the ending. Just the bleeding. The way we keep hurting and still go on.

We're not timeless. We're just broken in ways that don't heal.

But still—

We walk.

We breathe.

We remember.

And in a world that would rather turn us into symbols, that matters.

Because I know what we are.

We are human.

And we are alive.

AFTERWORD

Thank you for joining Ty, Nat, Amelie, and Echo on their journey through fear, memory, and what it means to still be human. *We Are Human* was born from the idea that even in a world stripped of empathy—beneath metal, circuitry, and control—there remains a pulse. A quiet, stubborn heartbeat that refuses to fade.

This story is, at its core, about survival—and what comes after. About the cost of being remade, and the courage it takes to claim your body, your mind, and your name again. Writing it pushed me into some dark places, but it also reminded me of the strength that lives inside those places. If it did the same for you—if it made you feel, question, or simply pause—I hope it also offered a glimmer of light in return.

To every reader who made it to this page: thank you. Your willingness to walk through the wreckage with these characters means more than I can say. To my friends, family, and early readers who kept believing in this book even when it broke me a little to write it—your faith held it together. Truly.

A Note on Themes

We Are Human explores difficult and often painful subjects, including trauma, loss of bodily autonomy, psychological manipulation, and the search for identity after violation. These themes are integral to Ty's story but may resonate deeply—or painfully—with some readers. If certain moments left you uneasy or raw, please remember: you are not alone in that feeling. It's okay to step back, to breathe, to reach out.

Helpful Resources

If you or someone you know is struggling, the following resources are available:

- National Suicide Prevention Lifeline (U.S.): **988** or **1-800-273-TALK (8255)**
- Crisis Text Line: **Text HOME to 741741**
- SAMHSA Helpline (Mental Health/Substance Use): **1-800-662-HELP (4357)**
- For international support: **www.befrienders.org**

Disclaimer

This novel is a work of fiction. Any similarities to real people, places, or events are purely coincidental. The characters and their stories are creations of the author's imagination, written to explore emotional truths through speculative means.

A Reminder

Sometimes, the horror isn't in the experiment or the machine—it's in being told you no longer belong to yourself. But you do. You always have. No matter what you've survived, what you've lost, or how many times you've been rebuilt—your humanity is yours to keep.

If this story left something stirring in you, let it. Let it remind you that you are more than what's been done to you. You are alive. You are human. And that will always be enough.

Thank you, truly, for reading.

Respectfully Yours,

Lincoln James

ACKNOWLEDGMENTS

A special thanks to these fantastic people who helped make this book possible:

Adri
Ben
Bree
Cossy
David
Denise
Jack
Jessie
Joanna
Kamran
Keaton
Lee
Mariah
Mason
Maureen
Mike
Mila
Nadia
Nicole
Rob
Ross
Ryan

ABOUT THE AUTHOR

Lincoln James, your favorite author's favorite author, is known for his haunting love stories, vintage thrillers, and slow-burn suspense. His characters feel, ache, and bleed, often trapped between the past and the people who won't let them forget it. When he's not writing, James is a Communication professor in New York City and cherishes moments with friends and family, proving that the most thrilling tales lie in the love and laughter shared with those closest to us.